BOOK ONE: SEVEN SEALS

THE DAYS OF LOT

MARK GOODWIN

ACKNOWLEDGMENTS

I would like to thank my fantastic editing team, Catherine Goodwin, Sherrill Hesler, Jamie Pogue, and Claudine Allison.

PREFACE

…As it was in the days of Lot; they did eat, they drank, they bought, they sold, they planted, they builded; but the same day that Lot went out of Sodom it rained fire and brimstone from heaven, and destroyed them all. Even thus shall it be in the day when the Son of man is revealed.

Luke 17:28-30

Ten years ago, when I wrote *The Days of Noah*, I never could have imagined the world in which we now live. Certainly, the dawn of a cashless society, a one-world government, along with the technology and attitudes necessary to bring them about were on the horizon.

However, the evil, the darkness, and the godlessness of our society have progressed at a staggering rate. Ten years ago, we could not conceive of perverts having the power or authority to force themselves into our homes and remove members of our households to be used for their deranged purposes as was the case in Lot's time. But that day has come as evidenced by the story of Yaeli Martinez and untold multitudes like hers.

Yaeli Martinez, the daughter of Abigail Martinez, dealt with depression like many teens. The Los Angeles LGBT Center had a presence in the public school where Yaeli attended. They convinced Yaeli that gender dysphoria was the root of her problems, and she began talking to a counselor about transitioning from female to male.

When Abigail Martinez discovered what was going on with her daughter, she fought back. But LA County DCFS took custody of Yaeli and put her in a foster home so she could continue transitioning. Abigail was only permitted to see her daughter once a week, the visits were supervised, and she was not allowed to talk about God with Yaeli.

Once Yaeli turned 18, she began receiving puberty blockers and testosterone injections. However, the drugs, therapy, and gender-affirming care that Yaeli received from Los Angeles County did not cure her depression nor fill the God-shaped hole in her heart. In 2019, even more distraught than before the state's intervention, Yaeli stepped in front of a moving train with the purpose of ending it all. First responders collected her bits and pieces from the scene, leaving her mother without a corpse to which she could say goodbye or bury.

While perhaps not as shocking as Yaeli's ordeal, this story is being repeated all over America and becoming more common place by the day. The LGBT movement has become just as powerful as the perverts who controlled Sodom and Gomorrah.

At the time of this writing, California has two bills working their way through the legislative process. One is Assembly Bill 957 which includes gender-affirming care as a basic responsibility that parents must provide to their children or have them taken away by the state. The other is Assembly Bill 665 which would expand existing laws to provide gender-transition counseling and therapy to children over 12 without parental consent. We are living in the final chapter of planet earth. We are living in the Days of Lot.

For the Lord himself shall descend from heaven with a shout, with the voice of the archangel, and with the trump of God: and the dead in Christ shall rise first: then we which are alive and remain shall be caught up together with them in the clouds, to meet the Lord in the air: and so shall we ever be with the Lord.

1 Thessalonians 4:16-17

This is my third series on end-time events. My previous two sagas diverged from common eschatological schools of thought falling somewhere between the pre-wrath and intra-seal rapture camps. This series follows the common pre-tribulation view.

Nothing has changed in my understanding of end-times prophecy. I still see Scripture that supports all of those scenarios. But, unlike the virgin birth, death, and resurrection of Jesus Christ, and salvation being by grace through faith in Christ Jesus and not by our own works, end-times prophecy is not so clear cut, as evidenced by the multitude of interpretations. I don't expect to fully understand how all these prophecies fit together until they come to fruition.

Folks who get offended because you don't agree with their particular eschatological viewpoint are typically people who have latched on to one school of thought because it has been promoted by their favorite pastor or teacher. Very few of them have done their own research. Those of us who study the scriptures can easily understand how our brothers and sisters might come to a different conclusion than our own, and for the most part, can disagree without being disagreeable.

First and foremost, let's remember that this book is fiction. It is not intended to convert you to the pre-trib camp any more than my other books sought to convince you of a mid-trib, pre-wrath, or intra-seal rapture. This series is meant to provide a source of entertainment that will not defile your mind and spirit like most of the literary offerings from the world and, perhaps, spark your interest to study God's Word for yourself.

In Mathew 25, Jesus implies that His return is imminent. And if imminent, that means He could come to collect His saints before you finish reading this paragraph. So be ready!

I've recently heard another strong case for a pre-trib rapture pointed out to me on two separate occasions by two men I greatly respect. One is a personal friend and the other is an accomplished Bible teacher. It's the idea of Daniel's 70 weeks. The clock started on those 70 weeks or 490 years with the rebuilding of the wall around Jerusalem after the Jewish exile. The clock stopped at 69 weeks or 483 years when Jesus was crucified, resurrected, and the Church of Christ was born.

Daniel 9:24 specifically says that the 70 weeks are "determined upon thy people," which Daniel was a Jew. So, the prima facie interpretation would stand that this 490-year period pertains to the Jews. Also, the tribulation is called *the time of Jacob's trouble*, and Jacob being the birth name of Israel.

5

Since the clock stopped at the birth of the Church it wouldn't be much of a stretch to assume that it will restart when the Church is taken in the Rapture.

One of the dangers of the pre-trib viewpoint is the false belief that Jesus will come to get us before anything bad happens. In fact, the opposite is true. Jesus said, "In this world, you will have tribulation." The parable of the sower in Matthew 13 tells us that many will fall away when troubles come and challenge that erroneous notion.

Yet equally as dangerous is the idea that could spring up from rejecting the Messiah's imminent return. It's the peril of assuming that you have more time, using that as an excuse to continue in sin. *I'll get right with God tomorrow.* Your eschatology might be correct but a heart attack, a car accident, a stray bullet, or any number of things could cause your personal rapture to come quicker than you think; and you'd be wrong—dead wrong.

What I will say is that, with everything going on in the world, if He doesn't come back soon it won't be a surprise. And if all of this jargon about pre-wrath, pre-trib, mid-trib, and intra-seal raptures is Greek to you, good. Sit back and enjoy the story. But, as you read, remember these words.

Watch therefore, for ye know neither the day nor the hour wherein the Son of man cometh.

Matthew 25:13

CHAPTER 1

Lot dwelled in the cities of the plain, and pitched his tent toward Sodom.

Genesis 13:12b

Mason Lot peered out his office window on the 22nd floor of 14 Wall Street. He could see Federal Hall, the location where Washington had taken his oath of office, but couldn't quite make out the famous statue of George. One side of his mouth turned up as he considered the irony.

"Wouldn't you be proud?" He pondered what the old president and Freemason would think of 14 Wall Street which was capped with a ziggurat or stepped pyramid, a common symbol among practitioners of the Masonic secret society.

Despite his name, he was not a Mason, and much preferred the shortened variant *Mace*, largely due to his distaste of all things secret which he'd acquired since coming to work as general counsel at Poseidon Capital.

Mason recalled that the Tower of Babel had likely been a ziggurat. "God confused the languages and dispersed the nations in the first Babylon. Now in this latest iteration, we've brought them all back together."

He glanced at the black and white photograph on his wall of the lower Manhattan skyline. He focused on the tallest building which was located only a few blocks from his office. He muttered the first two words of the address. "One World…" He smirked. "The Tower of Babel—looks like we got away with it this time."

A knock at the door interrupted his pensive state and preceded a young man walking into his office. "Mr. Lot…"

Mason walked to his couch and sat down. "Please, call me *Mace*. What can I do for you, Liam?"

"I was looking over the Peleus fund and I'm having trouble understanding…"

"They say curiosity killed the cat." Mason patted the empty seat on the couch signaling for Liam to sit. "Peleus is a private fund. Olympus is the only fund you need to concern yourself with."

Liam sat down with a troubled expression. "Sir, as the CCO, this is something you'll want to know about. I could only access this month's trades—all prior months are locked. But these numbers are insane. Every short, every call, one after the other, winner, winner, winner." Liam scrolled down the spread sheet displayed on his tablet. "I mean, if these are legitimate trades, why didn't the Olympus fund follow the same strategy?"

"Like I said," Mason glanced at the tablet and then reclined on the sofa. "Olympus is the only fund you have to worry about."

Liam held out the tablet with insistence. "Peleus jumped from eighty-four billion to seven hundred fifteen in a matter of weeks. Sir, we're talking about ten standard deviations, in other words…"

"In other words, what?"

"Look, Mr. Lot." Liam closed his eyes tightly as if stressed. "Mace, I appreciate the job, but I don't want to go to prison. Let's call this what it is— insider trading. I don't know how the traders are getting their information. I don't know where they are getting their information—in fact, I don't *want* to know. But I can't work here if this is going on."

Mason spoke in a soothing tone. "Relax, take a breath. No one is going to prison and there's no need for you to leave. I knew we were going to have this conversation sooner or later.

"We didn't just reach out to you on a whim. Mr. Costa knows some folks over at BlackRock and we poached you with permission—and recommendations, I might add. When we reached out to you, it was because we were looking for a team player, someone with ambition. Mr. Costa heard you'd been very diligent and were looking to get on the trading floor. We offered you this position which allowed you to make a big vertical move without the risk and pressure that traders have to deal with."

"Traders make all the money," said Liam.

"Poseidon doubled your salary, right?"

"Yes, sir, and no offense, but in Manhattan, going from eighty grand to one sixty is the equivalent of moving from McDonald's to the Olive Garden. My rent is four grand a month."

"Which is easier to swing working at Olive Garden." Mason lowered an eyebrow.

"Yes, sir, but as a trader at BlackRock, I could hit five hundred my first year."

Mason laughed. "One bad trade at BlackRock, and you *will* be working at Olive Garden."

"Which beats the heck out of mopping floors at Rikers," Liam countered. "One visit from the SEC and…"

Mason shook his head. "I told you—we don't have to worry about that. I'm assuming if you've done this much snooping, you've figured out who Peleus's only client is."

Liam narrowed his eyes. "In-Q-Tel? It's supposedly a non-profit VC firm which makes all of this even more sus. I mean, who ever heard of not-for-profit venture capitalists? That's an oxymoron—like jumbo shrimp."

"Do you know who Q is?"

Liam sat back on the sofa. "What? Like the guy who makes all the gadgets for James Bond?"

"Yeah."

"Wait, are you telling me In-Q-Tel is some sort of government agency?" Liam inspected his tablet. "They *are* based in Arlington." He looked up. "So, what—does that somehow make it all legal?"

Mason took a deep breath. "Are you familiar with Iran-Contra?"

"I may have read a chapter about it in US history, but I don't remember the specifics. Some scandal, right?"

"The CIA was selling weapons to Iran and using the proceeds to fund the rebels in Nicaragua who were fighting against the Sandinistas—communists."

"What does that have to do with Peleus?"

"It's similar in that Peleus is providing capitol to In-Q-Tel in the same way the arms deals helped fund the CIA who in turn supported the contras."

"You haven't explained anything," Liam argued.

"In-Q-Tel is the VC arm of the CIA. They've helped Google, Facebook, SpaceX, and hundreds of other companies critical to the national security state. Think of it like the Fed. If you or I try to put a hundred-dollar bill in the copier, it's called *counterfeiting*. If the Fed prints money, it's called *monetary creation*."

"Mr. Lot, sir—you're a lawyer. This *isn't* monetary creation. If the CIA needs funding, they have to ask for it from Congress."

"It doesn't really work like that. It hasn't for a long, long time. They've done some pretty shady stuff to generate income, including but not limited to selling weapons and drugs. The Peleus fund is one of the lesser evils. It doesn't put anyone at risk. And you can be sure, the SEC is *not* going to come looking."

"You don't think it's stealing?" asked Liam. "I mean, Peleus is generating billions of dollars in a matter of days. That's draining value from other investors…"

Mason interjected, "Whom we're happy to service through the Olympus fund. We cranked out nine percent last year for our investors when the broader markets essentially chopped sideways. That's remarkable. You realize, every dollar created through other channels of monetary creation, whether that be through the Fed or the fractional reserve banking system, all of it dilutes the value of the dollar. It's like taxation, it's a necessary evil."

"Evil," said Liam. "I'm not so sure about the necessary part."

"Yes, I agree. But this is the real world and that's how it works. You can either find your place within the system or try to eke out an existence living off grid—eating bugs or whatever."

Liam exhaled. "What if some rogue SEC agent decides to come sniffing around, or what if a whistleblower decides to go to the press?"

Mason chuckled. "The security state controls the press. No one is going to run anything that doesn't serve them. And so, what if a rogue agent comes sniffing around? Peleus is the bread and butter of the most devious and powerful people on the planet. They're not going to allow some underling to threaten their sustenance."

Liam stood up and walked to the window. "Okay, so why me? What made me the prime candidate for this job?"

"You're thorough, loyal, motivated, and have shown that you understand the universe has a certain order; a balance, if you will—a delicate one that needs to be respected."

"Let's say I do agree to stay with Poseidon. When I accepted the terms, I had no idea what I was walking into. Would it be completely against protocol to renegotiate my terms of employment?"

Mason had anticipated this part of the conversation long before hiring Liam. "Keep in mind that you're the only other in-house counsel. I just turned fifty and plan on retiring at sixty."

Liam turned around. "Am I being groomed for CCO?"

Mason lifted his shoulders. "C-Suite by thirty-five. Not too shabby, right?"

Liam's eyes grew wide. "Not at all. But still, that's ten years of—discretion. Could we discuss a little higher compensation?"

Mason narrowed his eyes to insinuate he was displeased with the request, even though he'd expected it. "What's a little higher?"

"Two fifty?"

Mason thought he'd say three and was prepared to go as high as two-fifty. But Liam opened with that number. "I can give you two hundred and promise a five percent increase a year, for now. You're twenty-five years old, fresh out of law school. Not many kids in your position get an opportunity like this."

"Yeah, okay. I'm in." Liam clapped his hands. He pointed at the crystal decanter on the bar opposite Mason's couch. "Should we celebrate?"

"After work," said Mason. "This isn't some TV show where the lawyers drink whisky all day. We've got forms to file and work to do."

"Yes, sir." Liam looked at the floor as if embarrassed.

"Great. Anything else?" asked Mason.

"No, sir." Liam turned toward the door, then paused. "Actually, one more thing."

"Okay, let's have it."

"What happened to my predecessor? I heard some whispering by the coffee machine."

Mason felt bad for the girl who'd worked as his associate. "Megan Fisk. You've heard the story of Icarus?"

"The Greek god who flew too close to the sun?"

"Close. Icarus was mortal and not a god. His father was an inventor who made wings of beeswax and feathers. The design was intended for him and Icarus to escape the island of Crete where they were being held prisoner. Upon taking flight, Icarus got overly confident and flew higher and higher, despite his father's warnings. The sun softened the beeswax, and the feathers came loose. Poor Icarus came careening toward the sea and drowned. His father was unable to intervene.

"I warned Megan not to let herself be tempted. I've got four daughters of my own, one about the same age as Megan, so it was natural for me to want to protect her. Unfortunately, Megan started obsessing about the lucrative Peleus trades. She tried to find a workaround so she could cash in. She ended up wiring money to a past college roommate who mimicked a couple of the Peleus trades. Long story short, she forgot she was a mere mortal and that her wings were made of wax."

Liam's eyes showed his concern. "So, was she arrested for insider trading?"

Mason shook his head. "Nope. Heroin—half a kilo. It was her first offense, so she only got five years, but it's hard to come back from that kind of thing. She'll never practice law again. And if she ever talks to anyone about Peleus, no one will ever believe her."

Liam's face turned pale white.

Mason put his hand on Liam's shoulder. "I hate that it happened to her. I still put money in her account every two weeks—try to make prison more…" He shook his head. "Tolerable? I can't do much else for her. But I can help you. Stay in your lane and don't put your nose where it doesn't belong."

Liam lowered his gaze. "Yes, sir."

Mason felt the conversation had gone as well as could be expected. "You and I are mere mortals, and the gods aren't ones to be trifled with."

CHAPTER 2

Because that, when they knew God, they glorified him not as God, neither were thankful; but became vain in their imaginations, and their foolish heart was darkened. Professing themselves to be wise, they became fools, and changed the glory of the uncorruptible God into an image made like to corruptible man, and to birds, and fourfooted beasts, and creeping things. Wherefore God also gave them up to uncleanness through the lusts of their own hearts, to dishonour their own bodies between themselves: who changed the truth of God into a lie, and worshipped and served the creature more than the Creator, who is blessed for ever. Amen.

Romans 1:21-25

Mason unzipped his backpack and tossed his sweaty gym clothes into the washing machine as soon as he came in the door Thursday evening. He walked into the bedroom. "I'm home."

Adrianna called from the bathroom, "Oh, hey. I'm running late. Can you call me a car? We're all going out for Tiffy's birthday, so don't wait up."

Mason tightened his jaw and dialed the number on his phone.

"Good evening, Mr. Lot. This is Carl with Elite Car Service. How can I help you tonight?"

"Hey Carl, Mrs. Lot needs a car to pick her up from the apartment—as soon as you can get here."

"Jason will be there in ten minutes, will that be okay?"

"Sure thing. Thanks, Carl." Mason ended the call. "He said ten minutes."

"Who are they sending?" Adrianna inquired.

"Jason."

"Oh." She sounded disappointed.

"What's wrong with Jason?"

She walked out of the bathroom half-dressed and entered her expansive closet. "It would have been nice if they'd sent one of the cute ones—like Rodger—you know, since it's the girls."

Mason wrinkled his nose. "You're all married."

"Oh please!" She emerged from the closet with a short black dress. "It's not like you don't look."

"I don't rub your face in it."

"Whatever." She pulled on the black dress and went back into the closet. "Don't forget, Maria is off on Thursdays, so you'll have to fend for yourselves for dinner."

"We'll manage." Mason scrolled through his phone until he found the number for Nick's Pizza.

Adrianna exited the closet with a pair of black pumps that Mason had never seen before. "And no pizza! The girls get enough of that junk at school." She slipped on the shoes.

Mason snarled and blacked out the screen of his phone.

She grabbed her black Prada clutch and headed for the door. "Oh, by the way, Wynter has something she needs to talk to you about."

"Something important?"

"Yeah."

"And you already know about it?"

"Yeah."

"What is it?"

"You'll have to talk to her about it."

"No, give me a heads up!"

"I can't, I'm late." She pretended to kiss him from six inches away. It's what she always did when she didn't want to mess up her makeup.

"You should have led with that." He followed her to the door.

"All I can say is, be supportive." She opened the door.

"At least we don't have to worry about her being pregnant." Mason pressed his lips together.

Adrianna turned and narrowed her eyes. "Don't go in there with that attitude. Remember, they're our child."

"*They*? What's up with the gender-neutral pronoun?"

"I've got to go. Rodger will be waiting for me downstairs."

"It's *Jason*." Mason tightened his jaw.

"Don't remind me." Adrianna rolled her eyes and pulled the door shut.

Mason huffed and took his phone out of his pocket. He swiped the screen and dialed the number for Nick's Pizza.

***

Forty minutes later, the pizza arrived. Mason paid the delivery boy and closed the door. He placed the box on the dining room table. And called his two teenage daughters to dinner. "Wyn, Prairie, time to eat!"

Both girls went to Beachman School, a non-traditional private school on the upper east side, a few blocks south of the apartment. Prairie was fifteen, in tenth grade, and the quintessential girly girl. She was petite with blonde hair, into boys, makeup, and pop music. Prairie was pretty and had lots of friends.

Wynter was seventeen, taller than most girls her age, with black hair. She'd been quite feminine most of her life, even through her junior year when she'd experimented with a goth look. But, shortly after the beginning of her senior year, two of her closest friends decided they were boys. Wynter followed in their footsteps, cutting her hair short, tossing out all her makeup and black skirts, exchanging them for guy's jeans, teeshirts, and hoodies.

Mason felt sad about the decision and tried to talk to her on several occasions. But when he recognized that he was only driving a wedge between them, he abandoned his arguments, hoping the phase would pass as quickly as Wynter's gothic stage.

Mason had two more daughters, Daphne and Hope, who were both married and out of the house. Hope was the oldest. She'd recently graduated from Manhattan's prestigious School of Visual Arts and had landed an entry-level position at the Metropolitan Museum of Art. Hope's hair had once been brown, but more recently changed between blue, aqua, and pink with the latter being the most recent. Hope wore a nose ring and had several tattoos. Mason had been a fan of none of those things but found his protests were largely ignored. Hope's husband, Raphael Cullum, was also an artist and fourteen years older than Hope, which Mason liked even less than the tattoos and nose ring. But she made her own decisions and Raphael made his own money—more than Mason, in fact. So, he was largely incapable of swaying her verdict. Hope and Raphael had been married for two years and seemed deeply enamored with one another.

The same could not be said about Daphne and her new husband, Steve. The honeymoon had reached an abrupt end when Steven failed to come home one night after a wild night of drinking and cocaine with his buddies from the Goldman Sachs trading floor. Steve Jackson worked hard, brought home a big paycheck, and felt entitled to blow off steam without any questions from his wife. Daphne was in her final year at Columbia to earn her MBA and was unable to support herself if she left Steve. Mason offered to let her come back, but Daphne was driven and would have viewed coming home as a failure.

Prairie was the first to reach the dining room. "Hi, Daddy!" She grabbed Mason and held him tight. His heart melted. Prairie had always been the most affectionate toward him. He loved all of his daughters, and would never admit it out loud, but Prairie was *daddy's girl*.

"Hey, Sweet Pea. How was school?"

Prairie took a seat at the table. "Don't even get me started. Mrs. Vanderhorn was talking about all this climate emergency stuff. The lesson was on activism, and we were talking about Greta Thunberg and what a great role model she is.

"I simply asked a question about Greta's claims she made five years ago about only having eight years to avert a climate disaster. Supposedly, the polar ice caps were going to melt, and the sea levels were going to rise and all of that. It's something I looked up. But I asked Mrs. Vanderhorn why people are still buying overpriced apartments like ours in Manhattan. I mean, most of the island is only seven feet above sea level, right? So, if it's going to be a catastrophic event, shouldn't we all be trying to get out of here before Manhattan becomes the next Venice?

"Well, she got *all* riled up and started accusing *me* of being a climate denier. I wasn't denying anything, I just wanted to know what the plan was if we're all going to be underwater in three years. I mean, it doesn't much matter what America and Europe decide to do about emissions when we're only a fraction of the global population. China and India make up half the people on the planet and we all know they're not about to give up fossil fuels to switch over to solar and wind.

"I mean, if we're going to be underwater, we should all start buying property up in the Catskills. But what do I know? I'm just a dumb high school kid."

He ran his fingers through her hair as he listened. "You're not dumb at all, Sweet Pea. That makes perfect sense."

Wynter walked into the dining room wearing her signature smirk. "Does the pizza have meat on it?"

"Pepperoni, but you can pick it off," said Mason.

"It's contaminated. I'll make myself some pasta." Wynter opened the cabinet, took out a large pot, and began filling it with water.

"You used to eat meat." Mason got plates for himself and Prairie.

"I used to eat melba toast with pureed peas and carrots. But I'm not teething anymore. I haven't been for a long time, Dad. That's what happens. Kids grow up and they change." Wynter took out a box of farfalle pasta and poured it into the pot of water.

Mason sensed that Wynter's aggression had little to do with the pepperoni pizza. "Mom said you had something we needed to discuss." He sat down and began eating with Prairie.

"I want to get top surgery." She stirred some salt into the pot.

Mason's brain tried to make sense of the statement. "Top surgery—why do you need surgery? And what's top surgery?"

"A double mastectomy—so I can continue transitioning."

Mason's mouth hung open. He dropped the pizza on his plate. "A mastectomy? You don't have cancer, do you?"

"I'm a boy, Dad. And I'd like you to quit referring to me as your daughter. My preferred pronouns are he, his, and him."

Mason felt like he was dreaming. None of this seemed real. "You're *not* a boy."

Wyn glared at Prairie. "What did I tell you."

Prairie's voice got louder. "Wyn, give him a chance. He's old. That's how he was taught to think."

Mason knew Prairie was attempting to stick up for him, so he didn't take the comment as an insult. "That's how we raised our children to think also."

Prairie let her pizza sit on her plate. "At school, we're taught to support people who need to transition. Maybe you should take some classes on inclusivity and diversity, Daddy. They didn't teach this stuff when you were in school. It's not your fault, but now it's affecting your relationship with your…" Her eyes shifted between Wynter and Mason. "…child." She seemed to have chosen the word that was least likely to offend either of them.

Mason suddenly realized he'd not been involved in the girls' education. He'd allowed Adrianna to oversee all aspects of school selection, grades, and making sure homework was completed. Prairie had always been the level-headed one. He'd never expected her to take such a line with him. "Wyn is not a boy. She's my *daughter*."

He turned to Wynter. "Baby, I love you very much. I understand that some of your friends are going through this—stuff. And right now, it probably seems like a good idea. But trust me, it's not. You're confused. We can schedule an appointment with a therapist and talk through this.

"High school is a weird time. And I also understand that the culture has made this thing about transitioning to another sex popular. But it's not realistic. You were born a girl and you can never be a boy. The only thing you'll accomplish is permanently scarring and mutilating your beautiful body."

"That's not true," Wynter argued. "Lots of people successfully transition. And I've already been to counseling about it. My therapist supports my decision."

"When did this happen?"

"About four months ago." She stirred the pasta in the boiling water. "I've seen a medical doctor as well. I started taking hormone therapy drugs last month—testosterone."

"You can't do that without my permission!" Mason yelled. "What doctor is prescribing testosterone to you without parental consent?"

Wynter pointed the wooden spoon at her father. "I don't need *anyone's* permission to be the person I am."

He rebutted, "If you want to wear jeans and t-shirts, cut your hair short, and toss out your makeup, that's fine. It's a phase, you can come back whenever you want. But you're talking about permanent injury! You can lose your hair from taking testosterone! You could get facial hair! Have you thought about what happens when you change your mind and want to be a girl again? You could end up with a five o'clock shadow and a receding hairline. There's no coming back from that. Don't even get me started on this mastectomy business!"

Prairie began crying. "Daddy, you're yelling!"

"Yes," he replied. "Your sister is making a life-altering mistake! It's the kind of thing that upsets me because I love her."

"You don't love me." Wynter turned off the burner for the pasta and walked out of the kitchen. "If you did, you'd respect my decision."

"Wyn!" Prairie got up from the table and followed her sister to the bedroom. She knocked on the locked door and shook the doorknob. "Wyn, let me in!" She persisted for several minutes.

Prairie returned to the table. "Daddy, you have to go talk to her. You have to tell her that you'll at least think about it."

"I'm not going to think about it. There's nothing to think about. God made Wynter a girl and that's the end of the conversation."

"God?" Prairie narrowed her eyes. "When did you start believing in God?"

"I've always believed in God. When did you stop believing?"

Prairie picked at her pizza but didn't eat much. "About the same time I stopped believing in Santa. You don't take it seriously, right? It's just a myth."

"God's not a myth," Mason argued. "We've always taken you girls to church. I had no idea you'd stopped believing in Him."

"We go to church on Christmas and Easter, the same days that Santa and the rabbit come. I assumed it was all part of the same fraud, like the grown-up version of Saint Nick and the Easter Bunny."

Mason Lot said nothing. He was completely blindsided by his failure as a father.

CHAPTER 3

For this cause God gave them up unto vile affections: for even their women did change the natural use into that which is against nature: and likewise also the men, leaving the natural use of the woman, burned in their lust one toward another; men with men working that which is unseemly, and receiving in themselves that recompence of their error which was meet. And even as they did not like to retain God in their knowledge, God gave them over to a reprobate mind, to do those things which are not convenient; being filled with all unrighteousness, fornication, wickedness, covetousness, maliciousness; full of envy, murder, debate, deceit, malignity; whisperers, backbiters, haters of God, despiteful, proud, boasters, inventors of evil things, disobedient to parents, without understanding, covenantbreakers, without natural affection, implacable, unmerciful: who knowing the judgment of God, that they which commit such things are worthy of death, not only do the same, but have pleasure in them that do them.

Romans 1:26-32

Mason Lot sat on the sofa next to Prairie as the two of them watched a movie later that evening. He found little interest in the film. His mind was plagued by the issue with Wynter and he could see no clear path through the debacle. He looked at the television screen on occasion but spent most of his time staring down the hallway toward Wynter's locked bedroom door. "I'm going to get another slice. Do you want one?"

Prairie nodded with a smile and without looking away from the film. Mason was glad that her young mind was not nearly so tormented as his by the evening's discord. He got up from the couch and retrieved their plates. "Do you want yours warm?"

"No thanks," said Prairie. "Cold is fine."

Mason elected to eat his slice at room temperature as well. He plated the pizza, tucked a roll of paper towels under his arm, and carried the food to the coffee table.

The doorbell rang. Mason put down the plates and checked the time on his phone. "It's nine o'clock. Who'd be coming by at this hour on a school night?"

Prairie lifted her shoulders. "I'm not expecting anybody."

Mason walked to the door and looked through the peephole to see an NYPD badge. "It's the police."

Prairie got up from the couch to see what was going on.

Mason opened the door. "How can I help you, officer?"

A thin person with androgynous features stepped out from behind the officer. "My name is Carter Reed. I'm with OCFS. I have a court order to remove Wynter Lot from the premises. He'll be remanded into OCFS custody."

"What did she do?" Mason was bewildered. "I'm sure there's been a mistake." Mason tried to close the door, but the cop put his toe in the doorway. "You can't just take her away without a hearing."

Mason took out his phone and dialed Ian Kirk's number. "I'm calling my attorney."

Ian answered, "Mace, it's been a while. What's going on?" Ian Kirk had attended law school with

Mason but specialized in family law whereas Mason had pursued business law.

Mason leaned against the door to prevent the intruders from entering. "OCFS is at my place right now with NYPD. Wynter is in some kind of trouble. They won't tell me what's going on."

"Let me talk to them," said Ian.

Mason handed the phone to Reed.

"This is Carter Reed with OCFS." The thin person looked aggravated at having to explain their self. "No, sir. We're removing Wynter because he's requested to be removed. Wynter is undergoing the lengthy process of gender reassignment and Mr. Lot has shown a persistent pattern of non-affirming behavior. This type of environment is toxic and can cause irrevocable harm to a transgender person, especially for those at Wynter's vulnerable age.

"I have paperwork signed by a judge for Mr. Lot and I'll be happy to send copies to your office, if you'll contact me with a request."

Reed furrowed their brow. "Good day, Mr. Kirk." Carter Reed ended the call and handed the phone back to Mason. Reed took out their own phone and placed a call. "Wynter, hi. This is Carter. We're at your front door. Whenever you're ready, you can come out." Reed smiled. "Okay. I'm here."

Wynter came out of her bedroom with a backpack and a duffle bag. Mason turned to address her. "Where are you going?"

"The OCFS shelter. Then after school tomorrow, I'll go through intake for the LGBTQ house where I can be around people who understand me."

"I understand you, Wyn!" Prairie became upset. "Daddy is just old-fashioned. He'll come around. You'll see."

Wyn hugged her sister. "He won't. If I'm in the custody of OCFS, New York will pay for my surgery. But it has to be completed before I turn eighteen. Dad isn't going to pay for it. We'll still see each other. You'll come to visit. Then, once I'm on my own, we'll see one another all the time."

Prairie sobbed. "Oh, Wyn, don't leave!"

"Do you feel safe?" Carter asked Prairie. "If not, we can provide housing for you."

Prairie narrowed her eyes at Reed. "What? Of course, I feel safe! My dad is the best!" She let go of Wyn and took her father's hand, stepping behind him.

"Wyn!" Mason pleaded. "Don't do this!" He eyed the two NYPD officers. One had his hand on a Taser and the other had unsnapped the leather strap securing his pistol in his holster. Mason wanted to put up a fight, felt that he should, but knew it could end in Prairie being taken from him as well.

***

An hour later, Adrianna stormed through the door having come home early from her night out. She pitched her expensive clutch on the table and kicked off her fancy heels. "Mace, what have you done?" She glared at him.

"What have *I* done? How is this my fault? You knew what Wynter was going to ask me and decided to keep me in the dark. Did you know she's been speaking to a therapist about changing her sex? Did you know she's been taking testosterone? What else have you been hiding from me?"

Adrianna waved her hands. "Don't try to blame this on me. What part of *be supportive* did you not understand?"

"Mom! Daddy! Please! Both of you, just stop it!" Prairie demanded. "Wynter is gone. Fighting about it isn't going to help."

Mason had no desire to make things worse for Prairie by quarreling. "I spoke with Ian. He's going to file an injunction first thing in the morning. We'll get her back. But I want both of them taken out of that school."

"What?" Prairie protested. "All my friends are at Beachman! I've got two years left!"

Adrianna put her arm around Prairie. "We're not taking you out of Beachman. Daddy is just upset right now. Ian will help us get Wynter home, we'll find a compromise that all of us can live with concerning her transition, and everything will go right back to the way it was."

"Wynter is *not* transitioning into a boy. She's our daughter, and I will not allow it!" Mason contended.

"I don't know, Mom," said Prairie. "I don't think Daddy or Wyn are going to bend on this one."

Adrianna scowled at Mason. "That's enough for tonight. I'm going to bed. I think it would be best if you slept on the couch."

Mason stormed off, collected his things from the master bedroom, and took them to Wynter's room. By no means was he going to sleep on the sofa when there was a perfectly good bed not presently occupied.

***

Wednesday morning, the CEO of Poseidon, Roy Costa, called Mason into his office. Costa reclined in his chair as Mason entered the room. "You look like garbage, Mace. Rough night?"

Mason's eyes were bloodshot, and he'd not shaved. "Family drama." He walked to the window and stared out at the neo-gothic spire of the Trump Building just a few doors down.

"I heard." Costa sipped his cappuccino and flipped through the pages of the Wall Street Journal.

"You heard?" Mason made an abrupt about-face. "From who?"

Costa glanced up for a second and quickly back down. "Don't worry. It's not in the Journal—yet. Which is why I called you in."

"What are you talking about?"

"I'm talking about the legal action you're taking."

"Is my house bugged?" Mason felt his face turning red.

"Our—principals…" Costa paused to sip his cappuccino. "…hold anonymity in very high regard. Anything that might pull them into the public eye quickly becomes a glaring red blip on their radar screen." Costa glanced at his phone. "AI monitors everything that's said around these things. Surely you've figured that out by now. But back to what I was saying, this business with the injunction needs to go away."

"Roy! They took my kid! Like—like—a home invasion or something! That's my little girl. I can't sit idly by. This perverted system has convinced her to cut her breasts off! Can you believe that?"

Costa stood up from the sofa. He walked over to Mason and put his hand on his shoulder. "Mace, I hear ya. I really do. But you've got to let this go. You know how these queers are. It's like they have their own little mafia. They run the court of public opinion—the papers, the news, even City Hall—you just got a personal demonstration of what kind of clout they wield."

Costa shook his head with a sympathetic smile. "It's not the kind of attention we need around here."

"Then I'll go prepare my resignation." Mason started toward the door.

Costa followed him. "It ain't that easy. You're a C-Suite officer. You can't just up and jump ship. This isn't news to you. I was very clear about how all of this works when I promoted you."

Mason paused in the doorway. "Roy, this is my little girl. I can't just let it go!"

Costa took a firmer tone. "You're gonna have to. Or find another way to go about it. A way that doesn't involve the courts, the newspapers, the cameras, and doesn't have a bunch of cross-dressing faggots marching up and down Wall Street protesting Poseidon. Because if any of that stuff happens, Wynter's operation is going to be the least of your troubles. You understand who we work for. You've seen what they can do when someone needs to go away. You've got Adrianna, Prairie, and your other two girls to think about. This is the kind of thing you can't come back from. Take the rest of the day off. Go squash this thing with the courts and get your head together."

CHAPTER 4

For their vine is of the vine of Sodom, and
of the fields of Gomorrah: their grapes are
grapes of gall, their clusters are bitter: their
wine is the poison of dragons, and the cruel
venom of asps.

Deuteronomy 32:32-33

Mason got out of the taxicab in Elizabeth, New
Jersey, just south of the port, and paid the driver in
cash. He crossed Trumbull Street to a sprawling
five-story brick building that had been subdivided
and leased to multiple businesses. Mason entered an
unassuming restaurant that occupied one of the
spaces.

A hostess who was much too pretty and dressed much too nice for a hole-in-the-wall restaurant in this neighborhood said, "Welcome to Mama De Luca's. How many are in your party?"

Mason looked around. "Is Gio here?"

"Giovanni?"

"Yeah."

She looked at the bald, heavyset man behind the bar then back to Mason. "Um. I'm not sure. I could ask. Who may I say is inquiring?"

"Mace—Mason Lot."

She directed Mason to the bar. "If you'd like to have a seat, I'll find out if he's around."

"Thanks." Mason took a seat at the bar.

"Can I get you anything?" The bartender looked more like a bouncer than a true mixologist.

"Pellegrino with lime, if you have it."

The beefy Italian nodded and retrieved the sparkling water from a nearby cooler. He opened the bottle and began pouring it into a stemmed glass. "Would you like to see a menu?"

"No thank you," said Mason.

Minutes later, a stocky man with black hair, a gold watch, a gold chain, and several gold rings came to the bar. "Goombah!"

Mason recognized the voice and smiled. He got off the barstool and hugged the sawed-off mobster. "Gio."

"I thought maybe they revoked your passport to New Jersey. How long's it been?"

Mason shook his head. "Too long."

"So, what's going on? Did you eat yet?"

"No."

Gio snapped his fingers. "Gina, I'm going to eat in the office with my old friend here. I want you to wait on us. Bring us an antipasto, some bread, and a bottle of that Chianti I got down in the basement."

"Yes, sir, Mr. Palermo. Would you like some menus?"

Giovanni paused for a moment. "No. Just tell Vinnie to make us pasta for two." Giovanni waved for Mason to follow him. "Where's your phone?"

"I left it at the office," Mason replied.

Giovanni shook his head. "If I could convince these knuckleheads around here that they don't need to take that stinkin' device with them every time they go out for a cannoli, I'd be runnin' this town."

"So you're *not* running Newark?" Mason jested.

"The *old man* is runnin' Newark. And he won't let anyone forget it." They walked through the dining room, then took a private elevator to the second floor. The space was completely open but with several dedicated areas designed for specific functions. A magnificent desk sat near a window overlooking the old Jersey neighborhood. A giant table that sat fourteen seemed to be equally suited for a dinner party or a board meeting. The loft contained a large sitting area with a large-screen television and pool table next to a self-service bar.

Mason gazed at the spread in awe. "Wow! Is this your office?"

"What? I gotta be on Wall Street to have a nice environment to work in?" Gio asked.

"I guess not." Mason touched the fine Italian leather of the sofa as he walked by the sitting area.

Giovanni pointed to the table. "Take a seat. Gina will be up in a few with some food. You know my boys are going to St. Michaels now. Valentino graduates this year. Father Paul is still there."

Mason pulled out a chair at the massive table and took a seat. "Oh, no! Don't even say that name to me. That time he caught me with two ounces of *your* weed, I thought I was done for."

"But what happened?" Gio held his chin high.

"I don't know. Nothing ever came of it. Mercy triumphs over judgment, I guess."

"Come on. You don't believe that. You know what happened, right?"

"No, what?"

"Are you serious? You don't know?"

"No!"

"My pops leaned on him." Gio gave a quick shrug.

"Your dad threatened Father Paul to get him not to hand me over to the police?"

"I thought you knew." Gio lifted his hands.

"How would I know? You never said anything."

"I didn't think I *had* to. I thought you'd put two and two together."

Gina knocked before entering with a plate of cured Italian meats, and assorted cheeses. She placed a basket of bread on the table and opened the

Chianti. She set the table with silverware and side plates, poured the wine, then left without speaking.

Giovanni placed his napkin in his lap, made the sign of the cross, then took a piece of focaccia from the breadbasket. "So, what brings you back to Jersey?"

Mason sniffed the wine before tasting it. "I hate to admit it, but I'm in a jam."

Giovanni took a long gulp of his wine. "Okay, spill it then. What's happenin'?"

Mason tried not to get emotional. He spent several minutes explaining his recent troubles to his old schoolmate.

"What can I do to help?" Giovanni listened with concerned eyes.

The elevator door opened, and Gina emerged with two plates of pasta. Mason remained silent while Gina served them and topped off their glasses with Chianti.

She cleared the antipasto dishes. "Should I bring another bottle, Mr. Palermo?"

Giovanni lifted his shoulders. "Mace, what do you say? Can you drink a little more?"

Mason shook his head. "I probably won't finish this glass."

Giovanni winked at Gina. "He'd have never turned down a second bottle when we were younger—trust me on that."

Gina gave an obligatory smile and returned to the elevator. "Then I'll leave you gentlemen alone so you can talk."

Mason waited for the elevator doors to close. "I need a couple of your boys to grab her from the foster home where she's living. Take her to a safe house and keep her under lock and key until I can figure out a way through this mess."

Giovanni was quiet for a moment. "Wow! I never thought I'd hear a request like that from you."

"I don't have a choice. They're going to mutilate her body if I don't do something."

"You're serious about this."

"Serious as a heart attack," Mason replied.

Giovanni's jovial demeanor faded, and he became forlorn. "I wish I could help you. I really do. But my hands are tied on this one, I'm afraid."

"What are you talking about?" Mason felt baffled.

"The old man—he says we can't have nothin' to do with Poseidon. He'd lose his mind if he even found out yous and me were havin' lunch. And it ain't just my own skin I'm trying to protect. My pops is a made man. He's the one who brought me into the organization. If I slip up, they'll take it out on the both of us. That's how they keep people in line these days.

"Back when all this stuff with the banks started and it became obvious that they were going to switch over to a central bank digital currency, all the families in New York and New Jersey started scrambling to buy legit businesses and get as much paper into the system as possible without being detected. We even got all new accountants—the guy

I got stuck with is always trying to show me how to reduce my tax liability. I'm like, buddy, I ain't trying to cut no corners here. I want to pay as much in taxes as possible.

"But I digress. The reason I brought it up was because I told the old man about you. I was going to bring a pile of cash down to you to stick in that Olympus fund. The old man cut me off before I even finished talking. Let me tell you something. He ain't afraid of nobody—Colombo, Gambino, Genovese—he'll go toe-to-toe with any of 'em.

"But I mention *Poseidon* and the old man looked like he was going to have a stroke. I don't know who you're workin' for, Mace. But whoever they are, they must make our people look like a bunch of choir boys."

Giovanni took another long gulp and finished his wine. "Besides, if Wynter goes missing, you'll be the first suspect. If your boss is telling you to leave this alone, you better do what he says. If you get whacked, you ain't gonna be able to help her nor anyone else in your family."

"If I don't put a stop to this, what kind of father am I?" Mason lost his appetite. "Can you get me a gun?"

"Be reasonable, Mace. This ain't you. Not for nothin' but you don't have the—skill set...to pull this kind of thing off."

"I'm well aware of that." Mason drank more of his wine than he should have. "But I'm out of options. I must protect my little girl. They've brainwashed her and she's not thinking straight. If she goes through with this, she'll regret it and it will be too late.

Mason stood up from his chair and walked toward the window. "I thought by having her in a private school we'd be immune from all this nonsense. Everyone knows about the craziness in the public schools, but you'd think if you're willing to pony up forty-K a year for tuition, you're essentially buying a pass from the insanity. I guess I should have put them in a Catholic school. I let Adrianna make all of those decisions."

Giovanni got up from the table and walked over to stand by Mason. "Saint Michaels has an entire class on diversity and inclusion. I'm not sure anyone can avoid it unless you keep your kids home and teach them yourself. I used to think those homeschoolers were a bunch of kooks, but I'm not so sure anymore."

"Will you help me—with the gun?" Mason pleaded.

Giovanni took a deep breath and put his hand on Mason's shoulder. "How about this? Jimmy Feathers has got some guys inside NYPD. He can probably get into the OCFS system and find out who Wynter's doctor is. If we get to the doctor, we can put the kibosh on the whole transition process."

Mason felt a glimmer of hope. "What, like send the doctor a threatening letter?"

Giovanni lifted his shoulders. "Hundreds of people are involved in bad car accidents every day in New York City. If a doctor is out of work for six months, his patients will have to see someone else. Elective surgeries get pushed to the back of the line, especially if we're talking about procedures the government is funding.

"You said Wynter's whole strategy is to get the city to pay for everything before she turns eighteen. No doubt, it's not a bad plan on her part. But once you subject yourself to the machinations of the municipality, you step into a bureaucratic quagmire that is inherently bogged down by red tape. One missing signature on a form can delay a project for months. This isn't the private sector where your doctor gets T-boned by a delivery truck one day and you have an appointment with somebody else a week later. This is government on top of government on top of government.

"Runnin' into this thing half-cocked and trying to abduct your own child isn't the way to go about it. You find your enemy's weakness and use it against them."

Mason considered the offer. "But T-boning the doctor with a delivery truck? That's kind of brutal, don't you think?"

Giovanni patted Mason on the back. "You've got a lot of people to blame for all of this. The school teachers who fed Wynter this horse hockey, OCFS who took her by force from your home, even society at large for accepting this tripe. But if there's one person you can point your finger at for helping Wynter mutilate her body, it's the doctor managing her transition. This ain't no innocent bystander, Mace.

"And let me tell you somethin'—no doctor better think about takin' a knife to change the gender of one of *my* boys. Cause I got my own knife. And I got *places* to take that doctor—places down in South Jersey where nobody will hear him scream. Nobody but me, that is. Trust me, if it were my kid, that doctor couldn't wish for anything better than to get T-boned by a delivery truck."

Giovanni exhaled deeply as if to calm himself. "At any rate, it's the best way to keep this atrocity from happening to Wynter."

Mason nodded. "Okay, thanks. What do I owe you for all of this?"

Giovanni held open his arms for a hug and embraced Mason. "You're like family to me. There's nothin' I wouldn't do for you. You don't owe me anything."

"Thank you." Mason was touched by his old friend's willingness to help.

"But," said Giovanni. "If you ever wanted to return the favor…"

If Mason had been talking to any other gangster, he'd have seen this last statement coming. However, he believed the exception to be in good faith. "Name it. I'll do anything."

Giovanni put one hand on Mason's shoulder. "This thing with the banks, the currency, and all that, you've got your ear to the tracks on this stuff.

If you hear something rolling down the rails, give me a heads up."

"Gio, you know enough about the people I work for to understand that I can't make any trades on the information I hear."

Giovanni shook his head. "I ain't askin' for that. I know enough about the people you work for that I wouldn't take a tip like that even if you gave it to me. I'm just askin' that if you hear the big one coming, you'll let me know."

Mason frowned. "Well, the big one is coming."

"Yeah, yeah, I know. But more specifically—when they're about to detonate the charges." Giovanni took a small black pouch out of his desk drawer and handed it to Mason.

"What's this?" Mason felt the weight. "Is it a burner phone?"

"Ha! There ain't no such thing." Giovanni shook his head. "Phones will co-locate. The FBI uses that feature to track who you're associating with. It's a burner *tablet*. It doesn't connect to cellular service. Only use it on public Wi-Fi, and only on a network you never use with your phone. There's an index card inside with an email address and a password. The pouch blocks all electronic signals so when you take out the tablet, power off your phone and slip it inside the pouch before you turn on the tablet—just to be safe. Shoot me a message if it looks like it's all about to come tumbling down."

Mason nodded. "I can do that."

CHAPTER 5

The lofty looks of man shall be humbled, and the haughtiness of men shall be bowed down, and the LORD alone shall be exalted in that day.

Isaiah 2:11

Mason arrived back at 14 Wall Street shortly after four o'clock Wednesday afternoon. Portia Olyphant, Poseidon's Chief Financial Officer came storming out of her office. "Mace, where have you been all day?"

"Handling some personal business. Roy gave me the day off. I just stopped by to pick up some things I left in my office."

"Have you not seen what's going on?"

"With what?"

"The markets. Check your phone! I'm trying to stem a mass exodus from the Olympus Fund. I need your help."

"Peleus has been short since Monday. You had to know something was coming down the pike."

"Something, but not of this magnitude. All three circuit breakers had been tripped by two o'clock. Trading for the day stopped two hours early! Tell me this isn't news to you! Where were you?"

He shook his head. "You saw the options the Peleus Fund was buying. You should have hedged. Anyway, the Olympus Fund is just a beard."

"The traders were specifically told *not* to hedge Olympus." She pressed her lips together.

"Then what do you want me to do about it?"

"Get on the phone and help with consoling our investors. Olympus may be a beard, but if it goes belly-up, we'll have no cover for Peleus. This is serious, Mace. They're saying Goldman might not make it through the night."

Mason could think of nothing else except Wynter. "I'm compliance. Customer relations isn't in my scope. Get sales and marketing to start making phone calls."

"They're already on it." Portia scowled. "When your house is on fire you don't walk past the extinguisher just because you don't have an FDNY badge. This is all hands on deck!"

"Get Liam. I'm sure he'll be happy to chip in."

"He's a child, but trust me. I've already put him to work."

"Then get the traders to help. They're the ones who make the big bucks." Mason found his phone inside his desk drawer. He shoved it in his pocket and stopped at the doorway being blocked by Portia.

"You're *not* leaving!" She stood firm.

"Get out my way!" Mason demanded.

She crossed her arms and stayed put. Mason pushed past her. She followed him to the elevator. "Mason, if you walk out that door, I'll have you fired!"

"Good luck with that." He pressed the *down* key and waited for the elevator door to open.

She continued to badger him even as the doors closed. "Mason Lot, I don't care if Roy gave you the whole month off! This is an emergency..." Her voice trailed off into an indistinguishable garble.

Once he reached the ground level, Mason took out his phone to see just how bad the market route had been. He hoped it would be enough to distract him from his preoccupation with Wynter's situation.

"Eight thousand points! Wow!" Mason stopped walking when he exited the building's revolving door onto Wall Street.

He heard a loud thump, similar to the sound associated with a vehicle that had backed into a barricade or another car, but without the tell-tale crunch. A woman screamed. Mason lifted his eyes to see what she was looking at. The body of a man about Mason's age wearing a gray suit lay on the brick pavement of Wall Street fifty feet away. He surveyed the area to look for a shooter, but of course, he'd heard no gunshot.

Onlookers took out their phones and began filming the lifeless corpse. Mason looked up toward the top of the New York Stock Exchange building that was directly across the street from him. He saw an open window on the eleventh floor.

Mason hurried to the man who had a puddle of blood forming around his head. "I bet this guy was in finance for 9/11, the 2008 crash, and COVID. He survived all of that but today was more than he could take." He checked for a pulse, but the man was dead. Mason took out his phone and made a call.

"911. What's your emergency?"

"Hi, a man is lying dead in front of the NYSE on Wall Street, right before it intersects with Broad. It looks like he may have jumped."

"Did you check for a pulse?"

"Yes. He's dead."

"We'll have someone there within the hour. Can you stay with the victim?"

"For an hour?"

"If he's already dead, it's a low-priority call. It's been a busy day, sir."

"I can't stand here for an hour."

"Okay. Can an officer reach you at this number if they need to ask you any questions?"

"Yes, but I've told you everything I know."

"I'll make a note of that. Have a good day, sir. I've got a full switchboard that I need to get to."

"Yeah, have a good day." Mason ended the call and frowned at the man near his feet.

Mason continued up Wall Street. He scanned the high floors of the buildings he passed for open windows or people near the edges of the roofs. He was more concerned about getting hit by falling stockbrokers than checking the financial news.

Once he reached Water Street, Mason hailed a cab. He closed the door and took out his phone. "Midtown, please. Eighty-fifth and Second Ave."

An ambulance ran a red light with its sirens blaring. The cab driver slammed the brakes, nearly colliding with the emergency vehicle. Once again, imminent peril overtook Mason's curiosity about the markets and he put his phone down.

"The world is going crazy, huh?" asked the cab driver.

"Yeah, seems like it." Mason watched the ambulance racing toward South Street and realized it was not responding to the dead jumper on Wall Street.

"You work down here?" the cabbie inquired.

"Yeah."

"Must have been a rough day. Most of the time, I envy you guys. Wonder what it would be like to have a fancy office, wear a five-thousand-dollar suit, eat at a restaurant with white table clothes for lunch—not today. I'll keep my taxi.

"Guy on the radio said the market might not even open tomorrow. Ain't heard of the stock market closing without it being a holiday or something since September 11th. Were you in the city on 9/11?"

"I was in Newark. I saw the smoke."

"Smoke for days," said the cab driver. "Felt like the end of the world."

Police sirens screamed southbound on Water Street. The cabbie stopped long enough to see where the patrol cars were coming from and going. "Today kinda has the same feel."

The cab driver continued cautiously toward midtown. "So, you must work for one of these big hedge funds. Where do you recommend hiding out until the smoke clears?"

"I'm not a trader. I work in compliance."

"Oh, okay." The cabbie nodded like he understood but furrowed his brow like maybe he didn't.

Mason felt safe enough to pull out his phone once more and scroll through the news feeds. He frowned at the top story which told of absolute bedlam in the foreign exchange markets.

"You reading about the meltdown?" the cab driver asked.

"The BRICS Plus nations: Brazil, Russia, India, China, South Africa, and Saudi Arabia, have formalized a shared central bank. They launched a gold-backed trade currency a couple of years back, but this is significantly more comprehensive."

Mason continued scanning the article. "They've also launched a new digital common currency that will replace their respective domestic paper currencies. It's like the euro for residents of the BRICS nations.

"They planned this," Mason mumbled. "The BRICS new central bank has already issued account cards to the citizens of the member countries. They rolled this out as seamlessly as a new flavor of ice cream.

"The new BRICS central bank digital currency will be backed by gold—it's financial warfare," he explained. "The dollar, the euro, and all the other Western currencies are backed by nothing but burgeoning debt and governments that spend money like celebrity housewives."

The cabbie frowned in the rearview mirror. "So, what does that mean—for people like me?"

"Higher prices, for one thing—much, much higher. It could cause supply chain disruptions…"

"Recession?"

Mason corrected, "Depression. For most of the past century, our standard of living has depended on the US dollar being the world's reserve currency. We've been able to export worthless pieces of green paper in exchange for resources and labor inputs. That all ended today—at least for half of the globe, it did."

The cabbie hit the brakes and stopped short. "The cops have got Pearl Street closed off. We'll have to find a way around this mess."

Mason again ignored the news of mayhem in the markets and shifted his attention to situational awareness. "It looks like they're waving vehicles through."

"Yeah," the driver acknowledged. "But they're takin' their sweet time about it."

Mason kept watch as the taxi inched forward at a glacial pace.

"Okay, okay," said the cabbie. "They've got the ramp entrance to the Brooklyn Bridge blocked off. It seems to be moving once we get beyond the underpass."

The taxi picked up speed as they passed below the steel girders of the flyover. Mason watched the Brooklyn Bridge exit ramp as they drove by. "The bridge must be closed coming from Brooklyn also. I don't see anyone coming off."

The cabbie replied, "Only three reasons they close the Brooklyn Bridge. Number one, construction. But DOT puts out a bulletin on that and taxi companies are in the loop. So, it ain't construction. Two, a bomb threat, or three, a jumper."

Mason frowned, figuring the odds were against a bomb threat, given his previous encounter at the NYSE. Rush hour traffic was brutal, as usual, but they encountered no other out-of-the-ordinary slowdowns for the rest of the ride home.

He had the cabbie drop him off a few blocks from his apartment. He powered off his phone, took out the tablet, connected to the public Wi-Fi of a nearby coffee shop, and sent Giovanni a message.

You probably already know this, but the walls just came down. We're not coming back from this one. If you have any last-minute financial preparations you need to make, I'd do it now.

CHAPTER 6

It is well enough that people of the nation do not understand our banking and monetary system, for if they did, I believe there would be a revolution before tomorrow morning.

Henry Ford

Mason walked into his apartment Wednesday evening. Adrianna was standing in the living room with a glass of red wine in her hand watching the financial news network. The empty bottle was on the coffee table behind her.

Prairie was in the kitchen eating leftover pizza. "Hey Daddy!" She wiped her hands on a paper towel and came to meet him.

"Hey, Sweet Pea." He squeezed her tight.

She kissed him and returned to her pizza. "Did you talk to the lawyer? Is Wynter going to come home?"

Mason sighed. "It's complicated. But trust that I'm doing everything I can."

Prairie pressed her lips together. "That means she isn't coming home."

Of all his children, Prairie was the least likely to fall for a platitude, so he didn't try. "I'm afraid not, Sweet Pea. At least not anytime soon."

Adrianna noticed that Mason was home. She turned with a look of despair. "Mace, are we going to be okay?" Unlike Prairie, Adrianna was digging for a platitude.

"We'll be fine. This is all part of the normal market cycle," he said.

Prairie narrowed her eyes in unbelief. "Normal market cycle? People are standing in line to get a window to jump out of."

Mason lowered his brow and shook his head signaling for her to not further upset Adrianna. "I'm going to get a shower. Would you like me to order dinner first?"

"I'm not hungry," said Prairie.

"Because you filled up on leftover pizza." Mason frowned.

Prairie shrugged and glanced at the empty wine bottle. "Mom obviously wasn't going to make dinner."

"Do whatever you want. I probably won't eat much." Adrianna slugged back the rest of her wine and picked up the bottle to carry to the kitchen. She tossed the empty and pulled a second bottle from the rack in the cupboard.

Mason didn't want to eat alone. He smiled at Prairie. "What if I order Korean?"

Her eyes lit up. She put the slice of pizza she'd been working on back in the box and placed the box back in the refrigerator. "Can I order?"

"Sure." He took out his credit card and handed it to Prairie. Satisfied with the outcome of their dinner plans, he proceeded to the bathroom and showered. Afterward, he put on his sweatpants and a tee-shirt. Before leaving the bedroom, he noticed the pill bottle on Adrianna's bedside table.

Mason walked over to inspect the medication. "Xanax." He spun the bottle around. "Do not mix with alcohol." He put the bottle back on the table and went to the living room.

She had opened the second bottle of wine and served herself a generous pour. "How did this happen? I thought the Fed and the FDIC had the problems with the banks worked out."

Prairie came to sit on the loveseat with a glass of wine.

"What are you doing?" Mason scolded.

"I asked Mom. She said I could have a glass."

"Adrianna! Why would you say that? And on a school night?"

Adrianna turned around as if unsure of what he was talking about. "I didn't tell her she could have any."

"Yes, you did, Mom!" Prairie argued. "I said, *hey, Mom, is it okay if I get a glass?* Then you said, *go ahead, honey.*"

"I didn't know you were talking about the wine. I wasn't paying attention." Adrianna seemed unsure about the conversation.

"You weren't paying attention." Prairie looked at Mason as if expecting him to reprimand her mother.

"Just go pour it out." Mason pointed to the kitchen.

"No, don't pour it out." Adrianna stood up and took the glass from Prairie. She poured it into her own glass, taking the empty one to the dishwasher.

Prairie whispered to Mason, "You'll wish you'd let me drink it before the night's over."

"How can they let all these smaller banks fail?" Adrianna returned gesturing toward the TV. "Look, Long Island Trust, I had a car loan with them right after college. That's over fifty banks that the FDIC has taken over today."

She turned to Mason. "They're saying the government isn't going to step in this time. Accounts that are over the FDIC-insured limit will lose everything over two hundred and fifty thousand. How much do we have in the bank?"

Mason looked at Prairie and then back to Adrianna. "We can talk about that later."

Prairie wrinkled her nose. "What? Do you think I'm going to go blab at school about how poor we are?"

"Poor?" Mason wasn't expecting that response.

"At *my* school, we're poor."

"What do you think *poor* is?" Mason quizzed.

Prairie lifted her shoulders. "I don't know. I figure you make less than two million a year. Probably less than one point five. I bet you take home less than a million after taxes—especially after you pay New York City income tax."

Mason tightened his jaw, uncomfortable about her acute assessment.

"Am I right?" she prodded.

He turned his attention back to Adrianna. "Our cash is at Chase. It's not going anywhere. And it's under the limit anyway. We're insured."

"So I *am* right." Prairie crossed her arms.

The doorbell rang.

"It's dinner!" Prairie hurried to answer it.

Mason welcomed the interruption. Prairie brought plates and they ate in the living room.

"Help me understand this, Mace." Adrianna's speech was beginning to slur. "What's happening?"

Mason turned down the television and explained the nature of the most recent banking meltdown. "A large chunk of the assets listed on a bank's balance sheet typically consists of US Treasuries and high-grade corporate bonds. For the better part of the past decade, the Fed has kept interest rates near zero. Then, during COVID, the Fed and the US government nearly doubled the money supply. That caused inflation numbers to skyrocket. The only tool the Fed had for bringing inflation under control was raising interest rates. So that's what they did.

"But, in taking the Fed funds rate from a quarter of a percent to five percent in about a year, they inadvertently caused massive losses on those banks' balance sheets in the form of unrealized losses. The losses had yet to materialize so no one paid much attention."

Prairie interjected, "Until Silicon Valley Bank."

"That's right. But once they went under, the cat was out of the bag," said Mason.

Adrianna sipped her wine. "But that was a long time ago. I thought they fixed all of that."

"They papered over it," said Mason. "And by the time SVB blew up, they'd already painted themselves into a corner. The regional bank crisis bailouts, by definition, pumped more money into the system causing inflation to blaze hotter again. The Fed found itself back where it started with no way to combat rising consumer prices except to hike rates. If they did that, it would create more instability in the banking system. If they did nothing, inflation would cross the point of no return. And all of this was against a backdrop of the de-dollarization trend."

Prairie interrupted once more. "Which America started by kicking Russia out of the Swift system forcing them to sell oil in currencies other than the dollar."

"I'm afraid so," said Mason. "And many other countries were eager to get away from the global reserve currency which they felt put them at a disadvantage."

Prairie pointed to the television. "Then this happened. BRICS announced their own central bank digital currency. They knew it would create havoc in the West, right Daddy?"

Mason picked at his plate. "That's right. Today's move put the dollar in freefall. US Treasuries are a dollar-denominated asset, so they're cratering also. That's pushing up interest rates on treasuries and exacerbating the unrealized losses with the banks. Because of SVB, high-net-worth account holders were onto the fragility of the banking system. They're pulling deposits left and right.

"What BRICS pulled off today will have a hyperinflationary effect on the dollar. If the government starts bailing out these banks, it will be like pouring gasoline on the fire."

Adrianna chugged her wine and poured another glass. "So we're not okay."

Mason put his hand on her shoulder. "We're as okay as anyone else. Probably more so than most."

"What if the fund goes under?" Adrianna asked. "What will you do?"

He moved the wine bottle out of her reach. "Poseidon manages a private wealth fund also. It was well hedged against today's losses. We're not going anywhere."

Prairie narrowed her eyes. "Are you sure about that, Daddy?"

"Yeah. We'll be okay."

***

Thursday morning, Mason's alarm sounded. He shut it off so it wouldn't wake Adrianna who was snoring heavily. He checked his phone to see a message from Roy. *Markets are closed today. Plus, we've got protestors setting up tents again in the park. They're on the sidewalk all the way down Broadway, up against the fence around Trinity Church. Caused some damage last night. Broke windows outside of TD Bank on the corner of Wall and Broadway and set fire to a trash heap in front of the Trump Building. Could get worse before it gets better. We might be working from home for a while.*

Mason texted him back. *Thanks for the heads up. I'll pass the word along to Liam. Let me know if you need anything.*

Mason thought about going back to sleep. But he worked on Wall Street, so he felt obligated to get up and monitor the damage. He went to the kitchen and started a pot of coffee. He turned on the television and lowered the volume.

He read the ticker at the bottom of the screen. *New York City Schools are closed for the rest of the week due to ongoing civil disruptions. Wyn and Prairie will be happy to hear about that.* His stomach sank as he realized Wyn wasn't home. *Prairie will be elated, anyway.*

Beachman followed the schedule for public schools in holidays and closures. He walked softly to her room, picked up her cell phone, and swiped the screen.

She opened her eyes and whispered, "Daddy, what are you doing?"

"Turning off your alarm. No school today."

"Why?"

"This stuff with the banks. People are protesting and causing trouble."

"Okay. Thanks." She rolled over and pulled up the covers.

"Sure." He kissed her head, walked out, and closed the door quietly.

Once back in the kitchen, Mason poured a cup of coffee and took it to the couch. He watched the talking heads prognosticate about the extent of the crisis, the future of the markets, and the reactions of the US government to the ongoing debacle.

His phone buzzed. He looked at the screen to see a message from Daphne. *Hi, Dad. Hope all is okay at your firm. Rumors are swirling at Goldman. They may lay off three-quarters of the trading floor. Steve wants to know if you can get him a job if he gets let go.*

Mason didn't like Steve and wouldn't lift a finger to help him. He dialed Daphne's number. "Good morning."

"Hi, Dad."

"Is Steve around?"

"No, he went down to the gym here in the building," she said. "Why? Did you want to talk to him?"

"I wanted to talk to you. I was just asking if he was there."

"He's a wreck over this whole thing."

"Yeah, everyone on the street is shaken up."

"So, are you guys going to be okay?"

"Poseidon will be fine. We don't have much exposure to finance."

"Can you get him a job then?"

"We'll probably make some cuts. I doubt anyone will be looking for traders anytime soon. But *you're* welcome to come home—if you need to. We'd love to have you here."

She sighed. "Did Wyn come home yet?"

"I'm afraid not. Do you have class today?"

"I haven't checked yet."

"If you don't why don't you come by?"

"If it's a madhouse out there, I don't want to get caught in the chaos."

"I could send a car to pick you up."

"Is that an invite for Steve also?"

Mason gritted his teeth. "Sure. Why not?"

"Alright then. Maybe we'll see you later. Otherwise, tell Mom and Prairie I said *hi*."

"Okay, love you."

"Love you too." Daphne ended the call.

Mason put the phone down and turned up the volume on the television.

***

An hour later, Prairie came into the living room carrying a cup of coffee. Mason frowned at her beverage choice but said nothing.

"What's going on?" she inquired.

"The Secretary of State is about to give a press conference."

"The Secretary of State? What does she have to do with the markets?"

Mason sipped his coffee. "The way BRICS rolled out their CBDC was malicious. It's obvious they wanted to create financial turmoil in the West."

"Kinda like revenge by Russia for the US booting them out of Swift? Or China for the US sticking our nose in their business with Taiwan?"

"We've got a knack for ticking people off."

"I doubt this press conference is going to be about de-escalating the tension."

Mason put his arm around her. "You're probably right."

Prairie typed on the keyboard of her phone. "Is it okay if I go over to Marco's to study since I don't have class today?"

Mason didn't like the idea. "The city is unstable. I want you to stay around the house today."

"Then can he come over here?"

"How old is Marco?"

"Seventeen."

"Isn't he a little old for you? Why don't you have one of your girlfriends come over?"

"If Wynter was here and she wanted to have a boy over, you'd be so glad that she wasn't gay, you wouldn't grill her about it. You'd be thrilled. You'd probably send a car to pick the guy up."

He stitched his brows together. "I don't think that's accurate."

"Anyway, Marco is the only person at my school that I can discuss geopolitics with. His dad is the Italian ambassador to the UN. I certainly couldn't talk about that stuff with any of those silly girls at my school."

"I thought you liked the girls in your class."

"Daddy—they're *kids*."

He understood her need for intellectual stimulation but feared she was growing up too fast. "If he comes over here, your bedroom door stays open."

"Thanks, Daddy!" She typed away on her phone.

"It's starting." Mason turned up the television volume.

Secretary of State Lola Miller stepped to the podium. Her eyes were red, and she looked like she'd been in a rush to get ready for the presser. "Good morning. After much deliberation between the president, DOD, and the State Department, the United States has decided to take action against the BRICS member countries.

"The disruption caused by BRICS was deliberate and hostile. How they rolled out their new central bank digital currency was designed to destabilize the US dollar and wreak havoc on US and allied markets.

"The rollout was done in the middle of the night and without warning. The fact that the infrastructure and payment systems were activated without informing the Bank of International Settlements or the International Monetary Fund serves as proof of the malevolent intentions of the BRICS Plus member countries. This constitutes an act of financial warfare and cannot be ignored.

"In the past, the United States has generously supplied military hardware to several of the BRICS Plus members. US companies have supplied fighter jets, military helicopters, drones, high-altitude missile defense systems, missiles, radar systems, as well as man-portable weapons to several BRICS Plus members such as the United Arab Emirates, Saudi Arabia, Mexico, Brazil, South Africa, and India.

"An undisclosed provision of the United States agreement with US military manufacturers such as Lockheed Martin, Raytheon, and Boeing is that they include a kill-switch microchip in all military hardware sold to foreign governments. Since we have determined the action taken by the BRICS nations to be tantamount to an act of war, we believe it is in the United States' best interest to trigger these kill switches, rendering that hardware impotent so it cannot be used against us in further acts of aggression by the BRICS alliance."

"So much for cooler heads prevailing." Prairie stood up from the couch. "I've got to get ready. Marco will be here in an hour."

Mason watched her walk away, wishing that she could remain his little girl just a little bit longer.

CHAPTER 7

And I saw when the Lamb opened one of the seals, and I heard, as it were the noise of thunder, one of the four beasts saying, Come and see. And I saw, and behold a white horse: and he that sat on him had a bow; and a crown was given unto him: and he went forth conquering, and to conquer.

Revelation 6:1-2

The protests of Thursday morning grew into riots by that night. Schools remained closed on Friday and civil unrest increased through the weekend. On Sunday, the National Guard rolled into the streets of Manhattan to restore order.

The Sunday morning news announced that the federal government alongside the British and European central banks had reached a solution to bring stability back to the markets.

Mason, Adrianna, and Prairie watched the television with great anticipation, in hopes the crisis was abating.

Blair Cornelius, host of Global Broadcasting Company's Sunday morning show, *This Week*, interviewed her first guest, US Treasury Secretary Miles Ramsey. "Mr. Secretary, thank you for taking time out of your very busy schedule to speak with us this morning. I'm sure you've been burning the midnight oil to see us through this terrifying ordeal. But I, for one, am very grateful for your efforts."

Ramsey had dark circles under his eyes. "Thank you for having me, Blair. And thank you for the kind words, but I must confess, it's been a team effort."

"Of course, and what has the *team* come up with in regard to the banking and currency crisis that began Wednesday morning?"

Ramsey loosened his tie, as if too tired to care about his appearance on national television. "Anytime a public official prefaces his statement by saying *we're trying to make the best of a bad situation*, I think people feel apprehensive, but in this case, it's more than a cliché. I'm truly pleased with the workarounds we've been able to institute.

"One of the things we started seeing long before Wednesday was high-net-worth account holders repositioning their wealth into short-duration government bonds such as the three-month T-Bill and many of these depositors were utilizing the TreasuryDirect website.

"Accounts at TreasuryDirect are only for US Bonds so they don't offer a savings, checking, or money-market-type function. So, what we've done is link the FedNow digital payment system to TreasuryDirect to make transfers instantaneously. However, FedNow is only set up to accept accounts from private institutions. We came up with a way to integrate the remaining US banks with the FedNow digital payment system. Once the process is complete, account holders will be able to move funds seamlessly from their TreasuryDirect account to their FDIC-insured bank accounts."

Blair sat back on the large sofa on the show's set and crossed her legs. "As long as those funds stay under the FDIC limit."

"That's correct," Miles Ramsey replied.

"But what about the banks that have folded?" she asked. "What are those depositors going to do?"

"Those banks will be absorbed by one of the four remaining banks. It's a lot of data, but we hope to have everyone's accounts transferred, up and running no later than Friday. That will give us next weekend for everyone to sort of adjust and we'll be ready to reopen markets on the following Monday."

Blair Cornelius opened her eyes wide. "Oh, so you're planning to keep markets closed all week. Wait—did you say *four* remaining banks?"

"I did." Ramsey nodded. "Chase, Citi, Bank of America, and Wells Fargo."

"That's big news. Are you saying all the others are gone?"

"All the banks are still here. They've just been absorbed by one of the four I mentioned."

"You didn't mention TD Bank. I assume that's because they're Canadian."

"Unfortunately, TD also failed. Chase will be integrating those accounts into their system."

"Just the American accounts, obviously."

"The Canadian banks as well. This crisis is global," said Ramsey.

"And the Bank of Canada was unable to throw them a lifeline?"

"This was a tectonic blow to the entire world banking system, but the US, Canada, Europe, and Great Britain have worked together to produce a viable solution that keeps everything running smoothly. Like I said, every bank account that existed on Wednesday of last week is still here. The only difference will be the letterhead on your statements. But it's going to cause a log jam and be counterproductive if everyone tries to log on to their account right now. By Wednesday, you'll see a redirect for your online banking account that will take you to your new bank. Then, you should be able to access all the features of your accounts by the end of business on Friday.

"I'm not saying all the branches will stay open, obviously. Especially in the larger cities, you'd have instances where you could have three or four branches of the same bank on the same block. That wouldn't be efficient, so I expect to see a significant amount of consolidation."

Blair Cornelius seemed to be processing the news. "But four banks, that's some serious mergers. You said they'll be linked with the new FedNow payment system and TreasuryDirect. But they're independent, other than being member institutions of the Federal Reserve. Is that correct?"

"Mostly." Ramsey nodded. "They'll be *partner* banks."

"But this isn't a nationalization of the banking system, is it? Can you define what a partner bank is?"

Miles Ramsey waved his hand. "It's a legal term that would bore most of your viewers. All of that information will be posted on the Federal Reserve's website by tomorrow evening. Folks are welcome to go read it. I'd do it right before bed as it will probably put you to sleep. But no, I wouldn't say it meets the definition of nationalization."

"When we check our accounts, folks who were under the two-hundred-and-fifty-thousand-dollar FDIC insurance threshold will be made whole, regardless of which bank they were with before the crisis. Is that correct?"

"You'll still have the same purchasing power, yes."

"Hmm. Sounds like a caveat is hidden in that statement somewhere," said Blair Cornelius.

Ramsey seemed reluctant. "It involves the currency. We've decided that Federal Reserve Chair Hassan Alami would be the one to speak on that issue. He'll be giving a press conference this evening."

Blair continued to pry. "You can't drop a cliffhanger like that Mr. Secretary. You're opening up the subject to all sorts of wild speculations that will be much worse than the truth. Talk about misinformation, the Treasury and the Fed will be doing damage control for the next month. Please, for our viewers' sake and your own, elaborate on what you mean."

Ramsey swallowed hard as if he'd just stepped in a pile of dog feces. "The crisis has put all global currencies under an extreme amount of stress. The dollar wouldn't have survived in its current form. We'll be transitioning to a digital dollar."

"You mean like a central bank digital currency? Wouldn't you need approval from Congress to do something like this?"

"Executive order 14067 was passed back in 2022 which authorized exploration of a US CBDC. This digital dollar will function as the local currency for the US and Canada."

"Local? What about internationally? Will the dollar still be a reserve currency?"

Ramsey's forehead beaded up with sweat. He checked his watch. "I've overstayed. We have so much that we're still working on with this. I'll try to answer your question but then I really must get back to work.

"The IMF has long issued credit in units called Special Drawing Rights or SDRs. While SDRs are not technically a currency, the IMF has developed a digital currency based on SDRs called the Universal Monetary Unit or UMU. To make it more recognizable as a digital currency, they're calling it Unicoin. The US-Canadian digital dollar will be pegged to Unicoin for stability—as will the euro, the pound, and all the other IMF member countries that haven't joined BRICS."

"Your next guest will be more up to speed on the inner workings of Unicoin than me. I've been buried in the minutia of our domestic monetary system. And I'm afraid I must get back to it right away."

Blair shook his hand. "Thank you for your time, Mr. Secretary. You've been incredibly informative and more helpful than you might imagine."

"Thank you, Blair. I've enjoyed speaking with you and I apologize that our time had to be so short."

The screen cut to a commercial for a new anxiety medication.

"This guy should win an Emmy!" Prairie exclaimed.

"Why do you think that?" Adrianna asked.

"His acting—like the Fed and Treasury didn't see any of this coming. Give me a break! Don't you think it's a little too convenient that they already had FedNow built out to act as the infrastructure for a CBDC and that they'd already developed a digital dollar under that executive order from 2022?"

Adrianna rolled her eyes. "You're starting to sound like your father. Everything isn't a conspiracy."

Prairie turned to Mason. "Did you know about that? This executive order 14067?"

"I've heard of it." Because of his job with Poseidon, Mason understood that the CIA must have seen this coming, whether the Fed and Treasury did or not. But he suspected Prairie was correct in her assumptions. He glanced at his phone that was always listening. Unfortunately, he could not elaborate on her hypothesis but was delighted that she was thinking for herself.

Prairie glared at the TV. "And Unicoin? That sounds an awful lot like *unicorn*—like all of this is some sort of magical upgrade."

Prairie crossed her arms as she watched the next guest take a seat on the sofa across from Blair Cornelius. "Who is *this* clown?"

"I've never seen him, but I'm afraid we're about to find out," said Mason.

Blair gushed over her new guest. "Ange de Bourbon, what a pleasure it is to have you here in the studio with me."

The man was in his late forties, fit, had a strong jawline, had perfect hair that was combed back and teased out a bit on the top, with piercing pale blue eyes. He spoke with a distinct French accent which the decerning ear would have known was from France rather than Canadian, and which the French would have known was Parisian. "The pleasure is mine. Thank you for having me."

Blair Cornelius looked as though she might salivate as she continued the interview. "So, I'll have to admit, before Friday, I wasn't familiar with you or your accomplishments. I suppose the best way to describe my first impression of you is the man who everyone knows, but nobody has heard of."

Ange de Bourbon gave a playful smirk that turned into a witty smile. "Okay, if you say so. I hope that's not an insult."

"Oh, and you're funny too. Of course, it isn't. I'm just making an observation. You're so— mysterious. I mean, we've never read about you in the society column, and you've managed to avoid the muckraking typically associated with politics. But as I started researching you for the interview, it turns out you're close friends with Bill Gates, the Clintons… Two weeks ago, you had the Prince and Princess of Wales stay with you at your castle in the

French countryside." She put her hand over her heart. "You have a castle!"

He nodded. "Harry and Meghan were there also. But technically, the château belongs to my family."

"*How* did you get all of them to coexist under one roof?"

He laughed. "Blessed are the peacemakers, right?"

"Yes, but that's second-coming type stuff right there. Wait—you're not the Messiah, are you?"

He winked at her, smiled, and leaned forward. "I'll let you be the judge of that, Blair."

She giggled. "Okay, okay, I'm going to wrap up your bio so folks can get a sense of who you are, then we'll get into the interview. We have *a lot* to discuss.

"You're on the Board of Trustees at the World Economic Forum, you also serve on two boards of philanthropic foundations. One is listed as the second largest private donor to the World Health Organization, the other foots the bill for the annual Bilderberg Group meeting, covering everything from lodging and travel to meals and entertainment.

"Back to the bit about the World Economic Forum, you were at Oxford with Dr. Yuval Harari, is that right?"

"Yes, Yuval and I are very close."

"I've heard rumors that you introduced Yuval to Klaus Schwab, is that true?"

"We all have circles of friends that overlap. It's hard to say."

"Your friendship with Klaus goes way back, is that correct?"

"My mother was an early investor with George Soros' Quantum Fund—she helped to get it off the ground in terms of seed money. She and George became close. She is still very involved with George's Open Society Foundations. He introduced her to Klaus."

"You have an interesting last name. I assume your father is from the House of Bourbon. They trace their ancestry back through the kings of France, Louis the XIV, and all that."

"And a few other European monarchs." He lifted his eyebrows playfully.

"What about your mother? Is she of royal descent?"

"No, not really. She came from a banking family."

"Oh? Which one?"

"Rothschild."

"Well, they're considered royalty where I'm from." Blair laughed. "Alright, we have to take a break. Then, when we come back, we'll hear what Ange de Bourbon has accomplished to keep us all from economic ruin."

Adrianna put her hand over her chest. "Can you imagine—all that money, and influence—having the royals come stay at your castle? It's like a fairy tale!"

Prairie stood up from the sofa and rolled her eyes. "Yeah, he's a regular Prince Charming." She walked to the kitchen and opened the cupboards. "Is it okay if I walk down to the bakery to get some donuts?"

Mason got up to stretch. He stood by the large floor-to-ceiling window overlooking East 85th. He could see a tan Humvee with a machinegun turret parked on the corner of 2nd Avenue. "I'd rather you didn't."

She filled her coffee mug. "We've been cooped up since Wednesday. It's reminiscent of the COVID lockdowns. That's probably why Wyn turned gay. You should let me out of the house before *I* start taking puberty blockers."

Mason snapped. "That's not funny! Your sister is in real trouble. If anything, it's because of that school I'm paying an arm and a leg for! She would've been better off locked up in the apartment."

"Mace!" Adrianna snarled. "Don't say that! It's Prairie's school also. And don't make it sound like we're throwing away money. It's an investment into their future." She turned her attention to Prairie. "Your father didn't mean that. The topic of Wynter is just a sore subject—for all of us." She glared at Mason. "Don't be so harsh on Prairie. She's dealing with the separation from her sister in her own way. And for a teenager, that usually involves sarcasm."

Mason walked to the kitchen to get another cup of coffee. "Your mother is right. I shouldn't have yelled. How about you eat a bowl of cereal to tide you over and then I'll walk to the bakery with you after this interview. I'd just feel better if you weren't out on the street alone with everything that's been going on."

She hugged him. "Sure, Daddy. And I'm sorry. I shouldn't have joked about Wyn."

CHAPTER 8

For thou hast said in thine heart, I will ascend into heaven, I will exalt my throne above the stars of God: I will sit also upon the mount of the congregation, in the sides of the north: I will ascend above the heights of the clouds; I will be like the most High.

Isaiah 14:13-14

"The show is back on." Mason leaned back on the couch.

Prairie brought her cereal to the living room and sat between Mason and Adrianna. "Great. Let's see what kind of eutopia Prince Charming has in store for us."

Blair Cornelius faced the camera. "We're back with *This Week* and my guest is Ange de Bourbon. We're talking about the thing that is on everyone's mind, the financial crisis, and what is being done so we can all get back to normal.

"Mr. de Bourbon, just before you came on, I was speaking with the Treasury Secretary, Miles Ramsey, and he intimated that the US dollar would no longer exist—at least not in the same capacity that it has for so long."

Ange de Bourbon spoke with an empathetic tone. "What I'm going to say will be hard to hear for some. And please, don't take it as a reprimand toward America. I love this country and its people with all my heart. But change is inevitable and more often than not, change is disruptive. My ancestor Louis XVI learned that the hard way. But I would be remiss if I didn't point out that Robespierre failed to grasp how delicate these situations can be as well. He was on the winning side, but his lack of finesse cost him his head, the same as the monarchs.

"All that to say that it's important for the leadership who are helping us navigate these turbulent waters to be neither tone deaf as King Louis and Marie Antoinette were nor oppressive hardliners as Robespierre was.

"But here is the reality Americans will have to come to grips with. After World War II, it was agreed at Bretton Woods that the dollar would be pegged to gold and would serve as the world's reserve currency.

"Obviously, there is great honor in being chosen as the guardian of the globe's currency, but, as we have learned, there is also great temptation. The US was unable to resist the allure of printing a few extra dollars which essentially amounted to free money that could be spent on whatever they wished. And like most indiscretions, it's a little easier the second time, and even easier the third, and fourth, and so on.

"However, we had people like President de Gaulle who noticed that there seemed to be a few more Federal Reserve Notes floating around than there was gold to back them up. This prompted him to lose faith in the Bretton Woods Agreement and he began turning in these suspicious slips of paper in order to repatriate France's gold.

"His assumptions were proven right when other countries followed suit and in 1971, Mr. Nixon was forced to close the gold window and thereby halted US dollar convertibility into gold on demand, officially defaulting on the Bretton Woods Agreement.

"This put the dollar into a tailspin. The US sent Henry Kissinger to Saudi Arabia to broker a deal in which global oil sales would be priced in US dollars in exchange for military support for the Kingdom. This petrodollar system stopped the bleeding and arrested the dollar's freefall.

"That agreement has been under stress for some years and came to a definitive halt on Wednesday, when Saudi Arabia along with the other BRICS nations launched the trade group's own digital reserve currency that will be used exclusively for trade among member nations.

"The action was perceived as being hostile and I won't disagree with that. But at the same time, if we are to move forward through disagreement, we must put ourselves in the other person's shoes. A little compassion and understanding will go a long way.

"So many of these developing countries and emerging markets that have chosen to join the BRICS system have felt the West has unfairly controlled the IMF, Bank of International Settlement, and even the UN. Whether you agree or disagree, you cannot say this argument is without merit.

"Many citizens of these countries have worked harder for longer hours and live in conditions considered to be abject poverty by Western standards. Certainly, there are other elements at play, but this perceived injustice, be it real or imaginary, must not be discounted in the BRICS nations' decision to develop their own currency.

"My hopes are that the swift retaliation taken by the US in disabling member nations' military hardware does not escalate into a greater conflict."

Blair Cornelius lowered her brow. "That's something I hadn't considered. But in the interest of not heading down a rabbit hole, I'd like to ask you about the terms of the new US-Canadian digital dollar. Secretary Ramsey said it would retain the purchasing power of the old dollar, but made it sound like it could be restructured in nominal terms."

"Yes, that's correct. A new digital dollar will be worth roughly two-seventy-five in old dollars. Europe went through the same thing when they converted to the euro, but it still bought about the same amount of goods and services."

"About," said Blair. "Prices sort of rounded up, didn't they?"

"We could see some of that, but if things start to spiral, we're prepared to step in with price controls."

"Price controls? Who would be in charge of that?"

"The IMF and BIS—Unicoin."

"But they don't have authority over domestic pricing. The US is a free market. So is Canada, Europe, and Britain, for the most part."

"It's part of the Unicoin agreement. Much of the price stability, especially around things like corn which makes up a tremendous portion of the standard American diet, has been subsidized by the government. Without the dollar being the reserve currency, those subsidies will be hard to fund."

"But they could be funded through taxation."

"At current debt levels and interest rates, the US will have very little tax revenue left over after servicing the debt. The other Unicoin nations have asked the US to accept austerity measures that ensure America will not become a burden on the rest."

"You're right," said Blair Cornelius with a long face. "This is hard to hear."

Ange de Bourbon pulled his brows together in a sympathetic expression. "I think the best way to look at this is like—you've been winning the lottery. When the dollar was awarded global reserve currency status, it was like America won the lottery. Now, those winnings became depleted but then in the 70's, you got the petrodollar arrangement. It's like you hit the jackpot again.

"That's come to an end, but consider your good fortune. You've been given roads, and internet, and computers, and homes, and cars, and food, and all these glorious trappings that would have cost so much more had the dollar not been the reserve currency.

"Sure, it's heartbreaking that you didn't hit the lottery a third time, and that you'll have to adjust your standard of living, but you're still so far ahead of the rest of the world. Imagine you and your neighbor both work at the same company making the same modest income. The difference is, you won your house in a lottery and your neighbor has a large mortgage. You may have a limited income, but you're still free to spend a larger portion of your weekly paycheck than your neighbor."

Blair Cornelius nodded. "That helps. Things will be changing but we have to look at it like the glass is half full."

"Give me a break!" Prairie protested. "He just said the rest of the globe is demanding we accept austerity measures and that we're going to have to start paying off this gazillion-dollar national debt we've managed to rack up. The glass isn't half full, it's not even half empty—we've got to hold it upside down and shake it to get the last drop."

Mason frowned, trying to anticipate what this revaluation would mean for their standard of living. "I don't think he's being honest about the purchasing power of the digital dollar. I wish we could anticipate the things we are going to need in the future and buy them now."

"Oh, listen to you!" said Adrianna. "The both of you! The man is trying—give him some credit. Even if we knew what we were going to need, where would we put it? We certainly don't have any space in the apartment.

"Besides, clothing styles change. It's not like you can buy that ahead of time. Food will spoil, so that can't be bought before we need it. What else is left? Transportation? The car service doesn't offer a pre-payment plan."

Mason sighed. "I know, I know. I was just thinking out loud. But one thing is for sure, these kinds of things are hard to predict. It can get worse than anyone thinks, and it can happen faster than anyone would imagine." He continued to ponder the issue to himself since he got no support from Adrianna.

Ange de Bourbon continued speaking. "And let's not forget, as bleak as this transition may seem, the new digital dollar will provide us with opportunities we've never considered before. The US can raise interest rates for account holders in one part of the country while lowering them in another. It could even be done on an individual basis to encourage or curtail economic activity as needed in that region or even drill down to specific neighborhoods. It doesn't have to be a one-size-fits-all solution any longer.

"And we've not yet begun to imagine the things we can accomplish with the digital dollar from a social standpoint."

Blair Cornelius wrinkled her brow. "How do you mean?"

"It can serve as the carrot *and* the stick. If an account holder is participating in positive behavior, perhaps an LGBTQ activist that regularly volunteers for Drag Queen Story Hour at their local library, we can thank them, as a society, by awarding them a higher interest rate.

"Your government has faced tremendous pushback in attempting to pass common sense gun laws. Let's say guns and ammunition dealers were excluded from FedNow and the digital dollar platform. Suddenly, you don't need legislation to cure this societal ill. Without a means of transacting business, they'll soon shutter their doors.

"If you recall the Canadian trucker riots years back, participants were simply locked out of their bank accounts. Of course, those who had cash could still find workarounds. But in a cashless system, the manner in which we can influence society to behave properly is endless."

Blair nodded. "You mean like a social credit score—like China's Sesame score. These issues all sound well and good, but you'll have a segment of the population that see these tools as overreach."

Ange de Bourbon rolled his eyes. "Of course. When the automobile came along you had people protesting because they wanted to stay with horse and buggy. But we didn't abandon progress over the preferences of a few naysayers who are determined to stay in the past.

"Imagine what this could mean for the planet. We'll be able to allocate how much people can spend on any single category of expenditures. If you've bought your quota of gasoline for the week, you'll have to take public transportation, carpool, or consider investing in an electric vehicle. And red meat, which produces so much methane to be absorbed into the atmosphere—we can put quotas on that so people will be nudged toward sustainable foods like plant-based options, insect proteins, or lab-grown meats.

"What about people who have suffered unfair treatment or disadvantage because of their skin color, gender identity, or sexuality? They could have their social credit score boosted as a form of reparations for their previous neglect.

"We are living in the information age. We have these amazing tools at our disposal. I believe we have a moral mandate to utilize them to shape our world into the progressive paradise that it can be, to protect our planet for generations to come, and to build upon social inclusivity, diversity, and equality for all. For him who knows the good he should do and doesn't do it, it is a sin."

Blair seemed unfamiliar with the verse borrowed from the Book of James. "You know, that is *so* wise. I'd never thought of it like that."

CHAPTER 9

But the men of Sodom were wicked and sinners before the Lord exceedingly.

Genesis 13:13

Mason watched the financial news on the television mounted on the wall across from the elliptical glider as he finished his workout Tuesday morning. He'd quickly reverted to the routine that he had used during the COVID lockdowns, using the small gym in his condominium rather than the huge fitness center located on the ground floor of his office building on Wall Street. One week had passed since the financial crisis had begun and the solutions were still in the implementation phase.

Mason checked the time on his phone and slowed his pace. Adrianna should be gone to Pilates by now. Mason wiped the sweat from his head and got off the exercise machine.

He and Adrianna had learned their limits of being around each other during COVID so Mason took a proactive approach to schedule his time in such a way that would minimize the friction. Mason took the stairs rather than the elevator back up to his apartment for the added cardiovascular benefit. He was winded when he reached the front door. He walked inside and saw Marco's shoes near the entrance. Mason frowned and made sure Prairie's door was indeed open. "I'm home," he said, hoping to interrupt any romantic activities that may have been going on.

Just then, Wynter's door opened. He felt confused, wondering if Prairie and Marco had decided to use her room to make out.

"Dad?" Wynter walked out. Her eyes were red from crying.

"Honey!" He rushed to her, wanted to hug her, but he was wet with sweat and stinking. "Oh, honey! Let me get a quick shower."

She nodded.

"I'll be right out." Mason hurried to the bathroom and got into the shower, not even waiting for the water to get hot. He rushed to wash his hair and body, got out, and rapidly dried himself just enough to not be dripping wet. He pulled on his pants, grabbed a shirt, and put it on as he returned to Wynter's room to find her still sobbing and sitting on her bed next to Prairie.

Wynter dried her eyes and said to Prairie, "Give me and Dad a chance to talk alone for a minute."

"Sure." Prairie hugged her sister and stood up to leave.

Mason whispered, "Is Marco here?"

Prairie paused in the doorway. "Yeah."

"Leave your door open."

"Yes, sir," she replied.

"I want to come home." Wynter embraced her father.

He pulled her close. "Okay. Do you want to talk about it?"

"I don't know. It's not going to happen—my surgery that is."

"Oh." Mason kept his enthusiasm hidden.

"The physician who was handling my case died."

"Died?" Mason's stomach tightened. "What happened?"

"He was hit by a delivery truck. The driver was texting."

Mason's heartbeat quickened. "You mean like a car wreck? Was the doctor driving?"

"No. Walking across the street."

"I see." Mason had not wanted anyone to die. He'd understood that the doctor would merely be incapacitated.

"All the other physicians that work with the state on minor transition surgeries are filled up. They won't be able to get me in before I turn eighteen."

Mason didn't know how to respond.

She wiped more tears from her eyes. "Anyway, I left the house."

"You notified OCFS, right?"

"No," she said. "I just ran away."

"Honey, you can't do that. We have to go

through the system. They have legal custody of you. If they find you here, we could be charged with kidnapping, and it will be nearly impossible to get you back after that."

She began crying again. "I can't go back. Jamie, the house mom, or overseer, whatever you want to call her. She's a biological male. She lets all the kids at the LGBTQ house drink, use drugs, and do whatever they want.

"After Doctor Rivera was killed and it became obvious that I wasn't going to get my surgery, Jamie got me and her some pot and a bottle of vodka. We got trashed and I passed out. When I woke up, she was, he was…" her voice cracked, and she began bawling uncontrollably.

Mason's face turned red. He needed no further explanation. He held his daughter while she cried. "It's okay. You're not going back there. I'll take care of this. I'll take care of everything."

Minutes later, Wynter said, "I'm sorry, Dad. This is all my fault."

"Sweety, none of this is your fault. But we need to move. Right now, you're a runaway. If the police find you here, it won't end well. Pack a bag, whatever you can find. I'll be right back." Mason got up and went to Prairie's room. "Marco, I hate to be rude, but you're going to have to leave. I have to take Wynter somewhere and Prairie isn't allowed to be home alone with a boy."

"Daddy! He didn't do anything. Don't take this out on Marco!" Prairie argued.

"I know, but it's an unforeseen situation. I'm sorry."

"Yes, Mr. Lot." Marco was polite and got up to leave.

"Let us go with you," said Prairie.

Mason shook his head. "You can't come."

"What if I leave too—until Mom gets home?" Prairie pleaded. "Or we can go to Marco's."

Mason felt bad for embarrassing her like this, but the situation was dire. "What if you guys go have a coffee across the street until Mom gets back?"

"Sure." Marco looked at Prairie. "That's fine with me."

Prairie huffed. "I guess that's my best offer."

"Good." Mason held up his phone and opened the Ring doorbell camera app. "Don't come back before one of us gets home. I'll know, and I'll never trust you again."

"Yes, sir." Marco stood tall as if at attention.

He handed a credit card to Prairie. "Get whatever you want. And don't wander around. The streets still aren't safe."

Mason went to his closet in the master bedroom to get shoes and socks. He grabbed his keys and a tube of one-ounce gold eagles stashed in a wooden box. He removed his phone from his pocket and frowned. It was the only method he had of being sure Prairie would not sneak back in the house with Marco while no one was home. "I hope she doesn't try anything. I can't have this thing tracking me all over town." He tucked the phone below a stack of sweaters on the top shelf and exchanged it for the tablet that Giovanni had given him. Mason checked to be sure no one was watching and took a wad of hundred-dollar bills from a shoe box.

Mason put on his shoes and hurried to the door. "Okay, we have to go! Everyone out. Prairie, that means you. Come on!"

"I'm coming!" she huffed. "Relax! Give me a chance to put some shoes on before you kick me out of my own house."

Mason's retaliation was on his lips, but he held it so as not to offend young Marco. The two teens soon emerged from Prairie's room and walked out the front door.

"When will you be home?" Prairie inquired.

"A couple of hours—it's hard to say."

"Alright then—see you when I see you." She sauntered down the hall toward the elevator.

"Be safe," Mason called. "I love you."

"I will. Love you too." She rounded the corner and was out of sight.

Mason called out to Wynter. "We need to go. Just grab a few things. We can buy anything else you need later."

Wynter exited her room, turned out the light, and looked back inside. She paused as if wishing she could stay. "If I could go back in time, I'd do everything differently."

Mason took ownership of his role in her bad decisions. "Me too, sweetheart. I'd have been more involved—I'd have found a better school, better environment…"

"Don't blame yourself, Dad." She carried her pack to the door.

Mason gave her a pair of sunglasses and a ball cap. "Put these on. We're going to avoid cameras as much as possible."

"Yeah, okay." She pulled the cap over her head and started down the hall.

Mason closed the door and put on his ball cap as well. He caught up with Wynter and the two of them got into the elevator.

"I need your phone," he said. "OCFS can use it to track you."

"Can I at least get my contacts out before you toss it?"

He felt terrible for her. "I'm afraid not, sweetheart. Anyone you contact can be interrogated by OCFS. They'll think they're doing you a favor by helping OCFS find you."

"Okay." She handed him her phone.

Once they arrived on the ground floor, Mason led the way to the exit. "We'll go out the side door." They emerged from the building on Second Avenue. "Follow me."

"Where are we going?" Wynter kept her head down and stayed close to Mason.

"Somewhere safe."

"More specifically," she said.

"Downtown." Mason looked behind them for a southbound bus. "First we need to get a MetroCard."

"I have a MetroCard," said Wynter.

"One that wasn't bought with a credit card in my name."

"Oh," she said.

"There's a check cashing place three blocks up. Come on. Let's pick up the pace."

The two of them hustled south on Second until they arrived at the location. Mason walked inside.

A Pakistani man smiled. "How can I help you?"

"I need a MetroCard with a hundred dollars on it, please." Mason took some money out of his pocket.

"Sorry, we don't take cash."

"You're a check cashing store! How do you not take cash?"

"New system. No more cash. If you want to cash check, we give you pre-pay Visa with digital dollar."

Mason gritted his teeth. "There's a one-month amnesty period for cash."

"Okay. Take your cash to the bank and come back with debit card. Then you can buy MetroCard."

Mason leaned forward. "How much?"

The man looked past the door as if to see if other customers were going to come in. "30 percent."

"Fine." Mason handed the man two $100 bills.

The man's eyes shifted from side to side. "I can't give you change."

"Okay, then. Put the rest on the MetroCard. What's that? $140?"

The man nodded and took the cash.

"What about a pre-paid Visa? Will you sell me one of those for the same percentage?"

The man studied Mason as if he suspected him of being a cop. "Yeah, okay. I'll do it. But card is extra. How much you want?"

"Two $500 cards."

"Fifteen total."

Mason pressed his lips together in aggravation and counted out the money.

The man took the cash, loaded the cards, and

passed them to Mason. "Okay, buddy. Have a good day."

"Yeah, you too." Mason nodded for Wynter to follow him, and they left the store. Mason looked up the street. "Here comes a bus. Hurry!"

They jogged to the stop and arrived at the same time as the bus. Before getting on, Mason casually let Wynter's phone slip out of his hand and fall to the street where it would be run over by the bus once it started moving again. He climbed the stairs and swiped the card twice. He and Wynter made their way to the rear of the vehicle.

Wynter sat down on the back seat. "What's downtown?"

"PATH."

"We're going to Jersey? I thought you said you were taking me somewhere safe. You grew up there. You should know how dangerous that place is."

"That's right. I grew up there. So I know how to get by without getting into trouble. We're going to get you a place to lay low for a while—until we can get all this sorted out. Do you need to see a doctor?"

"For what?"

"Because…" Mason swallowed hard, unable to vocalize his concerns. "…of what happened."

She turned away from him as if ashamed. "No. I'm okay."

He put his arm around her, pulled her close, kissed her cheek. "It's not your fault."

She bit her lip and appeared to be holding back tears. "Then why do I feel so guilty?"

CHAPTER 10

For in the time of trouble he shall hide me in his pavilion: in the secret of his tabernacle shall he hide me; he shall set me up upon a rock. And now shall mine head be lifted up above mine enemies round about me: therefore will I offer in his tabernacle sacrifices of joy; I will sing, yea, I will sing praises unto the LORD. Hear, O LORD, when I cry with my voice: have mercy also upon me, and answer me.

Psalm 27:5-7

Mason and Wynter got off the bus at the World Trade Center. The entire financial district was flooded with Occupy Wall Street protestors who were angry about the banking collapse and seemed certain they were going to get the short end of the stick.

Mason led Wynter through the crowd to the PATH station. From there, they took the train to Newark, New Jersey, and then a cab to Elizabeth City.

The taxi pulled up in front of Mama Luca's Italian restaurant. Mason took money out of his pocket. "Are you still accepting cash?"

"For a couple more weeks, I guess." The cabbie shrugged.

Mason handed the man a $100 bill. "Keep the change."

"Thanks. Have a good one."

"You too." Mason exited the vehicle.

Wynter got out. "Why are we here? Are we going to eat?"

"Are you hungry?"

"I could have a little something. It smells good."

"It's authentic Italian. My friend from high school runs the place." He put his arm around her and led her to the entrance.

Gina was at the hostess podium. "Good afternoon, Mr. Lot."

"They know you by name here?" Wynter whispered.

"Is Gio around?" asked Mason.

"Have a seat at the bar. I'll go get him." Gina walked through the restaurant.

The bartender recognized Mason. "Pellegrino with lime?"

"Please," said Mason. "Two. And can we see a menu?"

"Sure thing." The bartender served the sparkling waters and handed them two menus.

"Mace!" Giovanni walked up to him. "Good to see you."

"Good to see you as well. This is my daughter, Wynter."

She forced a smile and shook Giovanni's hand. "Nice to meet you."

"Walk with me." Giovanni signaled for Mason to follow him.

Mason put his hand on Wynter's shoulder as he stood up. "Order whatever you want. I'll be right back."

"Okay," she said.

Mason followed Giovanni through the kitchen and to the elevator that led up to his office. "You didn't say you were going to kill the guy. I thought the plan was to put him out of commission for a while."

Giovanni lifted his shoulders. "We did the world a favor. Imagine how many other kids we saved from going through what Wynter almost had to endure. Besides, when you cripple a guy, he ain't got nothin' better to do than sit around and blame people for his predicament. He sues people, testifies in court, and all that. When a guy dies, nine times out of ten, the family just wants to move on and that's that."

"I suppose I'm not accustomed to all this." Mason walked into the sprawling office apartment.

"But I'm guessing you're not here to chastise me because the good doctor is no longer with us."

Mason lowered his gaze. "Something happened to Wynter. I need a safe house and a gun."

Giovanni sat down at his desk near the window. "Again, with the gun?"

Mason sat on the leather sofa across from the desk and relayed the story to Giovanni. "I can pay." He handed him the tube of gold coins.

Giovanni held the plastic tube in his hand. "Heavy. But I'm not taking your money."

"Please, Gio. I really need your help."

Giovanni pushed the tube of coins across his desk to Mason. "And I'm not giving you a gun. Let me take care of this. Where is this LGBT house?"

"Hell's Kitchen, but I'm her father. I need to be the one who does it."

Giovanni snatched the tube of gold American Eagle coins from the edge of the desk. "Fine. Give me one of those." He removed the cap and extracted a single coin. He put the top back on and slid the container back toward Mason. "Now, you've officially paid for a contract on this scum bag. You're the one handling this."

Mason pressed his lips together. "That's not what I meant."

"Look here, Mace. If you pull the trigger, is it the gun killing the guy or you?"

"I see what you're getting at, but I need to do this." He looked at the floor. "It's my fault that it happened to her."

"Buddy, it ain't your fault. It's this pervert system we got going here. It's that piece-of-filth tranny who runs the house. Anyway, if you go over there and pop this fag, then what? Do you think the cops ain't gonna figure out it was you? Then who's gonna take care of Wyn?"

Giovanni lit a cigar. "Let me handle it. I'll make it look good. I'll send Micky the Arm over there and scoop this sissy up. We'll take him down to South Jersey, build a fire in a metal drum then lock that queer up in a shed with the fire burning inside. He, she, it,—whatever, ends up dying from smoke inhalation.

"Then, we take him back to the house and burn it down, fag and all. An autopsy will show he passed from asphyxiation."

Mason objected, "The house is full of teenagers. You can't do that!"

"We'll do it in the daytime. The kids will be in school. We'll scoop him up right after they leave in the morning. The whole place will be a pile of ashes by the time the bell rings. Easy peasy." Giovanni opened the drawer of his desk.

He tossed a key on the desk. "This is to an apartment on Emmet."

Mason collected the key. "Emmet? Is that in Newark?"

"Yeah, South Ironbound. It ain't Midtown Manhattan but ain't nobody gonna bother her there. She don't need to be goin' outside no how. That's what layin' low is all about. The apartment itself is nice, furnished, highspeed Wi-Fi, plenty of streaming services for the TV so she can just stay inside and veg out."

"Okay, thanks."

Giovanni pulled a key fob. "There's a white Ford Interceptor SUV parked out back. Take it. Keep it as long as you need it."

"You mean like the police vehicles?" Mason wrinkled his brow as he picked up the fob.

"Yeah. It's got black rims and everything. Ain't nobody gonna make eye contact with you while you're driving that. Half the people out there are doin' something dirty. The other half just get nervous around cops."

"You've put a lot of thought into all this."

"It's what I do for a living. And if I mess up, I don't get a pink slip like you."

Mason frowned at the thought of his old schoolmate's demise. "I appreciate all of your help. Let me know if I can ever return the favor."

Giovanni walked him to the elevator. "I don't want no stock tips or anything. But I know you hear things. Give me a heads-up if you come across anything I need to know."

"Of course. Thanks again." Mason stepped into the elevator by himself and nodded goodbye to his old friend.

Giovanni stuck his hand between the elevator doors before they closed. He reached behind his back and pulled out a pistol.

Mason's eyes grew wide.

Giovanni handed him the weapon. "Take it. I've got more."

Mason didn't want to get his fingerprints on it. "Is it loaded?"

"It'd be useless if it wasn't."

"Why do I need that?"

Giovanni lifted his shoulders. "Every time you come over here, seems you're asking me for a piece. Maybe you'll leave me alone long enough to get some work done if I go ahead and give it to yous."

Mason grinned at the teasing. He took the pistol and examined it. "Is the safety on?"

"It's a Glock. The safety is don't put your finger on the trigger until you're ready to shoot."

Mason tucked it in his jeans. "Thank you."

"But seriously, don't do nothin' stupid." Giovanni let the elevator doors close. "Take care."

"You too," Mason called out. Once back on the ground level, he traversed the busy kitchen and returned to the bar.

"Hey, Dad." Wynter had a plate of calamari and a bowl of ravioli. "Are you going to eat anything?"

He sat next to her. "No, but take your time. Finish your lunch."

"The food here is amazing! At first, I thought this was some dump that was used by the mob to launder money or something. But then I figured you'd never consort with people like that. Plus, if it was that type of place, they'd probably serve pre-packaged food like a chain restaurant."

"Yeah, right." Mason lifted one side of his mouth and ate a piece of her calamari.

After lunch, he paid the tab in cash and the two of them walked out to the rear parking lot. He pressed the *unlock* tab on the key fob and the headlights of the Interceptor came on.

"Is that a cop car?" Wynter asked.

"Same model, but no."

"Why would your friend get a ride like that?"

"He probably got a good deal through the police motor pool. I think he knows some guys."

"Oh." She wrinkled her brow. "Where are we going?"

Mason told her about the apartment. "We'll stop and get you some groceries on the way. There's a Walmart right over the bridge in Kearny. I'll get you one of those little tablets so we can communicate without using phones.

"Why does your friend have an extra furnished apartment?"

"For guests."

"In Ironbound?"

"Well," Mason tried to develop a plausible excuse. "He keeps it year-round, so I guess the rent is cheap."

"I bet."

***

Later that evening, Mason hauled the groceries, toiletries, and other items purchased from Walmart up to the apartment. As expected, the neighborhood left much to be desired, but Mason had seen worse. However, the building was brand new, and the unit was very nice. It was clean, the furnishings were all new, and the kitchen was well-equipped.

Wynter took her backpack to the bedroom and sat down on the bed. "Wow! This is a nice mattress."

Mason sat on the bed next to her. He set up her tablet and registered a new Tutanota email account for Wynter so the two of them could stay in contact. "This email service has end-to-end encryption, so no one can intercept our communications unless they physically get a hold of one of our devices."

She took the tablet and inspected it. "Why do you know all of this?"

He shrugged. "I've always been a big privacy advocate."

She narrowed her eyes. "I guess that means you don't want to tell me." She stood up. "I'm going to get a shower."

"Alright. I'll give you some space. Do you need me to bring you anything else?"

"Not that I can think of. I'll email you if anything comes up."

"Don't leave the apartment. Don't even open the door."

"What if I want to order a pizza?"

Mason frowned. "Alright, but don't go outside—not for anything." He handed her one of the prepaid Visa cards. "And check the peephole before you open it for the delivery person."

"I'll be okay," she said.

He retrieved the pistol from his jeans. "Take this. It's loaded."

"A gun?" She appeared startled.

"Yeah. Just in case."

"I don't have any idea how to shoot it." She hesitated but finally took the weapon.

"Point and pull the trigger, I guess." Mason regretted that he couldn't be more helpful. "I don't think you'll need a gun, but I'll feel better knowing you have it."

She placed the pistol on the nightstand beside the bed. "Okay. Thank you, for everything."

"Sure thing, sweetheart." He held her and kissed her forehead. "I'll try to get by tomorrow. But if you need anything, anything at all, email me. I'll come right over."

"Okay." She smiled.

He walked to the door. "Lock this behind me when I leave."

"I will."

Suddenly, the sound of an airplane flying low over the building caused the windows to rattle. Next, a loud boom preceded a violent shaking that felt like an earthquake.

"What was that?" Mason braced himself against the door frame.

CHAPTER 11

But as the days of Noah were, so shall also the coming of the Son of man be. For as in the days that were before the flood they were eating and drinking, marrying and giving in marriage, until the day that Noe entered into the ark, and knew not until the flood came, and took them all away; so shall also the coming of the Son of man be. Then shall two be in the field; the one shall be taken, and the other left. Two women shall be grinding at the mill; the one shall be taken, and the other left. Watch therefore: for ye know not what hour your Lord doth come.

Matthew 24:37-42

"Dad, look!" Wynter ran to the third-floor apartment's south-facing window.

Mason hurried to see what she'd spotted. His mouth hung open as he watched a massive smoke plume billowing to the sky.

"Was that the airport?" she asked.

He shook his head. "I don't know. The airport is about half a mile from here. That looks closer. Maybe the freeway."

"Like what? The pilot miscalculated the runway?"

"They don't make mistakes like that." Mason considered the tremendous loss of life. "Must have been an equipment failure."

Wynter sighed. "Those poor people. You don't think we could be under attack, do you?"

Mason thought about the military hardware kill switch that had been activated to destroy US-manufactured defense products sold to members of BRICS Plus. "I hope not. This looks like a textbook plane crash. It didn't hit a target like a building. But turn on the news and monitor the situation for a while. I need to get going. If it hit I-78, it's going to cause major traffic congestion. I don't want Prairie and your mom to worry."

He hugged her again. "I love you. I'm sorry I can't take you home. I wish we could all be together, especially when something like this is happening."

"I understand. But honestly, I could use a little alone time." She kissed him and closed the door.

Mason hustled down the stairs, got in the SUV, and drove north, hoping to catch I-95 before rerouted traffic from I-78 started clogging up the roadways.

No sooner had he taken the on-ramp than the interstate began slowing down. "You're kidding me!" Traffic inched forward for the next hundred yards, then Mason saw the reason for the slowdown. An older model silver Camry had hit the concrete wall separating it from the southbound lane. Two other vehicles had been unable to stop in time and had collided with the Camry. Mason watched as one of the drivers got out to approach the Camry, but he could not see anyone inside.

He eventually got past the bottleneck and continued North to the Lincoln Tunnel. Mason encountered yet another spot where the traffic came to a standstill. People blew their horns, but the clamor did nothing to alleviate the gridlock. Soon, the car in front of him inched forward. Mason craned his neck but still could not see the cause of the traffic jam.

After another ten minutes of stop-and-go at a glacial pace, Mason saw another unoccupied vehicle that had rolled into the divider wall and was blocking an entire lane of traffic. "What is wrong with people? Did everyone lose their mind on the same day?"

The congestion broke up and he finally made it to the Lincoln Tunnel. He paid his fare and entered the dark tube which ran beneath the Hudson River. A quarter mile into the mile-and-a-half-long underpass, traffic halted once more. People were getting out of their vehicles signaling that this roadblock was not breaking up. Mason likewise exited his vehicle and jogged ahead to see where the stoppage had occurred.

"This just keeps going and going and going!" By the time he saw the end of the congestion, he'd nearly reached the tunnel opening. Daylight peeked into the dim cave-like structure but was kept at bay by the darkness.

He saw a crowd of people standing around a police vehicle. "What's going on?"

"I don't know," said one of the onlookers. "The engine is still running but the cop is gone."

"Has anyone called 911?" Mason asked.

"I did," said a lady standing nearby. "I got a message saying all circuits are busy."

Mason looked around but saw no apparent solutions. He checked the door handle. "Locked." He looked at the bystanders. "Who has a tire tool?"

A man pointed to his taxicab eight cars back. "I got one in the trunk. What are you going to do?"

"Break the window and move the vehicle. If the NYPD has a problem with that, I'll pay for the replacement glass. But they shouldn't have cops abandoning their vehicles in the Lincoln Tunnel."

"Go ahead," said the woman. "I didn't see anything." She walked away as if not wanting to witness the possible crime.

The cab driver collected the heavy tool from his trunk and handed it to Mason. He lifted the tire iron and smashed the driver's side window. Mason gave the item back to the cab driver, reached in, and opened the door. He got inside the vehicle and drove it through the tunnel. Once out, he pulled the car to the side, wiped his prints from the steering wheel and door handles, then abandoned the automobile.

People began exiting the tunnel, honking their horns, and giving Mason a thumbs-up as they drove by in appreciation of his proactive measures. He ignored the accolades, preferring to go unnoticed as he jogged back to his vehicle. Soon, all those aware of his efforts had passed and the honks were coupled with obscene finger gestures and rude instructions for him to get off the road.

Mason was winded when he got back to the Interceptor. Traffic had broken up and now his vehicle was the one blocking the road. However, no one expressed their impatience with him as he got back into the SUV that looked so much like a law enforcement vehicle.

He finally made it out of the tunnel and onto West 42nd. He opted to stay on the main thoroughfares. They were more congested than the side streets of Manhattan, but they offered the best options for getting around abandoned vehicles should more such incidents arise before he got back to the Upper East Side.

Indeed, he saw two taxis and a delivery truck which appeared to have no drivers before he got to Park Avenue. Once he had to drive over the plastic poles separating the bus lane from regular traffic in order to get around a stalled vehicle. "This makes no sense!"

Mason turned on the radio and scrolled through the news stations while creeping slowly through heavy midtown traffic. "It's been an hour since that plane went down. They have to have something on it by now." He paused when he found the local GBC affiliate.

The commentator said, "The SEC's Garth Armstrong says he anticipates the markets to reopen on Monday of next week and that everything should be back to normal. He gave a press conference earlier this morning stating that all systems were *go*. In fact, the after-hours markets were allowed to open yesterday and pre-market trading today. Armstrong went on to say that the only reason regular markets would not be opening this week is that officials did not want to put the added strain of trading on the new FedNow system until it had a chance to get through the backlogs of money movements that are inevitable after such a long banking holiday."

Mason pursed his lips and continued scanning the stations. "That's the same stuff they've been talking about since the weekend. And it wasn't a holiday. It was a catastrophic failure of the monetary system."

He scrolled through station after station in search of information about the plane crash, but all the frequencies were parroting the same tripe, using almost identical scripts read by the various reporters.

Once he arrived at Park Avenue, he found it less congested than 42nd Street had been, but he still wasn't moving as fast as he wanted. Mason saw several more cars that were either abandoned in the middle of the Avenue, had stopped because they had rolled into an object like a lamp post, building, or another car, or were parked very irregularly with one or two wheels up on the sidewalk.

He found a parking garage on East 81st and jogged the final few blocks home.

CHAPTER 12

But know this, that if the goodman of the house had known in what watch the thief would come, he would have watched, and would not have suffered his house to be broken up. Therefore be ye also ready: for in such an hour as ye think not the Son of man cometh.

Matthew 24:43-44

He rushed to the elevator, then down the hall, and frantically shoved his key into the lock. Upon opening the door, he called out, "Prairie? Are you here?"

She came out of her room. "Daddy! Have you seen what's going on?"

The world was obviously being turned upside down, but he was relieved to know that at least Prairie and Wynter were safe. He embraced Prairie and gave her a kiss. "Is Mom home?"

"She's in the shower. Something's not right, Daddy. Look at this video."

He kissed her. "I know Sweat Pea. I'll look at it in a second. But first, I need to call your sisters. I want to make sure they're okay."

Mason rushed to retrieve his phone from the closet.

Prairie followed him. "Is Wyn okay?"

"Yes. She's safe."

"What's happening?" Prairie quizzed.

"I don't know exactly. We'll figure it out after I talk to your sisters." Mason called Daphne first, not only because she was younger than Hope, but also because she was the one with the least spousal support of the two.

"Hey, Dad. What's up?" Daphne answered.

"I was just calling to check in—make sure you were okay."

"Yeah, why wouldn't I be?"

"I was out earlier. I just got back in. I saw a few wrecks—I also saw a plane go down."

"You mean like a crash? Where did you see that?"

"Newark."

"Newark? What were you doing in Jersey?"

Mason instantly realized he was saying more than he wanted over the phone. "It's a long story. I just wanted to make sure you were okay. You haven't noticed anything strange?"

"No. I just got home from school a little over an hour ago." She paused. "Come to think of it, Hubert, the doorman at our building wasn't there when I came home. He's always there. If he has the day off, the building has other people who cover for him. He was there this morning. Steve and I used to joke that Hubert doesn't drink water or anything until he gets off work at 6:00 because we've never caught him taking a restroom break. But, you know, maybe he finally had to go.

"Anyway, Hubert's absence is no cause for concern. Have you heard from Wynter?"

"She's okay. We can talk about it later. Stop by sometime. I need to go. I want to give Hope a call."

"Alright. I love you, Dad. And don't worry so much. We're all capable of taking care of ourselves."

"I love you too," said Mason. "Talk soon."

Adrianna came out of the shower with a towel around her body and another around her head. "Who are you talking to?"

Mason had already dialed Hope's number.

"He's calling Hope—to make sure she's okay," Prairie whispered.

"Dad, what's going on?" Hope said over the phone.

125

"What happened to Hope?" Adrianna quizzed with concern.

Mason waved her off and mouthed the word, "Nothing."

"Hey, Honey," he said to Hope. "I was just checking in—I wanted to hear your voice."

She replied. "That's so sweet. Are you okay? How are you and Mom handling this thing with Wynter?"

"We're working through it."

"Good. Remember, the best thing you can do is be supportive. Wyn is going to do what he wants. The law is on his side with this one. If you fight him, the only thing you'll do is drive him further away. He called me last week. We had a long chat—sister to...I mean sibling to sibling. I believe it will all work itself out and we'll be stronger as a family after the storm has passed."

Mason felt uneasy about hearing Hope refer to her sister as a boy. He had too much going through his head to deal with that added tension. "I think you're right," he said to avoid a discussion. "I've got to go. I love you."

"I love you too, Dad. Tell Mom and Prairie I said *hello*."

"I will. Bye." He ended the call.

"What is going on with Hope?" Adrianna demanded. "Why didn't you let me talk to her?"

"Nothing—nothing is going on with Hope." Mason powered off his phone and stuck it back in the closet. "Follow me out to the balcony. I have something I need to tell you."

"Tell me now!" said Adrianna.

Mason pointed at the phone. "I can't."

Adrianna rolled her eyes. "Oh please, Mace. No one cares enough about what you say to eavesdrop over your phone—if that's even possible."

"I'm not going to argue with you. If you want to hear what I have to say, come to the balcony."

"I'm naked!" Adrianna protested.

"Then put on a robe!" he countered.

"You and your paranoia—I swear…" Adrianna went to get her robe.

Prairie held up her phone. "Can I show you my video now?"

"Yes, what is it?" Mason put his arm around her and looked at the screen of her phone.

She clicked the play button. The screen read *This video has been removed for violating our terms of service.* "It was just here!" she protested. "I don't understand. It didn't violate anything."

"What was the video?" Mason asked.

"It was a plane crash."

"At Newark?" he quizzed.

Prairie said, "No. Some suburb north of Baltimore. It crashed right into a strip mall. It was like the pilot had completely lost control. What were you telling Daphne about a plane going down?"

He pointed to her room. "Put your phone up and come out on the balcony. Is Marco still here?"

"No!" She took her phone and tossed it on her bed. "It was the strangest thing. He got a text that his father's security detail was coming to pick him up from the coffee shop. They showed up in two black SUVs, like something out of a movie. They got out and all of them had black suits, black sunglasses, the whole nine. They told him it was an emergency extraction, and that he had to go back to Italy right away. They wouldn't tell him when he was coming back.

"Those guys knew something, but they weren't saying a thing about it. I think all of it is connected."

Adrianna came out in her robe. "You've got Prairie buying into all of this conspiracy stuff now. Really, Mace. It has to stop."

"Mom! What am I supposed to think? It was like one of those things when the Secret Service grabs the president and carts him off."

"I understand honey, but we're not the type of people who believe in stolen elections and poison vaccines," said Adrianna.

Prairie rolled her eyes. "I know, Mom. We're the type of people who believe boys can have babies."

Adrianna scowled at her. "Why would you say something like that? You know what a challenging issue this has been for Wyn, for your father and me, for the whole family. Why would you joke about such a thing?"

"I'm not making light of Wyn's situation. I'd just like to pretend there's such a thing as reality for five minutes. Can we do that?"

Adrianna glared at Mason as if this meager eruption of teen rebellion was somehow his responsibility.

Prairie crossed her arms as she walked out onto the balcony. "I'm starting to think this whole thing with the gays and the gender identity stuff is a fraud."

Adrianna followed her through the sliding door. "When did you decide this?"

Prairie sat down on one of the patio chairs. "When I saw Wyn today. She was a wreck. I've never seen her so distraught. All these hormones and pronouns were supposed to make her feel better. But it's not working."

"You saw Wyn today?" Adrianna quizzed. "Where?"

"Here. Dad took her to a safe house or something."

"When were you planning on telling me this?" Adrianna glared at Mason.

He defended, "Right now! That's why I called you out to the balcony—so we could talk!"

"So…" She held her hands out with palms up. "Talk!"

Mason knew the information would upset Prairie. He sat next to her and took her hand. "Something happened to Wyn—at the LGBTQ house. The house mom, I think her name is Jamie, got Wyn drunk and high. Jamie is a biological male. She took advantage of Wyn while she was passed out drunk."

Prairie's eyes welled up. She covered her mouth. "Oh, no! Poor Wyn!" She began to sob.

Adrianna's face turned pale. She started to shake. Her mouth hung open. "My child! Where is she?"

"She's safe. She's in a private apartment in Jersey." Mason put his arm around his wife.

"Did you take her to the hospital? Did you call the police?" Adrianna pushed him away.

"I offered to take her to a doctor. She didn't want to go. If we call the police, they'll take her to another OCFS facility where she'll be at risk of the same thing happening," said Mason.

Adrianna stood at the edge of the balcony looking down at 2nd Avenue. She turned around quickly and spoke frantically. "You have to go get her! You have to bring her home!"

"We can't. She's a runaway." He was interrupted by a pounding at the front door.

"NYPD! Open up!"

Mason whispered to Adrianna and Prairie, "Not a word about Wyn!"

Both of them signaled their agreement with a nod.

Mason went to the door and answered it. "Can I help you?" Immediately, he recognized Wyn's skinny, androgynous OCFS case worker, Carter Reed.

Reed pushed past the police and through the door. "We have a search warrant. Please step out of the way. Is Wynter Lot inside the home?"

"No," he answered.

"Have you seen him?" Reed quizzed.

Mason refused to use a male pronoun for his daughter, but neither did he want to insight the wrath of this non-binary Nazi. Also, he knew Reed could pull the security footage from the building if they so desired. "Wyn stopped by. I assumed with permission. We talked."

"About what?"

"Wynter was upset. The doctor who was supposed to oversee all the medical procedures was injured or something. Wyn was concerned that the operation might not take place before her eighteenth birthday."

"His," Reed corrected.

"I'm sorry?" Mason said.

"You said *her* eighteenth birthday. It's *his* eighteenth birthday."

"Right," Mason acknowledged. "It was *her* for the last seventeen years. It takes a little time to break the habit."

Reed tightened their jaw and made a notation of the incorrect pronoun usage on a small tablet. "And the doctor was *killed*."

"Oh, I'm sorry to hear that."

"I'm sure you are." Reed smirked. "I'll have a look around. If you're telling the truth, we'll be out of your hair. If Wyn is here, you and your wife will be arrested for kidnapping. And Prairie, since she's a minor, will be placed into OCFS custody."

Mason's blood boiled. He eyed the pistol on the cop's belt, trying to figure out how to engage the retention mechanism to release the weapon. If Wyn had been in the house, he'd have died before allowing them to take Prairie.

The officer seemed to notice what Mason was looking at. "Can I help you?" he asked with a furrowed brow.

Mason looked up. "What's that?"

"You were staring at my gun."

"Was I? Sorry. I was just daydreaming. It's been quite a day. Did you guys hear anything about a plane going down at Newark International?"

The cop pressed his lips and gave his partner a knowing look.

"No?" said Mason. "What about all the abandoned cars in the city? What's happening with all of that?"

The second cop looked perplexed. He glanced at the first who gave him a subtle cue to remain quiet.

The second officer lifted his shoulders. "It's an ongoing investigation. We're not allowed to discuss it with the public."

"Are you talking about the abandoned vehicles or the plane crash?" Mason quizzed.

The first officer pressed his lips and grunted at the second as if he'd misspoken by even acknowledging there *was* an investigation. He turned his attention back to Mason and pointed to the sofa. "Go have a seat until the case worker has confirmed the person we're looking for isn't here."

He gave a polite nod. "I appreciate the fact that you folks have prioritized finding my child when the city is upended by everything else that's going on." Mason had gleaned all the information he could from the two NYPD cops. He complied with the order and sat quietly next to Adrianna and Prairie.

Minutes later, Carter Reed emerged from the hallway. "He's not here. We can go." Reed tossed a business card on the coffee table. "If Wynter contacts you again, you need to call me. Otherwise, it can be construed as contributing to the delinquency of a minor and you can be arrested. He is considered a runaway and isn't safe until we bring him back into the custody of OCFS."

Reed pointed for the officers to get out of the way and stomped arrogantly out the door. The second officer gave Mason an apologetic smile as he pulled the door closed on the way out.

CHAPTER 13

Howl ye; for the day of the LORD is at hand; it shall come as a destruction from the Almighty. Therefore shall all hands be faint, and every man's heart shall melt: and they shall be afraid: pangs and sorrows shall take hold of them; they shall be in pain as a woman that travaileth: they shall be amazed one at another; their faces shall be as flames. Behold, the day of the LORD cometh, cruel both with wrath and fierce anger, to lay the land desolate: and he shall destroy the sinners thereof out of it.

Isaiah 13:6-9

Mason walked to the door and locked the deadbolt as soon as the police and OCFS case worker had left.

"See, Mom! We're not crazy!" Prairie insisted. "The cop just admitted that something is going on and they're not allowed to talk about it."

"I don't care about any of that," said Adrianna. "I just want to see Wyn."

"We'll go see her tomorrow after I finish work." Mason returned to the sofa and put his arm around her.

"You're working from home. Why can't we go see her in the morning?" Adrianna asked.

"I'm working from home, but I'm still working. I didn't get anything done today. I can't play hooky two days in a row."

Adrianna huffed. "I'm helping Lexi plan her daughter's wedding. We're meeting the caterer tomorrow evening at six. I have to be back in the city before five. Can't you get some work done tonight? Then you can get an early start tomorrow and wrap up by noon so we can go see Wyn."

"I'm in school tomorrow," said Prairie. "I want to see her too!"

"Your father will take you to see Wyn another evening," said Adrianna.

"You can come with us tomorrow." Mason walked to the kitchen and looked inside the refrigerator.

"You're going to get me out of school early?" Prairie asked.

"You can take the whole day off." Mason looked for something quick and easy to prepare but saw nothing.

"No! She missed enough school during the protests last week!" Adrianna followed him into the kitchen.

"Something is going on and we're not being told what. I'm keeping Prairie home until I find out!" Mason closed the refrigerator door hard enough to make the jars and bottles inside clank together.

"Guys! Please! Don't fight!" Prairie pleaded.

Adrianna glared at Mason as if she wanted to push the issue further but seemed to know this was one of those times he could not be badgered into submission. "Fine. But just tomorrow."

"What are we having for dinner?" Mason asked.

Adrianna pulled a bottle of wine from the cupboard. "Between the information about Wyn and the police barging into our apartment, my nerves are too rattled to even think about cooking."

"Can we have Korean again?" Prairie asked.

"Honey, we just had Korean." Adrianna began opening the bottle.

Prairie countered. "Fine, pizza then."

Adrianna popped the cork and twisted it off the screw. "That's worse."

"So Korean it is." Prairie held out her hand for her father's credit card.

Mason pressed his lips together and pulled out his wallet. "Call me when it gets here. I'll be in my office." He handed her the card and headed down the hall to his home office.

He sat at his desk and fired up the computer. Mason had a dedicated T3 internet line that was hardwired and not connected to the apartment's Wi-Fi router. It was provided to him by Poseidon because of the sensitive nature of his work. The T3 line was not only fast, but it was also much more secure than a standard internet connection making it invisible to prying eyes.

He logged into his secure portal for Poseidon. *The spooks running the Peleus Fund know what's happening. Let's see if I can figure out anything from their trades.*

He frowned as he checked the positions being taken in after-hours trading.

They're short Goldman, Citi, Amex, and Morgan Stanley—those are all financials. That makes sense. It's going to be a long time before the currency crisis works its way through the system.

Bloomberg, CBS, Fox, ABC, NBC—obviously media companies are going to take a hit from falling ad revenue. But where's CNN? Why would they expect them to outperform?

L3Harris? They're a military contractor. It is the end of the world. If they can't make a buck, who can?

MetLife? I can see life insurance as being a tough gig going forward but there have to be a lot of smaller companies that are going to take the hit before MetLife. And these are all very near-term positions.

Macy's, Saks, Pfizer? These are companies from every sector. And they represent some of the strongest players in their fields. Why wouldn't they just short the S&P? That makes more sense than picking out the biggest and brightest to bet against.

He looked out his window toward the south, staring at the collection of skyscrapers downtown. "All these companies are based in New York City."

Prairie opened the door. "Daddy!"

Mason minimized the window. "Baby! You have to knock before you come in here. We've talked about that."

"I know, but I had to tell you."

"Tell me what?"

"The Korean restaurant. I called. The lady answered—sounded like she'd been crying. She said neither of her delivery guys has come back— they've been gone for hours and aren't answering their phones. Plus, she said two cooks are missing. She said if I wanted to order we would have to come pick it up, but they had only three people working so it would take a while.

"I asked her what she thinks happened to them. She said all four of them went to the Korean church on 59th and 1st Ave. She said something about the Rapture, then the line went dead. I Googled *the rapture*. The only thing I could find was some Netflix series about hip-hop, an old song by someone called Blondie, and an electronic music festival called *Rapture*."

Mason said, "I saw something about the Rapture on YouTube once. According to the guy making the video, Jesus would come back to collect all of His faithful followers right before the end of the world. But I went to Catholic School. We were never taught anything about that. And I've never heard the priest speak about it at church."

She replied, "We go on Christmas and Easter. Nobody wants to hear about the end of the world on Christmas and Easter, so that's probably not proof that he never taught on it."

Mason stared at his desk. "Still, you should have been able to find something about it on Google. Are you sure you spelled it right?"

She shrugged. "I don't know. Try your computer."

He opened a new window for his browser and typed the term into the search bar. "Huh. Nothing." He typed in a second search. "Maybe I can find that video on YouTube." Mason viewed the results. "It's gone."

"Kinda like that airplane video." Prairie stood in the doorway with her arms crossed.

Mason frowned. "Yeah. Kind of like that."

"So should I order pizza for dinner?"

Mason's phone rang. He looked at the number. "This is Roy from work. I have to take it. Order what you want. I'll be out in a while."

She blew him a kiss and closed the office door.

"Roy, hey. What's going on?"

Roy answered, "Mace, listen. We're moving the office to West Palm. With all these protests happening again, I think it's the best move. We saw how long the demonstrations lasted after the o-eight debacle. This thing with the dollar is going to hurt people a lot more than the great recession.

"Unfortunately, the people need a scapegoat, and that happens to be us as well as the rest of Wall Street. It doesn't make sense for us to keep banging a square peg through a round hole trying to make it fit. That's what it's starting to feel like with the office on Wall Street."

"Oh. Okay. That seems sudden."

"To you, I guess it does. But I was inches from pulling the trigger on a move back during the first Occupy Wall Street. I don't want to go through it again."

"What's the timeline on the switch?"

"I just leased an office. I'm down here now. I've got a tech crew coming in tomorrow morning to run all the cable and set up a secure network. We'll have OC-3 fiber optic lines, new desks, custom lighting—we'll be right by Rosemary Square. Did you know they have a Harry's here?"

"You mean like Harry's on Wall Street?" Mason asked.

"Yeah. We can go there for drinks after work on Fridays. It'll be just like the good old days. Goldman has an office about a block from here. They're calling West Palm *Wall Street South*."

"I'll have to give it some thought," said Mason. "When do you need an answer from me?"

"I'd like to be open for business Monday. But what's there to think about? Look. I'll give you a half million to relocate, plus I'll raise your salary to one point eight in pre-digital dollars. That's a thirty-percent raise. Factor in that Florida has no state income tax and you'll be taking home double what you bring in now. With all the shops and restaurants down here, Adrianna will never miss Manhattan.

"And real estate is very reasonable. What did you pay for your place?"

Mason said, "Seven and change."

"You can get a mansion down here for seven million. Or, if you prefer, you can get a nice condo right on the ocean for half of that. Probably double the space you have now," said Roy. "Come down here tomorrow, take a look around, and see what you think. You can't really make an informed decision if you don't know what you're comparing. You've been around traders enough to understand that simple concept."

"Alright," Mason acknowledged. "I'll talk it over with Adrianna."

"Mace, I understand this seems sudden. But you need to come down here and have a look around. I've got a place for you to stay while you look for a condo or a home. It's right on the ocean. Bring the girls. They'll love it. Make it a family thing. You need to come tomorrow. Okay?"

"I'll try."

"Don't try—do. Hang up the phone, pack a suitcase, and leave first thing tomorrow. I'm not saying this as your friend, I'm saying this as your boss. Sell it to Adrianna like that if you have to. Tell her you don't have a choice."

Mason understood Roy was trying to communicate something that he couldn't come right out and say. "Yeah, alright. I will."

"Good. I'll transfer the funds for the relocation into your account now. See you in Florida." Roy ended the call.

Mason took a deep breath and walked out to the living room. "I've got good news and bad news."

Adrianna had her feet up on the couch and was halfway through her first bottle of wine. "Tell me the good news. I don't think I can handle any more bad news today."

"I just got a raise," said Mason.

Adrianna sat up. "How much?"

"An extra 400K."

"That's better." She topped off her glass. "It's about time."

"Congratulations, Daddy!" Prairie emerged from the kitchen and hugged him. "But what's the bad news?"

Adrianna held up her hand. "Let's end the evening with the raise. We can talk about the bad news tomorrow."

"Unfortunately, it can't wait." Mason sat next to her on the couch. "Roy is relocating the firm to West Palm."

"Florida?" Prairie sat on the loveseat across from her parents. "As far as bad news goes, it could be worse." She seemed to contemplate the repercussions of such a move.

"Out of the question." Adrianna shook her head. "All of our friends are here. Our life, our family, everything we know is in New York."

"Well, it won't be much of a life if I don't have a job," said Mason.

"Nonsense. You can get a job at any shop on the street." Adrianna slugged her wine.

"We're in the throes of a severe economic crisis. No one on Wall Street is hiring," Mason argued.

"Every firm in the city has in-house council. You don't have to work in finance," Adrianna countered.

Mason stood up. "Come outside."

"Not this again, Mace." She emptied the bottle into her glass. "It's dark. It's cold. It's late September. You know how the wind whips through the buildings at this time of year."

"Then get a jacket. I have to tell you something."

Adrianna rolled her eyes and carried her glass out to the balcony. Prairie followed. Mason closed the sliding glass door and spoke softly. "The Peleus fund that we manage is a government operation to help fund the national security state. We get information that other people aren't privy to.

"Something is about to happen in New York. I don't know what, but I'm seeing trades that remind me of the airlines getting shorted on the day before 9/11. Not only that, but Roy knows too."

"He told you that?" Adrianna asked.

"Like I said, we're involved with the national security state. Our phones are monitored. Roy told me as much as he could. He insisted that we leave tomorrow."

Adrianna yelled, "I told you I have an appointment tomorrow!"

Mason opened the sliding door. "Lexi will have to meet with the caterer on her own, or she can reschedule. We're leaving first thing in the morning. I want both of you to start packing as soon as we get back inside."

"I'm not going anywhere." Adrianna slugged her wine and went back into the apartment.

CHAPTER 14

And Lot went out, and spake unto his sons in law, which married his daughters, and said, Up, get you out of this place; for the LORD will destroy this city. But he seemed as one that mocked unto his sons in law.

Genesis 19:14

Mason opted to take a taxi to Daphne's apartment rather than bother with finding parking for the Interceptor. He paid the cabbie and exited the vehicle. He found her Chelsea apartment building with no doorman and the door unlocked. He felt a sense of unease at being able to access the building so readily. Mason took the elevator to the

8th floor, then proceeded to Daphne's apartment. He knocked. No one answered so he rang the doorbell.

Shortly thereafter Daphne opened the door. "Dad, what are you doing here?"

"I just stopped by. Am I interrupting anything?"

"No." She looked inside at Steve who was sitting on the sofa, wearing earphones and playing a video game. "I was just studying. I have two quizzes tomorrow, Microeconomics and Statistics. I took too many classes this semester, but I want to get it over with—finish school so I can get a job."

"You'll get there," Mason assured. "Can I come in?"

"Oh, of course." She stepped out of the way.

He walked inside. "Is Steve still interested in a job?"

She turned to her husband who seemed oblivious to Mason's presence. She waved her hands to get his attention. "I haven't heard the latest news. You'll have to ask him. Why? Does Poseidon have an opening?"

"We will." Mason watched Steve who held up a finger signaling he needed a little more time to finish his game. "We're setting up shop in West Palm. Roy has had it with the Wall Street protests."

"As in Florida?" Daphne asked.

"Yeah. We'll need new traders. Most of our people aren't willing to relocate."

"I understand," Daphne replied. "We're not interested in moving either—especially not to Florida."

"Don't make a decision until you've heard me out."

Steve finally paused his game. "Hey, Mace. Good to see you." He put down his headphones and brought an empty glass to the counter where Mason and Daphne were. "Can I offer you a drink?" Steve opened the fridge, filled his glass with ice, then poured himself a whiskey.

"No thank you," Mason replied.

Daphne explained, "Dad has a job offer for you, but Poseidon is moving to Florida so I told him we wouldn't be interested."

"Yeah, seems things are solid at Goldman..." Steve sipped his drink. "...for the time being, anyway."

Mason had hoped the softer approach would work. "Can I speak to both of you outside?"

"Outside where?" Daphne quizzed.

"Outside. Downstairs. Out front of the building."

"Dad, you're freaking me out. What's wrong with you?"

"Nothing. Just—humor me. Come downstairs."

Steve looked at Daphne with confused eyes as if Mason were crazy. "Ah—sure. Why not?"

Daphne shook her head. "Dad, if you need to tell me something, tell me here. I've got a lot of studying to do. I'll be up until one or two as it is. How about I come by the apartment on Sunday? We can talk then."

"It has to be now—please!"

"Okay, let's go outside." She pressed her lips together and motioned for Steve to follow.

"Leave your phones here," Mason instructed.

"Dad, you're worrying me," she said.

"Please, honey. Just do it. You too, Steve."

They complied, then followed Mason to the elevator. Once they reached the exterior of the building, Mason told them about the plane, the abandoned cars, the short trades against the extensive tranche of New York City-based companies, and Roy's insistence that Mason get out of Manhattan the following morning.

"Something bad is going to happen and you need to leave the city. Come to Florida with us. We'll make a vacation out of it."

Daphne sighed. "Dad. I can't go on vacation. I'm drowning in schoolwork. I have those two tests tomorrow, a project for Digital Marketing due Thursday, and a paper due Friday. There's no way! Leaving town would derail the entire semester."

"Yeah, Mace." Steve sipped his whiskey and put his arm around Daphne. "Markets are open for after-hours and pre-market the rest of the week. They expect me to be there."

Mason nodded. "Sure, I understand. Daphne, maybe you could take your tests tomorrow, then we can pick you up. You can turn in your Marketing project early and email your paper to your professor. Tell them you're sick. People get sick."

She turned to go back to the building. "Not if they take eighteen hours in a single semester. When you carry a load like that, one sick day could mean failing a class."

He grabbed her wrist. "Please. Something is going to happen. You must listen to me."

She gently pried her arm away from her father. "I talked to Mom yesterday. She said this thing with Wyn has you pretty upset. I think the stress of that combined with everything that's happened in the markets has you rattled. I mean, your entire reality has been upended, who wouldn't be?

"You said you saw a plane go down. Maybe you did. I haven't heard anything about it on the news. But I think you could be misinterpreting the events. I think you're catastrophizing. You need to talk to someone. If I get the name of my therapist, will you call her? She's really good."

Mason raised his voice. "Honey, I don't need to see a therapist! You are in danger! You need to get out of the city! Wyn was there. She saw the plane crash. Ask her about it!"

Daphne turned around. "I thought you said the plane crash was today. OCFS is looking for Wyn. Do you know where he is? They need to find him. They're professionals. They understand what he's going through. If you know where he is, you need to call them. You're in no shape to be caring for Wyn. I didn't want to say this, but the reason Wyn left is because you didn't support him. I know it's not how you grew up, but times change, and you have to roll with the punches. We all love you, but we love Wyn also. And he needs your support. He needs all of us to be accepting, and loving, and he needs to feel like he is still part of this family regardless of his gender."

Mason's mouth went dry. He couldn't conceive how this conversation had devolved into him being blamed for Wyn's predicament. But he understood that Daphne was not about to be persuaded to leave town. "Okay. I have to go. Please, keep some things with you. If you hear anything out of the ordinary, be ready to get out of New York at a moment's notice."

"Sure thing, Mace," Steve lifted his glass as if toasting Mason's departure.

"And if you know where Wyn is, please call OCFS. They're the only ones qualified to help," said Daphne.

"Take care. I love you." Mason watched Daphne walk back inside the building and then hailed a taxi.

"Where to?" asked the cabbie.

"Christopher Street." Mason closed the door. Hope's apartment was in the West Village, the next neighborhood to the south of Chelsea.

"Christopher and what?" asked the driver.

"You can drop me on the corner of Hudson." That would give Mason a chance to walk a block and shake off some of the nerves from his encounter with Daphne.

They arrived in a matter of minutes. Mason paid the cabbie and got out. He walked up Christopher to the three-story brick building Hope and her husband, Raphael, owned. The top floor was a loft-style apartment where they lived, and the second floor served as their painting studio. The ground floor was rented out to tenants.

Mason pressed the call button. Hope answered. "Hello?"

"Hey, it's Dad."

"Come on up." The door buzzed.

Mason let himself into the building and walked up the two flights of stairs to her loft. The smell of marijuana wafted out when she opened the door to greet him. "Hey, Dad. Come in."

"Mr. Lot!" Raphael waved at Mason. He had a joint between his fingers, and he was talking on the telephone. He disappeared into the office which was the only room besides the bathroom segregated by walls from the rest of the apartment.

Mason forced a smile and waved back.

"Do you want a glass of wine?" Hope offered.

"No thank you."

"Have a seat on the couch. I'll be right there." Hope poured herself a glass of white wine and joined him in the living area. She sat next to him and spoke calmly. "How are you feeling?"

"I'm fine."

She stitched her brows together as if unconvinced. "Pot's legal now. Anyone can buy it in New York. They used to write prescriptions for it. Just because you don't need a doctor anymore doesn't mean it can't be used medicinally. You know, like if you're stressed or having a rough time."

"Where is this coming from? Did Daphne call you?"

Hope sipped her wine. "She did. Obviously, she was concerned about how you might be handling things."

"Hope, I'm not stressed. You know me. I handle things pretty well."

"Dad, your face started turning red when you said that. Yes, in general, you're a rock. But we all get a little overwhelmed at times."

"That's not what this is. Listen, I need to talk to you. Can you come downstairs with me?"

She shook her head. "No. I already know what you're going to say."

"Do you?"

"Something bad is going to happen in New York. Raphael and I need to leave the city. You saw a plane crash, people are disappearing, your boss gave you some coded message that he got from the intelligence community about a possible attack, but nobody knows what it is. And we can't talk about any of this over the phone because they're listening. Did I miss anything?"

Mason shook his head. "You got all of that secondhand. And it came in the form of Daphne building a case about me having a nervous breakdown or something of the like."

"Don't be mad at Daphne," said Hope. "If you'd come here first, I would have called her and let her know she was probably your next stop. Look, Dad. Everything is piling up. No one blames you—for having trouble adjusting to Wyn's decision about who he is…"

"That's *not* why I'm here!" Mason yelled. "You are in *danger*. Your life is in *danger*!"

Raphael came out of the office. He spoke in an almost whispered voice. "Hey man, be cool. No one needs to get upset. We're all copacetic here, man." He offered Mason a hit off of the joint he'd been smoking. "Take a puff. Step back. It'll help you get some perspective. Take the edge off and look at things in a fresh light tomorrow. It's never as bad as it seems at the time."

Mason held up his hand. "No, Raphael. Sometimes, it's worse than anyone thinks."

Raphael hit the joint and handed it to Hope. "Then in times like that, you have to let go and focus on the future. Every rain cloud passes. Hope shared with me a little bit about what you've been going through. And man, I've been there. The paranoia, the delusions, my own self-limiting beliefs, the illusion that the way I saw things were the way things were…"

Hope interrupted him. "Dad, I was off work today because the Met has been closed since all this stuff started with the currency. Raffy and I walked down to SoHo for lunch. The whole way there and the whole way back, we didn't see any abandoned cars or anyone talking about people disappearing."

He countered, "Daphne's doorman is missing. Ask her!"

"Dad, we can't run away like the world is ending because Daphne's doorman left work early. I think you are interpreting events to fit this apocalyptic narrative that your mind has invented to help you make sense of things you're having trouble understanding. That's all. Like Raffy said, it happens to the best of us."

Mason stood up and started for the door. "Something bad is going to happen to New York. If you're not going to listen, at least be ready to leave at the first sign of trouble. I love you, Hope, and I really wish you'd listen."

"I love you too, Dad. But I can't let your period of emotional trauma turn my world upside down. Neither can Daphne, nor Wyn, nor Mom. And I beg you not to drag Prairie into this chaos with you. She's young and can't make decisions for herself. It isn't fair to her. Get some help, or medication, or both. We'll all still be here when you get back."

"Peace out, brother." Raphael held up the two-finger peace sign as he walked Mason to the door.

Mason felt sad, like he'd failed, as a father, as a human being, as everything. He wanted to cry but was so horrified at the thought of what might become of his daughters that he could not. He descended the stairs and exited the building onto Christopher Street. He headed east, in the direction of the Stonewall Inn located only two blocks away. It was the iconic ground zero for the modern gay rights movement. Mason pondered how activists who'd wanted to be left alone to *do what we want* had become the political juggernaut that commanded others to *do what we say.* He thought about what these tyrants had done to his daughter and wondered if his libertarian leanings had perhaps been a little naive.

Rather than hail a taxi right away, Mason turned north on Hudson and walked for a while. He pulled the small tablet from his inside jacket pocket. He powered it on and then leaned against a lamp post while he logged onto the Wi-Fi of a nearby bar. First, he messaged Wynter. *Pack everything. I'm picking you up at 9:00 AM. We're heading to Florida for a few days. Prairie is coming. She's excited to see you.*

Mason saw no reason to get into the particulars of the conversation. Next, he messaged Giovanni. *Boss says to get out of NYC. Something bad is about to happen. Not sure if it could affect Jersey, but I'd take the family on a trip if I were you. I'm heading out first thing in the morning.*

He stowed the tablet in his jacket pocket and continued north on Hudson. The civil unrest that had broken out after the currency event had been quelled for the most part. Subsequently, the military's presence in Manhattan had been scaled down. Mason saw the first Humvee since beginning his stroll through the West Village. It was parked on the sidewalk, blocking the entrance to a small deli on the corner of Bleeker Street.

Mason observed the four guardsmen posted by the vehicle. They appeared bored and ready to be done with the uneventful post. Mason approached them cautiously. "Good evening, gentlemen."

The one wearing sergeant insignia stood up straight and pulled the butt of his rifle into his shoulder as if preparing for an attack. "What do you want?"

Mason held up his hands to show he intended them no harm. "Just wondering what you guys were being told—about the disappearances."

The guardsman standing next to the sergeant looked at him with worried eyes. The sergeant returned the glance with a slight shake of the head. The sergeant redirected his attention to Mason. "If you have a family member or know someone that isn't where they should be, wait twenty-four hours to see if they turn up, then if not, you may file a missing persons report at the nearest NYPD precinct."

"That's about what I was expecting." Mason turned and walked away. He felt the notification vibration on his tablet. He pulled it out of his jacket to see Giovanni's response. *Yeah, I got a thing tomorrow morning. Might be good for me to be gone for a while after that. Where are you going?*

Mason replied, *Florida.*

He also saw that Wynter had acknowledged his previous message with a *K*. Mason powered off the device and waved down a taxi.

CHAPTER 15

Then the LORD rained upon Sodom and upon Gomorrah brimstone and fire from the LORD out of heaven; And he overthrew those cities, and all the plain, and all the inhabitants of the cities, and that which grew upon the ground. But his wife looked back from behind him, and she became a pillar of salt.

Genesis 19:24-26

Mason and Prairie walked up the stairs to the apartment in Ironbound. Mason knocked and Wynter opened the door. Prairie embraced her sister. "I'm so sorry. I didn't know. When you came home, I ignored you because Marco was there. I didn't even see that you were hurting. I didn't even ask." She began to cry.

Wynter pulled Prairie close. "It's okay. You had company. If I would have asked, I know you would have sent him home."

Prairie looked up with remorseful eyes. "You're not mad at me?"

"Of course not. How could I be?" Wynter turned to Mason who was bagging up the food from the fridge. "Where's Mom?"

Prairie said, "Lexi's daughter, Sky, is getting married. Mom's helping her plan it. She and Dad had a knock-down-drag-out over her not coming. So the topic is kind of a sore spot for Dad."

Mason cleared the anger out of his throat before speaking. "She's going to take a plane tomorrow."

"Oh, right. I guess you guys could have flown down if it hadn't been for me." Wynter lowered her gaze. "Kinda hard to get a ticket for a fugitive from justice."

Mason placed the bags of food near the door. "You can't get a ticket today anyway. My intentions were to book Mom's flight for tomorrow. She may end up having to rent a car."

"Why can't you get a ticket?" asked Wynter. "The plane that crashed on the interstate shouldn't have even affected Newark. Did you try JFK?"

"I tried every airport within a hundred miles— LaGuardia, Philly, New Haven…"

Prairie interrupted. "So you saw the plane crash too!"

"Yeah!" Wyn pointed toward the interstate. "It hit right there. It shook the whole building. A giant fireball and smoke plume came up. I can't believe they didn't say anything about it on the news."

Prairie told of her experiences the day prior, the plane crash video that was quickly taken down, and Marco's rapid departure with his father's security team.

"Does this have something to do with why we're going to Florida?" Wynter asked.

"We'll talk about it on the way," said Mason. "Where is the pistol I gave you?"

"Still on the nightstand." Wynter looked toward the bedroom.

Mason nodded. "Prairie, help your sister load her belongings in the SUV. I'll be right down."

Keenly aware of the oppressive gun laws in New York, Mason extracted the magazine and ejected the shell from the chamber. He wrapped the gun in a bath towel and took it down to the car. He placed it in the rear compartment near the foil-wrapped shoe box containing his and Prairie's phones. He closed the hatch. "Did you get everything?"

"I think so," said Wynter. "I'll go double-check and lock up. Are we going to be gone a while?"

"It's hard to say," Mason answered.

"I'll go with her." Prairie trailed behind her big sister.

Soon, the Interceptor was loaded, seat belts were fastened, and they were on the road.

"Don't you need a map?" Wynter sat in the front passenger's seat.

"It's I-95 the whole way," Mason answered. He drove straight to the interstate on-ramp and headed south. Minutes later, they arrived at the I-78 interchange. Large portable road signs alerted motorists that I-78 was closed and that access to Newark International Airport had been shut down.

Mason tried to identify the crash site of the airplane but could not.

"Nothing to see here," said Prairie from the back seat. "Move along."

"Seems to be a lot of that going around," Wynter added.

***

Two hours into the trip, Wynter asked. "How long is this trip anyway?"

"The map said eighteen hours," Prairie informed. "But with no phones, it's going to feel like at least double that."

Mason watched yet another convoy of military vehicles passing by on the opposite side of the road shortly after passing Philadelphia.

"Where do you think those guys are going?" Prairie asked.

"Looks like Philly," Wynter answered.

"Most of the riots are over. You'd think they'd be *leaving* Philly," said Prairie.

"Unless they're getting ready for another event." Mason watched the convoy get smaller in his side-view mirror.

"Look, Dad," said Wynter. "Another overturned, burned-out semi."

"The trees and grass all around it are scorched too," said Prairie.

"And there," Wynter pointed toward the median. "More broken glass. Plus, the guardrail is twisted up like the one we saw back near Trenton."

"Looks like there were a lot of wrecks yesterday." Prairie pressed her face against the window as she peered out at the damage.

"Seems as though they've managed to clear most of the vehicles, except for the big rigs," Wynter said. "It's like they were in a hurry—like they're trying to cover something up."

"Do you think Daphne and Hope will have a chance to get out of the city?" Prairie inquired. "I mean once they figure out what's going on."

"I don't know Sweat Pea. I talked to both of them, but they're convinced I'm having a nervous breakdown. I told them to be ready to leave at a moment's notice. I've done all I can do." Mason marinated in his failure for the next leg of the journey.

The interstate was littered with recently-cleared accident sites all the way to West Palm Beach.

Mason continued to see military convoys along the route. All of this added to his sense of uneasiness about his wife and daughters still being in New York.

They arrived at the condominium Roy had rented for them shortly after 4:00 AM. The girls had napped during the trip, but Mason had not taken his eyes off the road except for restroom breaks and to fill the gas tank. The girls inspected the ocean-front apartment while he took a shower. Mason kissed them both good night and fell asleep dreaming that he was still driving.

***

Mason woke up at noon on Thursday. He came out of the bedroom to find Prairie and Wynter on the sofa watching an MTV reality show about delinquent teens using drugs, drinking, having wild parties, and sleeping around. "Can we see what's on the news?"

"Nothing," said Prairie. "We checked. It's like an information blackout or something."

Mason frowned at the program. "Then can you find something besides that to watch?"

"Can we go down to the beach?" Wynter walked to the sliding glass doors and looked down at the ocean.

Mason knew he couldn't expect them to stay locked up in the apartment. "I suppose. But stay right in front of the building in case I need to find you."

"We have phones." Prairie glanced at Wynter. "At least I do."

Mason saw that the foil-encased shoe box had been unwrapped.

Prairie noticed where he was looking. "I put yours on the kitchen counter to charge. I mean, you have to call your boss and tell him that you're here, right? Plus, you have to figure out how Mom is going to get down here."

"I guess you're right." Mason walked close to them so they could hear him whisper. "But don't say Wyn's name where the phone can pick it up. Don't text anything about her and don't talk about anything we've seen or about something bad happening in New York. I'm serious!"

Prairie seemed sufficiently concerned. "Okay, Daddy. We'll be careful."

"Can we have a credit card?" Wyn asked. "We didn't bring bathing suits and there's a surf shop across the street."

"And can we get something to eat while we're out?" Prairie asked.

The condo was angled so they could see the beach as well as the adjacent shopping strip. Mason looked down at the street to see a selection of restaurants, bars, and retail establishments.

Mason took out a credit card and handed it to Wynter. "What kind of swim apparel were you thinking of buying?" He worried about what she would wear up top if she decided to get men's swim trunks.

"A bikini, I guess," Wyn replied.

"So can we get her some cute girl clothes also if we see anything?" Prairie asked.

"Sure." Mason wasn't about to turn down that request. He opened the sliding doors and stepped out onto the balcony. "Looks like they have about everything you could need. Stay in this little shopping center."

"Okay, we will!" Prairie grabbed her sister's hand and hurried out the door.

Mason went to the kitchen and looked through the sparse food offerings that they had brought with them. "I need to make a list and go on a grocery run."

He wrinkled his nose at the choices of pre-ground coffee K-cups provided by the hosts but popped one in the machine and pressed the *brew* button. He found only a loaf of bread for breakfast items. Mason watched the coffee finish brewing then carried the hot beverage out onto the balcony. He examined the shops on the strip. "Bagels. I'll text Prairie and tell her to bring me one."

Mason sipped his coffee, placed the cup on the patio table, then went inside to retrieve his phone. He sent the message to Prairie. Just then, she and Wynter came into view. He watched Prairie check her phone as the two of them strolled down Ocean Drive.

"This wouldn't be such a bad life." He checked the price of other condos in the building. "It's like Roy said, half the price and double the space of what we have on the Upper East Side. But we certainly can't get a view like this in New York."

The condo was in Riviera Beach rather than Palm Beach proper. Mason checked to see the distance to the new office. "Seven miles. Twenty-three minutes. I never dreamed of getting to work that fast in New York." His mind drifted to Adrianna. "She won't like it." He recalled the harbingers which had driven him to come to this coastal paradise. "But she may not have a choice." He sent her a text. *Any luck getting a plane ticket yet?*

She replied shortly thereafter. *Nothing. It's like the airports are closed. I'll try again tomorrow. It's probably a computer glitch. I'm sure it will be sorted out by then.*

Mason felt his stomach tighten up. He typed out his response with great agitation. *You need to leave today. Rent a car.*

Her reply came quickly. *All the rental car places are in the airports.*

His fingers felt stiff as he entered the next message. *That's not accurate. There's an Avis downtown on Broadway and an Alamo right off Broadway, right around 11th or 12th, I think. You can stop halfway and get a hotel. North Carolina maybe. The condo is very nice. We're right on the ocean.*

He didn't want to type Wynter's name so he added, *Your daughter would love to see you. She needs her mom right now.*

He sipped his coffee and waited for her to text him back. When it came, he frowned as he read it. *If it's going to take me two days to drive, I might as well wait for the airports to open tomorrow. You know how much I hate road trips. Tell my CHILDREN that I love them. I'm going to yoga right now so I'm turning off my phone. I'll let you know tomorrow what time to pick me up at the airport.*

"No!" Mason wanted to throw the phone. He sent one last plea, hoping to reach her before she shut off the phone. *We talked about this. You need to get out of New York today!*

He waited for a reply, but none came. His heartbeat quickened. Mason turned on the television and found Fox News, hoping it would distract him from the sense of dread overwhelming him at the moment. He stared at the screen but paid no attention to what was being said. He tuned in just enough to realize the stories being covered offered no substantive value and went right back to ruminating about Daphne, Hope, and Adrianna.

He paced back and forth from the kitchen, to the balcony, to the sofa. More coffee was the last thing he needed given his anxious state, but nevertheless, he brewed three more K-cups over the course of the next hour and a half. His incessant worrying was eventually interrupted when Prairie and Wynter returned home.

"Hey, Daddy," Prairie chirped. "Here's your bagels. I brought you a couple."

"Thank you." He opened the white paper bag, split the bagel in two, and placed it in the toaster oven. Mason could feel the acid of the coffee churning about in his stomach along with the acid of distress. He needed to get something to soak it up right away.

Once the timer was set on the toaster, he turned to look at the shopping bags. "Looks like you girls found a few things."

"We did!" Prairie pulled a black bikini out of the first bag. "Wynter found this little number."

Little is right, Mason thought but made no comment.

"I got this." Prairie took out a second bikini featuring a pink floral print which wasn't much bigger than the black one. "We found some sundresses too." She took out a couple of short dresses. "This one is for Wynter and this one is for me." She held a white one with lace trim over herself. "I can't believe people are wearing white in September, but it seems all the rules are different in Florida." She folded the dress and put it back in the bag. "When in Rome…"

"Dad doesn't want to hear about dresses and bathing suits." Wynter took the bag containing her purchases.

"No, I do. They're all very pretty." Despite his reservations, Mason was thrilled to see Wynter buying feminine attire.

Prairie ignored her sister's comment and continued to pull out short sets, tank tops, and other Floridian apparel. "We need to go to a proper department store, also. Wyn has to get some makeup."

"Okay," said Mason. "But can she borrow yours in the meantime?"

Wynter lowered her brow. "Prairie is a blonde, Dad. I have black hair."

"Oh." It occurred to Mason that perhaps every girl might have their own color palette when it came to makeup.

"Did Mom call?" Wynter asked.

Mason would have preferred to look at clothes a while longer. "I texted her."

"And?" Wynter asked.

"Still no flights out. I asked—begged, rather, for her to rent a car and drive down. But she ended the conversation. She said she loves you both."

Prairie became distressed over this information. "Daddy, you have to make her come. We talked with the girl working at the bagel shop. It's bad. She said tons of people around here disappeared. Did you know they have a six o'clock curfew?"

"Six?" Mason inquired. "It was eight o'clock in New York when we had the riots."

"Yeah, but this is different," said Wynter. "So many people are gone from around here that thieves started going around and looting houses. Lots of the people who are missing left their houses wide open, lights on, television on, everything. Looters are going to houses and knocking on doors. If no one answers, they go in, clean the place out, even steal the cars from the garage when they leave."

"Wow." Mason listened closely to Wynter's account. "Does she have any idea what might have happened?"

Prairie answered. "She says it was the Rapture. Her aunt, grandmother, and cousin are all gone. They went to the same church. Plus, the ice cream shop is closed. She says the girls who worked there were always inviting her to go to church with them."

"Yeah, but Sweat Pea, we're Christian, and we didn't disappear. Maybe they have some anecdotal evidence that makes them believe that theory, but it's something else."

"I'm not a Christian," said Wynter. "I'm an atheist."

"And I'm agnostic," Prairie added.

"How can you be agnostic?" Wynter quizzed. "You're a logical person. You know there's not some all-powerful creature living in the sky that makes the flowers grow."

"I don't know that," Prairie countered. "And neither do you. And nobody can prove it either way, so agnostic *is* the logical answer. But with everything that I'm hearing, I'm leaning sixty-forty *for* there being something else."

Wynter interrogated her father. "And what makes you a Christian?"

"We go to church," Mason defended.

"Twice a year," Wynter countered. "Mom goes to yoga three times a week. Does that make her Hindu?"

Prairie turned to the television. "What just happened?"

Mason looked to see that the broadcast had cut to static. "I'm not sure." He walked to the coffee table and picked up the remote. He touched the guide button and navigated to the next news channel. "CNBC is out." His stomach sank. "ABC News— nothing."

Mason put the remote on the coffee table, pulled out his phone, and called Adrianna.

"Hi, you've reached Adrianna. I can't get to the phone right now…"

CHAPTER 16

And when he had opened the second seal, I heard the second beast say, Come and see. And there went out another horse that was red: and power was given to him that sat thereon to take peace from the earth, and that they should kill one another: and there was given unto him a great sword.

Revelation 6:3-4

Mason ended the call to Adrianna and put the phone back in his pocket. He picked up the television remote.

"Try CNN," said Prairie. "They're in Atlanta."

He scrolled down. His hand shook. His head felt dizzy. He sat on the floor, could not press the button to select the channel that would confirm his worst nightmare. Mason's breathing became irregular, his heart pounded in his chest, in his ears. He felt hot, then cold—shivered, felt like he was falling.

"Dad." Wynter knelt beside him. "Give me the remote."

He wrapped his arms around it, protected it like a precious jewel. "No."

"Please, Dad." Wynter tried to pry it from his hands.

"Just wait—hang on." He defended.

Prairie sat crying on the floor next to Mason. "Daddy, we need to know. Maybe it's nothing."

His eyes welled up. He knew it was not nothing. He put his arm around his youngest and pulled her close. Wynter eased the remote from Mason's hand as if she were stealing a dead antelope from a sleeping lion. She switched to CNN.

The reporter said, "Fed Chair Hassan Alami delivered remarks at a press conference this morning saying that 95 percent of all personal bank accounts have been fully integrated and are now…"

Wynter scrolled through the channels. "Where is GBC based?"

Numbness began to overtake Mason's initial emotional reaction. "Washington," he muttered.

Wynter selected GBC from the menu.

Terry Bergman, the daytime face of GBC was seated behind her desk. She wore her typical men's shirt with a sports jacket, short brown hair, and very little makeup. Her face became grave as she put a finger over her ear. "I'm getting a report in just now. My producer just wants to double-check—we don't want to put out any news that hasn't been verified, especially something of this magnitude… Okay, yes, GBC can confirm that there has been a massive explosion in New York City…"

Mason took out his phone and tried calling his wife once more.

"All circuits are busy…" He ended the call and put the phone on the floor.

Wynter wailed, "Mama! No! Please!" She screamed at the top of her lungs. "No!"

Mason held Prairie with one arm and put his other around Wynter to pull her close. "Shhhhh."

Both girls sobbed uncontrollably. Mason turned up the volume so he could hear over the loud painful cries of his girls.

Terry Bergman continued her report. "We are currently unable to reach the GBC New York news bureau located on 59th Street. Whatever caused the explosion appears to be affecting cell phone transmission, the internet, as well as satellite.

We have people at GBC right now trying to reach out to their counterparts at the various news agencies based in Manhattan to get more details about the explosion. The only thing we know right now is that all of them seem to be offline."

"Where is Fox?" Wynter dried her eyes.

Mason felt confused. He had trouble thinking. "Ahh—I don't know. 6th Ave and something. It's right by Rockefeller Center."

"Rockefeller Center! NBC is there. Where is that?" Wynter seemed to be building a case for her mother's survival.

"49th!" Prairie quickly latched onto the idea. "Ten blocks away from the GBC New York studio. So Fox, CNBC, NBC, MSNBC, and the GBC studio are all in a ten-block radius. Maybe it's just in that area!"

"Where is ABC?" Wynter inquired.

Mason shook his head. "I don't know. Sixty-something." The margins were getting slimmer.

"The park starts at 59th. Which side?" Wynter asked.

"West side." Mason swallowed hard. Any explosion big enough to hit all the known affected areas would likely have hit Chelsea.

Prairie seemed to notice his concern. She checked her phone. "It's 2:30. Daphne is probably still in school. Way uptown. I'll call her now."

Mason watched Prairie make the call. He reached for his phone and called Hope.

"All circuits are busy. Please try your call again…" He ended the call and looked at Prairie.

Her eyes were forlorn. "I got the same message."

"Okay, that just means the phones are jammed. Try texting," Wynter insisted.

Mason nodded. "Prairie, you text Daphne. I'll try Hope." *Text me when you get this. Are you okay?*

"And Mom," Wynter instructed.

Mason messaged his wife. *We heard there was an explosion. We're worried. Please call, text, or email to let us know you're okay.*

The three of them turned their attention back to the television.

Terry Bergman touched her ear again. "Alright, my producer is telling me that we've just received cell phone footage of the explosion which we believe to have occurred in New York City."

The video showed a massive fireball billowing toward the sky in what seemed to be slow motion.

Bergman grasped to find words to describe the video clip. "This–this…is, I'm speechless. Like many of you, I was in high school when 9/11 happened. And the shock, the horror, was so difficult to process. I suspect when all is said and done, today will be many times more painful to remember for our country than even that most fateful of days.

"But back to the recording, this was taken from Riverhead, Long Island. Guys, can you get me some information on how far away that is from Manhattan?" Bergman paused.

"Daddy, do you know?" Prairie inquired.

He shook his head and waited for Terry Bergman's response.

"That can't be right." Bergman pressed her earpiece as if she could not understand what was being said to her. "Alright. Maybe it is. I'm being told Riverhead is roughly 70 miles from Manhattan.

"Um, just for reference, I had an aunt who lived in Daytona Beach, Florida and we would visit her in the summer on occasion. I can recall seeing the fireball from a Falcon 9 lifting off at Kennedy Space Center which was probably about 60 miles away. It was incredible but nothing like this.

"But to estimate what could cause an explosion of this magnitude, and for it to appear to be so large from such a distance—I don't want to speculate but I can't think of anything else other than a nuclear bomb.

"Now to be clear, this is nothing more than me trying to grasp at straws as I try to make sense of what I'm seeing. However, I would highly advise that if you are in the path of this massive smoke plume we see, you should stay inside with your windows closed until further notice.

"My producer is telling me that the prevailing winds in that area go from west to east. That means anyone on Long Island should seek shelter indoors until you've received an all-clear from the Federal Government. I'm sure we will be hearing from them soon.

"We have another video for you. Everything we are showing you for the rest of the broadcast has the potential to upset sensitive viewers, so if that is you, or if you have small children, you may want to consider pausing the broadcast. This video is a clip from the Times Square live cam."

The video showed footage taken from the iconic location with people walking to and fro. Single people, couples, people who looked like tourists, many with backpacks. Some were sitting on benches, others stood checking their phones, all oblivious to what was about to happen.

Above them, jumbotrons promoted Broadway shows and sneakers, chocolate bars and TV shows, athletic apparel, and SUVs. Behind them, buses, taxis, scooters, and delivery trucks hustled and bustled along 7th Avenue. Then suddenly, a brilliant white flash drowned out all the color, all the lines, all the contrast that had made up the moving images of the city that never sleeps. The cars, the people, the advertisements, the buying, the selling, the coming and going came to a certain and instantaneous halt.

Mason hugged his two daughters. His mouth felt dry. He held his breath for the next words, the next video, or any indication of what had happened, who did it, and why.

"Right now, we have GBC's Chief National Security Correspondent, Gale Simpson with us," said Bergman.

The shot switched to a man with neat hair and a pressed shirt standing in front of the White House. A small mic was clipped to the lapel of his navy-blue jacket.

Terry Bergman asked, "Gale, have you been able to find out anything concerning the explosion in New York City?"

"Good afternoon, Terry," Simpson replied. "We have reached out but have not gotten a definitive response. Although the chatter would suggest that this was a nuclear explosion of some sort. We are still trying to assess exactly what happened and no one I have spoken to is ready to say if this was intentional or some kind of an accident.

"Indian Point is the closest nuclear reactor which is about 36 miles up the Hudson River from Manhattan. GBC is beginning to get other cell phone footage of that massive fireball you showed earlier. Most of them are very similar so we probably won't be showing each and every one of those videos, but they all have one thing in common. They are taken from a distance of greater than 65 miles. We can use the location of those videos, the angle of the sun, and whatnot to determine that the fireball does seem to originate from the Manhattan area. So, while we can't say that it wasn't an accident, we are confident that this explosion is not from the Indian Point nuclear facility."

"Okay," said Bergman. "It's important to start ruling things out as we work to get to the bottom of this terrible event. Gale, has your team been able to estimate the size of the fireball? It appears to be incredibly large given the distance at which the video was taken from."

"Yes," Simpson answered. "This next video is from Lakehurst, New Jersey. We estimate it was about 65 miles away from the explosion."

The next clip appeared to be almost identical to the first, with a gargantuan fireball mushrooming toward the heavens.

Simpson provided commentary. "This clip is a little longer than the first. As it goes on, we can see the smoke plume begin to drift in that easterly direction you mentioned earlier. And while we're on the topic, I'd like to reiterate the advice you gave for anyone east of Manhattan. Get inside now. Close your doors and windows and stay where you are until you get an all-clear from DHS or FEMA.

"Back to your question, Terry, our best estimates suggest the fireball was about three-quarters of a mile wide."

The television became silent.

Gale Simpson broke the quietude. "Terry, are you still with me?"

"Yes, Gale. I'm here."

"Okay, I thought I'd lost you for a moment."

"I'm just trying to digest what you told me," said Bergman.

"I know, I know," Gale Simpson spoke with an empathetic tone. "It's a lot to handle. It's nothing like any of us have ever had to cover. Manhattan Island is only about two miles wide, so it's difficult to imagine how any structures could have—I don't know, Terry. I don't want to start speculating on the damage without knowing exactly where the explosion occurred."

"I understand," Bergman agreed. "Do you have any way of predicting what size of a bomb would be required to produce a fireball three-quarters of a mile wide?"

"Again, Terry, we simply don't have the details to guess on that one. So many factors come into play there. Was it a ground-level detonation? If not, at what altitude was the detonation? All of those data points have to be filled in to…"

"I'm sorry to cut you off, Gale. But the White House Press Secretary, Marsha Cox is stepping to the podium. We're going to the briefing room now."

The screen showed a tall slender man in his late fifties wearing a short blue dress, black heels, and what appeared to be a blonde wig, approach the lectern. "Good afternoon." He spoke with a low, masculine voice. "At 3:19 Eastern, this afternoon, New York City was attacked by a nuclear missile which was launched from Russia. After I've delivered my remarks, DHS Secretary Morris

Haseley will be providing more details about the nature of this attack and the US's response.

"From initial satellite images, we believe that all of Manhattan, parts of the surrounding boroughs, as well as areas of New Jersey like Hoboken, have been utterly destroyed. We do not expect to have many survivors from these areas. The satellite images show massive structural damage and fires burning as far north as Hackensack, New Jersey, as far south as Sheepshead Bay in Brooklyn, out past JFK Airport to the east, and even into Newark west of the blast zone.

"Currently, FEMA, the National Guard, as well as the US military are being mobilized to go into the affected areas and assist those who need our help. But they will not be able to move in until the fires caused by the blast have subsided.

"The president is speaking with NATO allies right now and will be delivering an address later this evening. Our thoughts and sympathies go out to the families and loved ones of all of those who have lost their lives in today's attacks.

"The White House will be providing ongoing updates throughout the day as will the directors of various federal agencies tasked with handling today's crisis."

The aged transvestite introduced the next speaker. "Secretary Haseley, the podium is yours."

CHAPTER 17

And ye shall hear of wars and rumours of wars: see that ye be not troubled: for all these things must come to pass, but the end is not yet. For nation shall rise against nation, and kingdom against kingdom: and there shall be famines, and pestilences, and earthquakes, in divers places. All these are the beginning of sorrows.

Matthew 24:6-8

Department of Homeland Security Secretary Morris Haseley stepped to the microphone in the White House Briefing Room. His eyes appeared worried, but not afraid. "Good afternoon."

He glanced at his notes. "First of all, you should know that the president, his staff, and most of his cabinet have been relocated to an undisclosed continuity of government center. These centers are equipped with secure communications and all the necessary resources to sustain life for an extended period of time.

"Members of Congress located in Washington DC at the time of the attack were also taken to a COG center. US Senators and Representatives who are presently in their home states or away for other reasons have been encouraged to seek shelter at the nearest COG facility.

"Going forward, these briefings will continue but will be held remotely with the press." Haseley took a deep breath and looked down at his notes once more.

"As Ms. Cox said, New York City was struck by a multiple independently targetable reentry vehicle, or MIRV, carrying a thermonuclear warhead that the Department of Defense estimates to have been 4,000 kilotons. The warhead detonated at a height of 500 meters above street-level Manhattan, just south of Central Park.

"North American Aerospace Defense Command detected the launch of a Russian RS-28 Sarmat intercontinental ballistic missile or ICBM. The US immediately contacted Russia about the launch. We were assured that this was a test launch that had somehow not been communicated through regular channels.

"Nonetheless, the Department of Defense activated all available missile defense assets. We soon realized that the launch was not a test and prepared to engage the MIRVs once they were released.

"Without getting too deep into the details, the RS-28 ICBM is capable of hauling several MIRVs as well as decoys, which it carries through space, then launches back to earth's atmosphere once over the desired target.

"Our defenses are not effective on the ICBM itself as it is in outer space. We seek to annihilate the MIRVs with exoatmospheric kill vehicles prior to their re-entry. Defense systems are highly capable of eliminating these threats, even when we are dealing with multiple MIRVs as well as decoys.

"Unfortunately, the MIRV that got through today was a Russian Avangard hypersonic glide vehicle which travels at 20,000 miles per hour. That's roughly ten times the speed of a bullet from a gun. You can imagine how hard it would be to shoot a moving bullet, which is why the Avangard was able to defeat our missile defense systems.

"While the weapon was manufactured and launched by Russia, we do not believe they are the only responsible party. The president as well as the joint chiefs all agree that the missile strike against New York City was instigated by the BRICS Plus nations who felt slighted by our decision to deactivate military hardware sold to them when they were considered US allies.

"Ten minutes ago, the US responded to the attack with an array of weapons including Minutemen ICBMs, air-launched cruise missiles, as well as Trident II missiles launched from Ohio-Class submarines strategically positioned around the world. We struck Moscow with a 6,000-kiloton nuclear warhead for their leadership role in today's attack. We hit Beijing with a 1,000-kiloton bomb, and smaller 50-kiloton warheads assaulted Riyadh, Sau Paulo, New Delhi, Johannesburg, and Dubai.

"Our message is clear, and our resolve should not be tested further by the BRICS Plus federation which has now decided to establish itself as not only an economic coalition but also a military alliance. If you spray us with water, we will spray you with blood. If you do not wish to reap the consequences alongside your violent partners, we strongly suggest reconsidering your membership in this corrupt organization known as BRICS Plus."

"Daddy! This is World War Three!" Prairie held Mason's hand so tightly that her nails dug into his flesh.

He was still trying to process losing his wife and other two daughters. Mason was in no condition to deal with the onslaught of world war. But he feared Prairie was correct in her assessment.

"What are we going to do?" Wynter's sorrow seemed interrupted by the concern for her own life. "What if the Russians and the Chinese retaliate?"

Mason looked away from the television, tried to focus. He walked out to the balcony, gazed at the ocean, down at the shops. "Then this is the calm before the storm."

Prairie followed him outside. "Daddy, I'm scared."

Wynter stood with her arms crossed in the opening of the sliding glass door. "Where do you think they'll hit next?"

Mason swallowed hard, put his grief on hold, and charged toward the door. "Come on. We're going to make a grocery run before we do anything else."

Prairie and Wynter trailed behind him. Mason pressed the elevator call button. "When we get there, each of us will grab a grocery cart."

The doors opened and they stepped in. "What are we going to buy?" Prairie inquired.

"Mostly stuff that doesn't have to be cooked and doesn't need to be refrigerated." He pulled out his wallet and gave a credit card to Prairie. "Wynter, you still have the card I gave you earlier, right?"

"Yes," she answered.

"Good. If things look hectic at the grocery, we may need to check out in different aisles. We don't want to look like hoarders." The doors opened and Mason led the charge to the Interceptor.

The girls kept pace with him. "So, just anything?" Prairie asked. "Canned pasta, pop tarts, cookies, chips, bread, that kind of stuff?"

Mason frowned at the list of options but could think of few better choices. "Easy on the chips.

They take up a lot of space and don't provide much mass. It's mostly air in those bags."

"Pringles are stacked pretty closely in the can. Should we get some of those?" Wynter asked.

"That's fine. But let's try to get some things like canned soup that offer nutritional value as well." Mason unlocked the vehicle and they all piled in.

Prairie closed the door and buckled her seat belt. "Peanut butter is nutritious, and it stores well. Jelly too."

"Fine." He started the engine and raced out of the parking garage. The closest grocer was a mile away, over the bridge, directly across the intercoastal waterway from the condo. When they arrived, a line had already formed to enter the parking garage.

"I guess we're not the only ones who thought of stocking up," Wynter said.

Mason gripped the wheel, hoping the queue would move faster. "These people see the grocery shelves empty out every time there's a hurricane. This isn't the first rodeo for most of them."

Mason looked around. "In fact, you girls go ahead and get out. Get two carts and start filling them. I'll find a parking spot and meet up with you inside."

"Okay." Wynter unbuckled her seatbelt. "Come on, Prairie."

"And stay together!" Mason warned.

"We will. But please, hurry." Prairie closed her door and jogged behind her older sister.

The line of cars moved slowly, but steadily. Five minutes later, Mason parked the SUV in one of the last remaining spots on the uppermost level. He bailed out of the Interceptor and slammed the door. He rushed inside, grabbed at a cart, and began surveying the picked-over aisles.

He pushed his cart up the produce aisle and began filling the cart with what was available. "Apples, potatoes, celery." He picked up a container of lettuce. "Too much space. Not enough food." He put the lettuce back. "Carrots, these are dense. Nuts!" Mason scooped up several bags of pecans, pistachios, and walnuts. He found a few bunches of bananas. "These won't keep long." He took only two bunches. He placed a bag of oranges in the cart and pressed on. He found the meat aisle stripped. He frowned and pushed his cart to the frozen seafood aisle. "Three bags of shrimp. They have to be peeled and deveined." He dropped them in the cart.

"Daddy, what are you doing?" Prairie ambushed him from behind.

His heart jumped at her sudden appearance. "Stocking up."

"I thought you said to get stuff that didn't need to be cooked or refrigerated." Wynter pushed her cart to be next to his and inspected its contents.

"I told you guys to get that stuff. I figured if we have two carts of dry goods and a cart of fresh food, that would be a good balance."

"Oh." Prairie picked up the shrimp. "Then can we buy some pasta? There's quite a lot of that left."

"Sure," Mason replied.

"The bread is gone," Wynter explained. "Not a loaf, a bagel, or a bun left in the whole store."

"They still have flour," Prairie explained. "We could make bread. It would probably be good for us to have something to do, keep our minds busy."

"Okay," Mason agreed. "Get a couple of bags. And get baking soda as well as yeast if you can find both."

"I will." Prairie pushed her cart toward the flour. "Come on, Wyn. We'll see you at the register, Daddy."

"Alright." Mason pushed the cart toward the dairy aisle. "Butter, milk, and eggs, all gone." He pushed the cart toward the cheese. He found a few wheels of brie, goat cheese, some blue cheese, and several containers of crumbled feta, but all the typical block, shredded, and sliced cheeses, such as Swiss, cheddar, and mozzarella were completely sold out.

Having filled his cart with the limited number of available items, Mason pushed his cart to the checkout lane where he encountered yet another long line. Even the self-checkout registers had queues snaking into the aisles.

***

Despite the grocery being only a mile away, the undertaking had consumed two hours by the time they finished. Mason surveyed the bags of food stacked up on the kitchen counter and overflowing onto the floor.

Wynter stood next to him. "They were completely out of bottled water."

Prairie added, "Even the gallon jugs were sold out."

Mason walked to the sliding doors. He peered down at the strip mall and noticed a sign that said *Fish On*. "Did you guys happen to look inside that fishing supply store next to the bagel place?"

"No," said Wynter.

"Why?" Prairie asked. "Do you think they would have bottled water?"

"No. But they might have bait buckets. We could use those to store water." He headed for the door. "You guys get all the perishable stuff into the fridge. I won't be long. I'll help you organize the dry goods when I get back."

Mason hurried to the parking garage, wishing he had a cart or some other means to transport the buckets without having to move the SUV again. However, he did not. He returned to the Interceptor and drove to the tackle shop across the street.

Mason pulled into a parking space and the alert tone on his phone sounded. He pulled it out to see a pop-up message over his lock screen. Above the text was a red triangle with a red exclamation point in the center. Mason muttered the words as he read them. "Warning. NORAD has detected multiple missiles heading toward the continental US. Please seek shelter inside immediately and remain indoors until further notice." He read the rest of the message and clicked the URL which offered to provide additional information.

Once on FEMA's website, Mason scanned the information as quickly as possible. "Nuclear blasts can cause electromagnetic pulses which may disrupt cellular service, internet, and/or electric service for several miles, depending on the height and size of the blast.

"Fallout decays rapidly. Seven-ten Rule. For every sevenfold increase in time after detonation, there is a tenfold decrease in the radiation rate. After seven hours the radiation rate is only ten percent of the original and after forty-nine hours it is one percent…"

His reading was interrupted by the sound of screeching tires and crashing metal. He looked up to see a Maserati that had just slammed into a Toyota Camry which was backing out of a parking space. The Maserati backed up and drove around the Camry, squealing tires as it left the parking lot.

Likewise, the driver of the Camry sped off as quickly as possible, without getting out to check for damage. Mason saw people running to cars parked in the beach access parking lot. Doors slammed and horns blew while they all hurried to leave. Mason rushed out of his vehicle and dashed to the door of the tackle shop.

The attendant was locking the door.

"Hey, I just need to grab a few things," Mason pleaded.

"Bro!" The heavyset man with long hair and a beard turned the latch and pulled his keys out of the door. "Russia is about to blow us off the map! Didn't you get the alert?"

"Yeah, I did. But I need some buckets." Mason pulled out his wallet. "I won't be long. Five minutes."

The man started walking down the sidewalk. "Can't do it, bro."

"A thousand dollars. Five minutes!" Mason took out the cash and waved it in the man's face.

The man stopped long enough to add up the bills in Mason's hand.

Mason added, "Cash is still good for a few more weeks." He pulled out another wad. "Two thousand."

The big man snatched the money, walked back to the door, and unlocked it. "Take what you need."

"Thanks." Mason pulled the door open as the heavyset man hurried away. "I'll keep a list and come back to pay you when you reopen."

The man did not respond but continued running away. Mason quickly located the bait buckets. He found five, two, and one-gallon sizes. He stacked up all the fives and twos next to the door. He surveyed the rest of the store for items that could be useful. "Coolers!"

Mason stacked up ten of them beside the buckets. "That's about all I can fit in the SUV." He rushed to the Interceptor and drove it onto the sidewalk with the hatch only a foot away from the tackle shop door. He opened the hatch and loaded his goods inside.

Just as he slammed the hatch shut, he noticed a stand-up cooler with sodas and bottled water. "Jackpot!" He glanced at the front passenger's seat which was still empty. He loaded two more coolers with as much bottled water as he could fit, shoved them into the front seat, and returned to the wheel. He slammed his door and sped back to the condo without putting on his seatbelt. The alarm dinged, reminding him of his unsafe decision.

Mason growled at having to buckle up at such a stressful time, but his mind could not handle the incessant dinging of the alarm. He fastened the belt as he drove up the ramp of the parking garage.

CHAPTER 18

And I will shew wonders in the heavens and in the earth, blood, and fire, and pillars of smoke. The sun shall be turned into darkness, and the moon into blood, before the great and terrible day of the LORD come.

Joel 2:30-31

Mason walked in the door carrying several of the five-gallon buckets stacked up with a few of the two-gallon buckets nestled inside.

"Daddy!" Prairie held up her phone to show him the alert.

"I know, Sweet Pea." He handed her the buckets. "Start filling these up. Wyn, come with me. We have to get the rest of the stuff out of the SUV."

"But the message says to stay inside," Wynter countered.

He waved for her to follow. "Palm Beach isn't a likely target. If it is, being inside won't help. Going indoors is to protect you from the fallout. That won't come until sometime after the blast."

The lights flickered. Mason took a deep breath, looked outside, considered what targets might be hit in Florida. *Orlando, Miami, Jacksonville?*

He said to Wynter, "We're going to have to take the stairs. We can't take a chance on the power going out while we're in the elevator."

"Alright," said Wynter. The two of them rushed to ferry the coolers and remaining buckets back to the apartment.

Mason was winded when they completed the first run. He looked at the television which was still playing.

Prairie was filling a bucket in the kitchen sink. She left the water running and walked away. "I have to check the other buckets. Can you keep an eye on this one?"

"Sure." Mason walked to the kitchen and monitored the two-gallon bucket.

Prairie explained herself as she headed toward the bathroom. "I figured I should fill as many at a time as possible. I don't know how long we have."

"Good thinking," Mason called out loud enough for her to hear.

Wynter stared at the television.

"Turn that up." Mason exchanged the bucket which was nearly full for an empty one.

Wynter picked up the remote and the picture went blank. The lights went out. The refrigerator stopped humming. Everything became as quiet as the dead of night except for the sound of water gurgling from the tap to the bucket. "We still have pressure."

Mason left the water running and walked to the sliding glass door. He could see no mushroom cloud to the south. He opened the sliding glass door.

"Dad! No! Keep it closed!" Wynter begged.

"It's okay. Even if something was hit nearby, we have time before the fallout reaches us." He stepped outside and craned his neck over the balcony trying to look north.

"Do you see anything?" Wynter inquired.

"No. Nothing." He came back inside, closed the door, and returned to the kitchen to swap buckets once more.

"Should we try to get the rest of the stuff out of the SUV?" Wynter inquired.

"Yeah, maybe we should." He took his phone out of his pocket. "No signal but it still works."

"Why wouldn't it work?" Wynter asked.

"FEMA said a nearby explosion would create an EMP effect. I think that could fry the circuitry in a cell phone."

Prairie walked in and joined the conversation. She pulled her phone out of her pocket. "I have service."

He nodded. "You could be connecting to a cell tower on generator backup. Click the FEMA URL on the alert you received."

"Here." She handed her phone to him. "The bucket in the shared bath needs to be swapped out. It's almost full."

Mason took her phone and clicked the FEMA link. He read the update so the girls could hear. "5:55 PM Update. Nuclear strikes have been carried out against San Francisco, Los Angeles, Houston, Chicago, and Washington DC. No additional incoming threats have been detected at this time."

Prairie had shut off the water and stood quietly in the hallway listening to Mason.

Wynter looked at her sister, then at her father. "DC would be the closest. Why would our power have gone out?"

"I don't know," said Mason.

"Will the fallout come here?" Prairie inquired.

"I don't know that either." He continued reading the FEMA alert page. "Wait. Here's a plume estimator." He showed the graphic to the girls. "It doesn't look like any of the fallout is predicted to come this way."

"Good. But we still need to get the supplies, right?" Wynter asked.

"Yeah. Plus, there's no guarantee that we won't have another exchange." Mason walked with

Wynter to the door. "Prairie, keep filling those buckets. We'll be right back."

Mason used his phone to illuminate the dark stairwell. "I saw flashlights at the tackle store. I should have grabbed some. They were those big ones, with the square batteries."

"But they're closed by now." Wynter followed him down the stairs.

"The door is unlocked. If we don't get them now, they'll be gone." Mason hustled down the stairs.

They jogged from the building, down the street, to *Fish On*. "It feels like we're looting," Wynter whispered as they walked in the door.

Mason whispered his response. "The guy left the door open for me. I told him I'd keep a tab and pay him when they reopen—if they reopen."

"Then why are we whispering?" She spoke softly.

"Because you were whispering," he replied. "Let's get what we need and get out of here before a cop comes by and thinks we're burglars."

"Should we get fishing poles? And maybe some lures? This thing is probably going to last a long time." She picked up a casting net and examined it.

"Sure, but hurry up!" Mason found the flashlights. He took two as well as a multi-tool and a filet knife. Wynter handed him the casting net, three poles, and tackle box which she'd filled with lures, hooks, weights, and line.

He felt agitated at having to carry so much. "What are you going to carry?"

"Some of these shirts and hats. We might not be able to wash clothes for a while. This stuff is all synthetic, so it won't stink as bad as cotton. Plus, it's made for being outside in this climate."

He understood her reasoning. "Fine, but get it, and let's go!"

She loaded up a hat for each of them plus several shirts, then followed Mason back to the apartment.

***

An hour later, the buckets were filled with water, all the supplies from the vehicle had been carted up the stairs, and the dry goods had been arranged in the cupboards and cabinets. The busyness had ceased, and Mason's mind drifted back to Hope, Daphne, and his wife who'd likely all been vaporized in the attack on New York.

He thought about each of them, where they might have been at the exact moment of detonation, if they'd had a chance to realize that they were about to die. *Is there any chance one of them might have gotten to safety?* He walked to the glass doors and looked out at the ocean. He pulled his phone out of his pocket to see that he had one bar of service. He checked his messages but saw none.

Mason turned to Prairie who was sitting on the sofa and checking the latest FEMA update. "Still nothing from your mom or your sisters?"

Prairie bit her lip and gazed at him compassionately. "Daddy."

"I know." He turned back toward the Atlantic. "But I keep thinking, what if they were in a tunnel or the subway…" He considered these possibilities and thought about the radiated air that anyone in such a place would have to breathe eventually. He understood this would be a much more painful death with no prospects for survival. Mason found himself hoping they'd all been killed instantly.

Wynter came to stand next to him. "It's 90 degrees—in September! We'll cook in this apartment if we can't open the windows. Prairie just checked the fallout plumes. None of them are coming this way. Can we open the doors?"

Mason signaled for Prairie to bring her phone. She did and he examined the radiation forecasts provided by FEMA. "Okay. But we have to limit the amount of time we're on the phones. We can take them down to the parking garage to recharge in the Interceptor, but I'd like to keep those trips to a minimum as well."

Prairie put her phone in her pocket. "Daddy, how did your work know something was going to happen in New York?"

He signaled for her to put her phone on the coffee table and motioned for the two of them to follow him outside on the terrace. He closed the sliding glass door. "Both of you already know this, but I'm going to say it again. Don't breathe a word of this to anyone."

Both nodded. Mason continued, "Poseidon runs a fund for the national security state."

"CIA, NSA, DIA, those guys, right?" Wynter asked.

"Yeah, but I'd classify the national security state as more than the sum of its parts." He pressed his lips tightly together. "They operate outside of the normal rules of the game. Either they're allowed to function with no governmental oversight, or they have workarounds so that they are unaffected by Congress, the courts, or even the president when it comes to restricting their behavior.

"Also, the power brokers within the national security state are not limited to employees of the intelligence agencies. I have very few details about the whole thing, but my guess is that the intelligence community more or less serves as the henchmen for this organization and the leadership is completely separate."

Wynter ran her hand through her short, black hair. "But it's a US organization, right? How would they have known the Russians would nuke New York?"

Prairie crossed her arms. "And more importantly, if they did know why didn't they tell anyone? They murdered Mom, Daphne, and Hope if they knew and didn't warn the people."

Mason put his arms around them both and pulled them close. "I wish I had the answer to that one, but unfortunately, I don't."

"Could it have been a false flag?" Wynter asked. "Could the US have launched a missile on their own people?"

"Anything is possible," Mason replied. "But I don't see the motivation for such an attack. Sure, these people are capable of the evilest thing you can imagine. But they're calculated. They don't do anything without a purpose."

"It all started two days ago," said Prairie. "When the people disappeared and planes fell out of the sky. Marco's security team snatched him away from the coffee shop less than half an hour after the time you two saw the plane crash near Newark. Come to think of it, if the pilots disappear, that's a pretty good reason for the planes to crash.

"But back to Marco's security team, it's like they had a protocol for this event—like it was expected or something." She looked into her father's eyes. "Same thing with Poseidon. Roy called you that day and told you to get out of New York—like some sort of plan had been put in place— a plan that was triggered by the disappearances."

Wynter narrowed her eyes as she listened. "It's true. Everything happened inside of forty-eight hours. But how does it all tie together."

Prairie turned toward the ocean. "One thing is for sure. After the Russians nuked six of America's largest cities, no one is asking questions about the disappearances anymore."

Wynter leaned on the balcony rail. "If it *was* the Russians."

CHAPTER 19

And he shall confirm the covenant with many for one week: and in the midst of the week he shall cause the sacrifice and the oblation to cease, and for the overspreading of abominations he shall make it desolate, even until the consummation, and that determined shall be poured upon the desolate.

Daniel 9:27

"Daddy, wake up!" Prairie shook Mason's arm Friday morning.

He threw the covers off and sprung from the bed. "What is it? What's happening?"

"The power came back on!" she replied.

His heart pounded in his chest. "Oh." Mason was relieved to hear anything other than news of imminent peril. "That's good." His hands quaked as his body slowly processed the fact that he was not in danger. Wearing only a pair of gym shorts, Mason followed her into the living room.

Wynter stood in front of the television and scrolled through the news channels looking for any information.

Mason watched the TV out of the corner of his eye as he closed the sliding glass door and turned on the air-conditioning. The strong ocean breeze had been the saving grace allowing them to sleep the night before in the hot, humid climate, but the time had come to cool down the apartment.

"GBC is on!" Prairie declared.

Mason sat on the sofa to see what was left of the world.

A pretty middle-aged blonde woman spoke with a distinctly British accent. "This is GBC London broadcasting to the UK and now also to the US, I'm Diedre Collins and this is News Day.

"As most of you know by now, GBC studios in Washington DC were taken out in yesterday's attacks. Most all of the staff there were killed. My colleagues here at GBC London will be working around the clock to keep everyone informed of the latest developments, not only here in the United

Kingdom but also our dear friends in the States who have lost so much over the past twenty-four hours.

"My guest today is World Economic Forum board member and philanthropist Ange de Bourbon, who will be talking to us about how the world narrowly avoided total and complete destruction and how we move forward from here."

The camera panned out to show de Bourbon sitting next to Collins. She said, "I so enjoyed your interview with the late Blair Cornelius. I feel like I know you already."

Ange de Bourbon's eyes closed for a moment as if remembering a dear friend. "Yes, well that is a testament to her prowess as a journalist, and perhaps more specifically, an interviewer. She will be deeply missed. But I trust you will carry on the legacy left by Blair and all those at GBC who worked tirelessly to bring accurate reporting to their viewers."

Collins replied, "Those are big shoes to fill, but I'll put forth my most earnest effort. We have much ground to cover so let's jump right in, shall we?"

"I'm looking forward to it," said de Bourbon.

"Let's begin with yesterday's nuclear exchange. I was petrified. Perhaps my worst fear was that it seemed to be escalating. First, the strike on New York, which I've heard Russia is denying. Then, the retaliatory strikes on the various BRICS countries, and finally, so many of America's biggest and brightest cities—erased in an instant. We've not seen any photos of the remains other than satellite images which don't show the details. But even those—it's like my mind won't process the fact that I'm looking at New York or LA; it's like something from a video game or the cover of a post-apocalyptic novel.

"But my question is this. What stopped the dominoes from falling? The US Department of Homeland Security said yesterday that if you spray us with water, we'll spray you with blood. Certainly, the Americans are armed to the teeth when it comes to nuclear weapons. They have enough to destroy the entire globe many times over. Why did they not retaliate to the attacks on Houston, San Francisco, LA, Chicago, and Washington DC?"

Ange de Bourbon nodded pensively. "You're correct in your assessment, Diedre. We were traveling down a path from which there is no turning back. Fortunately, I was able to convene an emergency delegation of world leaders to put an immediate stop to the escalating violence between the US and Russia.

"As you know, I'm very active in geopolitics and have become close friends with many of the global influencers, particularly in Europe. Right after the explosion in New York yesterday afternoon, US President Blanchard began contacting the leaders from NATO member countries. President Blanchard urged them to sign a declaration of war against the BRICS Plus nations and to publicly condemn the strike.

"The Secretary General of NATO reached out to me because several member countries were voicing their concerns about a possible extinction-level event arising out of an escalating nuclear exchange. NATO's leaders, including UK Prime Minister Victoria Cromwell, French President Emile LeBlanc, and German Chancellor Hans Schmidt all urged President Blanchard to take a moment before responding to the strike on New York City.

"In fact, no other NATO member endorsed the American's decision for the counterstrike, particularly a strike against so many other countries that were not directly involved in the attack. The essence of NATO's existence is that an attack against one is an attack against all. However, this is not a permission slip for one member to unilaterally drag the entire organization into a nuclear conflict which is what nearly happened yesterday.

"Next, a few of us got together on an emergency teleconference, the leaders I just mentioned from France, Germany, the UK, as well as the heads of state from Canada, Italy, Belgium—we also invited Flavio Moretti, head of the Bank of International Settlements, and Charlene Magnuson of the IMF to join us, and my close personal friend, Amadeo Falcone..."

Collins interrupted him, "The CEO of Gnosis— that Amadeo Falcone? He runs multiple social media companies, payment platforms, satellite internet, biohacking, his latest venture is the Immortal Project, which seeks to make death a thing of the past. I won't pretend to understand it, but how does he have time to get involved with geopolitics?"

"If you want something done, ask a busy person," de Bourbon laughed.

"Is that a Hillary Clinton quote?" asked Collins.

"Uh, Benjamin Franklin, I believe," de Bourbon answered. "Back to what I was saying before, we agreed that in order to save the world from annihilation, we needed to present the Americans with some tough love. Essentially, we said that hostilities needed to cease or we would ban all relations, economic as well as military with the US. They'd find themselves alienated from NATO and cut off from Unicoin."

Diedre Collins opened her eyes widely. "So that's essentially everyone, except the BRICS Plus nations. Basically, play by the rules or be left out in the cold, with nothing—no trade partners, no functioning currency, and no support for future conflicts. It's quite the ultimatum. I'm sure the Americans were quite bemused. They're not accustomed to being on the receiving end of such compelling terms."

Ange de Bourbon crossed his hands. "Indeed, they are not. However, they can be reasonable, even if it requires some persuasion at times. President Blanchard agreed to a cease-fire. I presented his offer to Russia as well as the rest of the BRICS Plus nations. They accepted."

Collins said, "So it sounds like cooler heads prevailed in the end."

"For now," said de Bourbon. "But emotions, hostilities, and revenge still linger like a foul stench in the kitchen long after the fish has been cooked and the garbage has been taken out. It will be some time before these two groups are able to sit down and speak with one another without it triggering violent tendencies.

"What we need, what the world needs is order. We've had our share of global disorder for such a long time. Yesterday, obviously, brought us to the brink of planetary destruction, but beyond that, last week's financial chaos, the ongoing tensions around Jerusalem, and so much turmoil.

"What I have proposed is, instead of global disorder, we should put our heads together and replace it with a Global Order. My good friend, Klaus Schwab, at the World Economic Forum, has long advocated for a Global Reset. I believe this is our time for such a reset. It's time we rethink our old way of doing business.

"The leaders I spoke with yesterday and I have signed a charter for what we are calling the Global Order. We've extended membership privileges to NATO signatories as well as all Unicoin participant nations. But this is much more than an economic block or a treaty organization. It's a centralized governmental structure that will allow us to address the problems which are threatening our very existence.

Diedre Collins asked, "So this would be what type of government entity?"

"I believe it would be best described as a technocracy, where the governing persons have some level of expertise in a given field. So, as it stands, we have six heads of state, each representing their respective countries —these have extensive experience in governing. Then we have the leaders of the BIS and IMF, both of which understand the global economy.

"Amadeo, as I mentioned before, brings a wide array of knowledge in so many fields, health services, technology—but if you want to boil it down to a single talent, standing up new systems is really what he does best. If we're going to do something new, we need a person who has done new things before.

"Then there's me. I've been given so much over the course of my life—I've been mentored and taught by some of the greatest minds on the planet, to understand diplomacy, threats to the environment, the perils of a society that is out of balance as far as income equality and acceptance of individual views on gender, color, and sexual identity. But when I say *myself*, I'm not speaking solely of Ange de Bourbon, I'm including all the wonderous council that will be available to me as chairman of the Global Order Commission.

"And I don't want to stop there. I want to build on this concept, to develop an intellect inside of an artificially intelligent entity that reflects the collective values of the commission."

"It sounds exciting and Amedeo Falcone is certainly the person to help you get it rolling!" Diedre Collins exclaimed. "But it also sounds lofty. Is such a commission possible?"

"We've already signed the charter," de Bourbon explained. "I haven't slept since yesterday—none of us have, but we're doing important work and we must seize the opportunity we've been given. Otherwise, our planet will not survive."

Collins put her finger to her chin as if remembering. "You listed the members of this commission. One name that was glaringly absent was President Blanchard. Does that mean the Americans will not play a leadership role in this new entity?"

"Amedeo was born in America. What better representative could they ask for?" de Bourbon quizzed.

"I was referring to an elected representative—like Blanchard."

Ange de Bourbon offered a conciliatory smile. "Diedre, no one loves America more than me. But it's time to rethink global hierarchies. President Blanchard's decisions yesterday brought us to the precipice of doom—such a statement sounds like hyperbole, but I think you'll agree, in this instance, it is not.

"The United States was the custodian of the world's reserve currency for many decades. Their stewardship practices over that asset have been—found wanting, to put it generously. Not only by the BRICS Plus nations, but by Europe, Britain, and Canada as well.

"The remaining members of the IMF and BIS have allowed the Americans to save face by granting them the ability to adapt the digital dollar. Of course, that experiment was dependent on the Canada's participation. This morning President Tremblay expressed Canada's desire to implement the use of Unicoin rather than the digital dollar.

"The US will be forced to follow suit, otherwise their economy will go into a tailspin from which there is no pulling out." He folded his hands and shook his head as if sorrowful.

Diedre Collins said, "Forgive me for interrupting. But the US Central Bank has sort of hung their hat on this digital dollar, haven't they? How could they transition from digital dollars to Unicoin, especially in the wake of the nuclear exchange?"

"That won't be an issue," said de Bourbon. "The FedNow payment system is agnostic. It isn't dependent on a particular currency. It could switch from digital dollars to Unicoin in a keystroke. Likewise, account holders' balances would be converted instantaneously.

"America is going to have a very difficult period going forward. They've lost six major cities. The fallout over California alone will decimate much of their agricultural capacity for years to come. Much of America's fertilizer has traditionally come from Russia and China. Obviously, with the strained relationships, that resource will be limited even for agriculture in parts of the country *not* affected by fallout.

"The northeast, much of that section of the country will be unlivable. Those living near the blast zones who survived will be dealing with health issues, and unfortunately, many of them will not be with us for very long.

"Just under half of the country's oil refineries were located in the Houston area. And we didn't just lose the facilities. We lost the workers and a large percentage of the knowledge base. The US petrochemical industry may not recover for decades. And back to the fertilizer problem, domestic production for the US depends on natural gas, much of which previously flowed through Houston.

"So, on that level, the Americans have enough on their plate without fretting over the affairs of the world. They need to look after their own house for a while. And the Global Order will be here to help with that healing process.

"If you'll allow me to change subjects for a moment, I have some uplifting news."

"We would certainly welcome that," Collins replied with bright eyes.

"The conversations I had with world leaders yesterday, the gravity of what happened and almost happened..." de Bourbon paused as if pensively choosing his words. "It opened the door for dialogue. I was able to have conversations with leaders who have been historically reluctant to hear what I had to say.

"In my call for peace, I was able to get Israel and the Palestinians to put aside their differences. Israel has agreed to work with the Global Order in negotiating amiable boundaries for a new Palestinian state. In return, Islamic leaders have acknowledged the right of the Jews to have their own place on the Temple Mount in Jerusalem.

"As an expression of my personal gratitude for Israel's willingness to enter into these negotiations, I'll be funding the effort to rebuild the Jewish Temple on the Temple Mount, to exist peaceably beside Islamic holy sites."

"So you've brought Jews and Muslims together." Diedre Collins put her hands together prayerfully. "Blair Cornelius had the honor of interviewing you after you saved the world from economic ruin. I envied her for that. I remember her musing about you being the Second Coming." Collins swallowed hard. Her voice cracked. "But if she had lived to see this interview, I think she would see what I see. You *are* the Messiah. You've just saved the world from total ruination and mankind from utter extermination."

"Those are very kind words." Ange de Bourbon basked in her worship. "And I think Blair Cornelius would applaud you for the tremendous and important work you are doing here at GBC London."

"Thank you. I know you're busy saving the planet from itself, but please say you'll join us again soon. I enjoyed our conversation so much," Collins gushed.

"I most certainly will. Thank you for having me, Diedre."

CHAPTER 20

And when he had opened the third seal, I heard the third beast say, Come and see. And I beheld, and lo a black horse; and he that sat on him had a pair of balances in his hand. And I heard a voice in the midst of the four beasts say, A measure of wheat for a penny, and three measures of barley for a penny; and see thou hurt not the oil and the wine.

Revelation 6:5-6

"Who is this guy?" Wynter gestured toward the television with disdain. "I mean, no one had even heard of him a week ago. Now he's the self-appointed dictator of the whole world?"

Mason was more concerned with the realities Ange de Bourbon had illuminated than his previous lack of media attention. "Whoever he is, the man has a point. We're in for some tough times." Mason ignored the program and walked to the sliding glass doors.

Prairie came to stand next to him. "People are coming out of their houses."

Mason gazed at the street below. A couple of cars drove by the convenience market but kept driving once they saw it was closed. Three young people walked along the sidewalk of the coastal strip mall. They checked doors as they passed each shop. "They're going into *Fish On*."

Wynter came to join them. "Good thing we got what we needed yesterday."

"Yeah," Mason said. "But I feel bad. The guy wouldn't have left the door unlocked if I hadn't asked."

Prairie opened the patio slider and walked out. She bent over the balcony rail. Mason felt uneasy, not necessarily at her precarious position perched ten floors above the street, but in general. He put his hand on her back, ready to grab her and pull her in should she lose her balance.

Prairie pointed to a young man and woman trying to jimmy the lock on the front door of the bagel shop. "It probably won't matter by sundown.

Something tells me the national guard isn't coming to restore order this time."

Wynter joined them on the balcony. "They've got bigger fish to fry with six American cities leveled and the surrounding suburbs still on fire from the bombs."

Mason figured the girls' assessments were correct. "I need to text someone. I have to connect to a Wi-Fi that isn't associated with any of our phones."

Wynter peered at him with narrow eyes. "Who are you?"

"Are these the spooks that knew America was about to be nuked and didn't tell anyone?" Prairie asked angrily.

"No. It's no one as dangerous as all that." Mason walked back inside.

"Be careful, Daddy." Prairie followed him inside.

Wynter added, "Take the gun."

Mason shook his head. "No. Cops could show up to arrest the looters. I don't want to get mixed up in any trouble. You guys lock the door and don't open it until you hear my voice." He glanced at Wynter. "The gun is on my nightstand. But don't play with it. It's for emergencies only."

Mason found the small tablet stashed inside his luggage. He tucked it under his arm and headed for the door. "I'll be right back."

Mason walked to the elevator, pressed the call button, then thought about the possibility of another power outage. He left the elevator bank and took the stairs down to the street. He walked south on Ocean Drive, past the strip mall. Mason saw the Palm Beach Shores Resort and cut through the shrubs to get into the parking lot. He found a spot with few windows looking out at his location and powered on his tablet. Mason connected to the resort's Wi-Fi and messaged Gio.

Did you make it out?

Mason cut through the resort's beach access and out onto the sand. He checked to see that he still had a signal, then found a place to sit. He saw only two other people on the beach. They were too far away for him to make out any discernable features about the fellow beach combers. Seconds later, the tablet vibrated. Mason read the message. *Yeah. Thanks for the tip. I owe you big time. I got out with Ceeny and the boys. We're down here in Miami. Where are you?*

Mason typed out his response. *Palm Beach. Wynter and Prairie are with me.*

Gio soon responded. *Where's Adrianna, Hope, and Daphne?*

Mason's hand quaked. He'd been too preoccupied with keeping Prairie and Wynter safe to even grieve. The knot in his throat threatened to strangle him. He stuck his hand deep into the sand, dug his fingers down to where he could feel moisture, closed his eyes, wanted to scream, wanted to bawl, wanted to mourn.

Mason took a deep breath, pulled his hands out of the sand, brushed them off, and entered his reply. *They wouldn't listen. They didn't leave.*

Gio quickly messaged back. *Oh, Mace. I'm sorry.*

Mason's thoughts drifted away from the conversation. He remembered the early years, before Prairie and Wynter had been born, when Hope and Daphne had been babies. It seemed like another lifetime.

The tablet vibrated. He looked down and read the text. *We should probably meet up. It looks like things could get worse. I'm afraid if we don't make a move now, we won't have another chance.*

Mason typed. *Who do you know in Miami?*

Charlie the Crab, came the reply. *Remember that old lobster roll place on Bloomfield right before the park?*

Mason inquired, *Sort of like a sandwich shop? It closed down, didn't it?*

Yeah, Gio texted. *That was Charlie the Crab's spot. He's the nervous sort. The guy shakes and stutters all the time—like he's being interrogated. Even when he ain't doing anything wrong. That ain't a good quality to have in an organization like ours. The old man told him to get out of town—paid for him to open up his lobster roll shop down here. Plus, the Crab keeps a couple of safe houses down here for us, for when guys need somewhere to lay low for a while.*

Mason typed out a message. *I just listened to the news. I think you're right. Things are about to get tough. Sounds like the rest of the world is done with America. I think they'll be happy enough to watch us deteriorate into a third-world country. Barring a miracle, I assume that's where we're headed. Cities aren't the best place to be in most third-world countries. You should head out to the woods. Pick a place in flyover country where the radiation isn't going to hit and go there. Learn to farm, get some animals, and hunker down.*

Gio quickly replied, *Sounds like solid advice. What about you?*

Mason turned to block the glare from the sun on the screen of his tablet. *I'm waiting to see if I have a job. The people I work for always manage to find a way to make themselves useful. I'd do both if I could. But I don't see a lot of farmland around here.*

Gio messaged back, *If things get bad, we might need to look out for one another. Look around and see if there's anything nearby. I'd like to stick together if we can.*

Mason pulled up the map of West Palm Beach. He zoomed out to inspect the regions to the west. *Nothing but urban sprawl from here to the wildlife management area. Then it doesn't look like much until you hit lake Okeechobee.*

He looked south. *You can't tell where West Palm ends and Fort Lauderdale begins. Same thing with Miami. It's like one big super city all the way down.* Mason shook his head. *If we have any chance of not being devoured by the golden horde, we'd have to go north—northwest.*

Mason spied out a small town near the north side of the lake. *Okeechobee. I wouldn't want to be any closer to the cities than that.*

He sent Gio another message. *Looks like you're less than two hours away. Why don't you come up so we can talk? I might have some ideas.*

***

Later that afternoon, Mason called the realtor on a small property he'd seen listed in Okeechobee County, Florida.

"Hello?" a man's voice answered.

Mason was caught off guard. He'd expected an eager salesman on the other side of the call. "Um, yes, hi. I was looking for Ron—with OK Realty."

"This is," answered the man.

"Yeah, great." Mason looked at the address scratched out on a note pad. "I'd like to see the property on 110th Street. The house on four acres."

"Oh," said Ron. "Well, the thing is, everything is sort of up in the air right now. Nobody knows what's going on. I'm not showing property at this time."

Mason felt sure he'd connected with a bad apple. "Is there someone else at your agency that could show me the property? Or is there another realtor you recommend?"

"Nope," said Ron. "I reckon it'll be about the same with anybody you call. It was like that even before the bombs. The banks froze all lending until this business with the currency gets worked out. So lots of agents more or less went on hiatus last week. Most buyers got the message so even for those of us still working, our phones quit ringing. There isn't anyone else at OK still working except me."

Mason felt disapointed. "Thanks for your time. Have a nice day."

"You, too." Ron ended the call.

Mason began to call the numbers of other agents with listings in the area. Most calls went to voice mail. Some had messages that stated they were out of the office until further notice. Still others had notifications that their voice mailboxes were full and could no longer accept additional messages.

Frustrated with the process, Mason called Ron once more.

"Yeah, this is Ron." The man seemed to recognize the number.

"Hi, this is Mason Lot. I spoke to you a few minutes ago. Listen, I have cash. I'm not looking for a contract that would be contingent upon me securing a mortgage."

Ron replied, "Under normal circumstances, that would be just dandy. But as it is, the entire system has been turned on its head. I'm not even sure if I'd be able to deposit earnest money into a bank until this currency debacle gets cleared up. Then there's title. They won't schedule any closings until the banks figure things out. And considering the country was just nuked, no telling how long until things get back to normal."

"I'd take a quit claim deed. All we need is a notary, right?" Mason asked. "I can disperse funds from my account to the sellers via a bank wire. He can sign when the transaction clears. I'll do the same for your commission."

"That's very generous of you," said Ron. "But I'd never recommend a quit claim deed. How about you call me back in a couple of weeks? We'll see how things are looking."

"But you're obligated to present offers to the seller, right?" Mason persisted.

"I am. Are you making an offer sight unseen?"

"No. But I'd pay over asking if I like it after I see it."

"Call me in a few weeks. I'm just not available to show it to you before then."

"Are you familiar with gold coins, Ron?" Mason inquired.

"Some. Why?"

"I'll give you a one-ounce gold eagle coin for taking me around and showing me a few properties today. Before the currency crash, it was selling for three grand. I'll pay you before we see the first house. Just tell me where to meet you."

Ron was silent for a moment. "What time would you like to meet?"

"I'm in Palm Beach. I can be there in an hour and a half."

"I'll meet you at the 110ᵗʰ Street property," said Ron. "See you then."

Mason ended the call. "Girls, get your shoes on. We're going to look at a farm."

Prairie grabbed her flip-flops. "Does that mean we're not going to live on the beach?"

"We'll probably rent a place around here and buy a farm where we can go if things get worse. As far as I know, I still have a job." Mason shoved his phone in his pocket and headed for the door. "Wyn, come on. We need to go."

Wynter arrived wearing jeans and tennis shoes. "I had to change. I didn't want to go look at farms in a sundress."

Prairie looked down as if reconsidering her attire. "Should I put on something else?"

"You'll be fine. We're just looking. You won't be milking any cows today." Mason held the door open and motioned for them to hurry out. "But we need to move. Gio will be downstairs waiting for us."

Wynter lowered her brow. "Gio? You mean the guy from the restaurant?"

"Yeah." Mason locked the door. "Now let's go."

Wynter was first to the stairwell door. She held it open for her father and sister. "What is he doing in Florida?"

"I told him to get out of New York." Mason descended the stairs.

"I didn't realize you two were such close friends." Wynter followed close behind.

Prairie led the pack. "Why haven't I ever met him?"

"Mom—wasn't a big fan of Gio," Mason replied.

"Because he's a gangster?" Wynter asked.

"He's a restaurateur," Mason countered.

"A restaurateur who can provide guns, safe houses, loaner vehicles…" She paused. "Curious timing on my transition physician's demise. It seems to have occurred about the same time you rekindled your friendship with your high school chum."

The statement didn't sound like a question to Mason so he provided no answer.

Prairie stopped short, blocking the way. "So?"

"So what?" Mason inquired.

"Did he?" Prairie quizzed. "Did you have the mob rub out Wyn's doctor?"

"Of course not!" Mason pointed down the stairs. "Now move! We need to go!"

"I wouldn't be mad if you did," said Wynter.

Mason was happy to hear her say that, but no confessions would be made at this juncture.

They reached the ground level and Mason led the way out onto the street. He pointed to a black Yukon XL Denali. "That's Gio."

The driver's side window rolled down and Giovanni stuck his head out. "Paisano!"

Prairie walked close behind her father and whispered. "He knows you're not Italian, right?"

Mason answered in a low voice. "We grew up in an Italian neighborhood. Gio has always treated me like I was one of them. He always assumed that we'd work together in his family's business despite my constant reassurance that I wasn't interested."

"Oh, that tells me a lot," said Prairie. "But I suppose he makes a better friend than an enemy."

Mason did not commend her for her astute observation, even though it was, once again, spot on. He opened the back door of the SUV to see a stout young man sitting in the back.

Gio introduced him. "This is Valentino, my oldest. I think he was two last time you saw him, Mace."

"Good to see you." Mason waved. "This is Prairie and Wynter."

"Hi!" Prairie greeted Gio and Valentino. "I can sit in the middle." She got in ahead of her sister.

Wynter pressed her lips together. "I thought you hated the middle!"

"I have shorter legs. It only makes sense." Prairie buckled herself in next to the much-older boy.

Wynter looked at her father as if expecting him to say something. When he did not, she rolled her eyes and got in the vehicle. Mason closed the door and walked around to the front passenger's seat. Once inside, he fastened his seat belt and looked for a mirror to get eyes on Prairie and Valentino. Finding none, he sat back for the ride. "Where's Luca and Francine?"

"They stayed at the spot with the Crab." Gio put the vehicle in drive.

Valentino added, "Dad says it might not be safe out here for girls."

"Well," said Prairie. "Lucky for us, we've got you to keep us safe."

Mason could almost hear Wynter's eyes rolling again.

CHAPTER 21

And there shall be signs in the sun, and in the moon, and in the stars; and upon the earth distress of nations, with perplexity; the sea and the waves roaring; men's hearts failing them for fear, and for looking after those things which are coming on the earth: for the powers of heaven shall be shaken.

Luke 21:25-26

Mason stepped out of the SUV and approached the old cowboy standing in front of an older-model pickup truck. "Hi, are you Ron?"

"Yes, sir." The realtor shook Mason's hand. He wore Lee Jeans, boots, a large brass belt buckle, and a Stetson hat. "Unfortunately, I'm afraid I have some bad news."

"Oh?" Mason looked the property over.

"The seller says he wants to take the place off the market. I was afraid of this. That's why I wanted to hold off on showing anything," said Ron.

Giovanni walked up. "What? Is this guy trying to shake us down for more money or something?"

Ron seemed to not appreciate Gio's thick accent or his brash mannerism. "It ain't nothing like that. He's afraid of how the exchange rate is going to shake out after we've converted over to Unicoin. As it stands, the digital dollar is trading six to one to Unicoin. Factor in the conversion from dollars to digital, and a Unicoin costs roughly twenty-bucks. Best I can tell, it only buys about five dollars' worth of goods in old dollars. That's if you can find anything on the shelves worth buying."

Mason argued, "But the world is falling apart. If he holds on to it, he could very well end up getting nothing for it."

Ron shook his head. "You can't tell sellers nothing. I tried it after the bubble popped in 2008, and then at the top after COVID. All they know is John Doe sold his house for such and such, and all they can think about is how they're losing out if they don't get the same amount that John Doe got. They'll ride it all the way to the bottom—every time."

Mason handed the man a gold coin. "We're here now. What else can you show us?"

Ron held the coin. "I don't know. It's liable to be the same story all over town. You might best hang on to this. Call me back in a week or two."

Prairie examined the meager farmstead. "When we came through town, there was a line outside of the sheriff's department. What was that all about?"

"Missing persons." Ron frowned. "Once folks get the paperwork filed and process their claims through probate, we'll have plenty of properties on the market."

"That was all people reporting people who disappeared?" Wynter's eyes opened wide. "There must have been a hundred people in that line!"

Ron turned toward town. "Today is for people with last names beginning with E through H. Tomorrow will be I through L. If they miss their day, they'll have to wait until it cycles back around."

"You had that many people vanish?" Valentino asked.

Ron swallowed hard. "Maybe fifteen or twenty percent of the town." He looked up at Mason. "I take it you didn't lose as many where you're from."

Prairie answered for him. "We're from New York. We lost everybody."

"Sorry to hear that," said Ron.

"But not in the disappearances—before the bombs," said Mason. "It was just a few here and there."

"Makes sense," said Ron.

"How does any of this make sense?" Wynter demanded.

"Okeechobee is more like what folks used to call the Bible Belt. More so than New York City, anyhow."

"So you think it was the Rapture!" Prairie stared at him as if wanting to hear more.

"Either that or the aliens." Ron raised his shoulders. "Whichever it was, seemed to be mostly church-going folks that disappeared."

He leaned on his pickup and looked blankly up the road. "I could almost tell which houses would be empty—just from knowing folks from around town. I never saw some of 'em running back and forth to church. But still—something about 'em—I knew they'd be gone."

Mason was more concerned with securing a bugout location than solving the mystery of the missing people. "So the places where the owners have disappeared, do you know who is in line to inherit them?"

"A few, maybe," answered Ron. "Some of 'em didn't leave nobody. And some of 'em, everyone in the family is gone. Then others, the family member who is still here wasn't in the will. Could be a long time before those cases work their way through the courts."

"What about properties where the person inheriting it is pretty cut and dry?" Mason quizzed. "Do you think they'd be willing to rent a place with an option to buy? It gives them a source of revenue while they wait, plus they'll already have a buyer when the rest of the market gets hit with a glut of inventory. That's bound to happen once probate starts settling cases. I'll pay you ten percent of the first year's rent as a finder's fee."

Ron pressed the coin as if he could tell whether it was real or not by doing so. He seemed to conclude it was genuine and shoved it in his pocket. "Alright then. Give me a few minutes. I need to make some phone calls."

Prairie took the lull in activity as an opportunity to chat up Gio's son. "So, Valentino, are you in college? I mean, were you—before all of this?"

He shook his head. "My friends call me Val. And no, I'm—*was* a senior in high school. Sorry to hear about your mom."

"Yeah, it's tough. I lost my sisters too." She gazed at the ground.

"Not all of them." Wynter appeared annoyed at being cut out of the conversation.

"Obviously." Prairie forced a smile. "So, Val, think you can cut it? Trading in the city life to be a farmer?"

He looked around at the flat landscape broken up only by fences and thickets of palm trees and live oak. "I don't really have a say in the matter. Besides, it's not like we have anything to go back to."

"How is Miami?" Wynter inquired of him.

Val glanced at his father. "We've been locked down, so I haven't seen much of it."

Ron returned. "I've got a place for us to look at over on 144th. The owners disappeared. The daughter will get the place as soon as it clears probate. She has her own place and no interest in dealing with it. But it's as is. She doesn't want to be bothered with it at all. You'd have to box up the personal effects of the mom and dad for the daughter to go through later. You're responsible for the upkeep, utilities, and everything else."

"Fine by me," said Mason. "Let's check it out."

"Follow me." Ron returned to his truck and led the way.

Mason's group returned to the Yukon and drove to the next property several miles away.

When they arrived, Mason exited the vehicle and walked up to Ron. "How did you find out about this property being vacated?"

Ron looked at the sandy ground below his feet. "I—had a feeling they'd be gone." He straightened his posture and started for the front door. "They fit the description."

Mason tried to shake the uneasiness plaguing him about the vanishings. As soon as they entered the home, he was met with a decorative wooden cross hanging on the wall. Next to it, was an ornamental black iron sign. He read the words silently to himself. *As for me and my house, we will serve the Lord.*

Mason shook off the malaise to focus on the mission at hand. "It's well kept."

"Yep." Ron ticked off the property's attributes. "It's a three, two. Screened in pool, almost five acres fenced, furnished, of course."

Mason walked through the rooms with Giovanni.

"It's going to be a little tight," said Gio.

Mason replied, "You and Ceeny can have a bedroom, your boys can share a room. My girls can take the other. I'll sleep on the couch. It's a pull-out."

Gio lifted his shoulders. "I got the Crab too."

"Oh, I didn't realize he was coming."

Gio frowned. "The guy is down there all by himself. His business is done for. He ain't got nowhere to go."

"Do you have anything larger?" Mason asked.

Ron said, "There's a five, four a few streets over. But it's only two acres, and the pool isn't covered. Probably won't be as cheap as this place. But otherwise, it's about the same situation. The owners are gone and their son is out on his own. Let me give him a ring." Ron excused himself.

Mason didn't like the smaller lot but realized they needed more room. He looked at Giovanni. "Do you think we could grow enough food for all of us on two acres?"

"I couldn't grow enough food for all of us on a hundred acres," Gio replied. "Farming ain't really my thing."

Mason pressed his lips together, knowing it also was not his thing. "We'll figure it out. Maybe I'll sleep on the floor in the room with the girls. Charlie can have the sofa."

"If you do that, then you guys take the master. We can tie a mattress to the roof of the Yukon when we come up from Miami so you won't have to sleep on the floor." Gio looked around the house as he thought.

Ron came back into the house. "He said we can go look if we want."

Mason asked, "What about something with animals?"

"What kind of animals?" Ron lowered one brow.

"The kind you eat," Gio replied. "Cows, chickens, pigs. Did anybody up and disappear and leave behind a working farm?"

Ron answered, "If they did, the heirs will be much more likely to take over the property. With times being what they are, I expect farm animals will quickly become a prized commodity. It doesn't take a genius to figure that out. Heck, if I knew of a deal like that, I'd have already locked it up for myself.

"I'm sure y'all heard what they're saying on the news about transportation, fuel shortages, agricultural production loss, supply chain freezing up. This is going to make COVID look like a kid's birthday party, complete with clowns, ponies, and pinatas."

"Yeah," Mason sighed. "That's why we're here."

"I figured as much." Ron took his phone out and looked at the number. "Here's someone calling from Miami right now. Come to think of it, that inventory glut might get bought up pretty quick."

Mason asked, "How much is the woman asking for this place?"

"She said four grand. I reckon that was old money." Ron looked at the ceiling. "That'd be roughly two-fifty in Unicoin per month, assuming the conversion settles at six to one for digital dollars."

Mason nodded. "Three hundred Unicoin for your finder's fee then?"

"That would be just fine," Ron said.

"Okay. We'll take it." The place was not what Mason had hoped for, but the rural location would give them a fighting chance as conditions continued to deteriorate.

CHAPTER 22

Flee out of the midst of Babylon, and deliver every man his soul: be not cut off in her iniquity; for this is the time of the LORD's vengeance; he will render unto her a recompence.

Jeremiah 51:6

Mason pulled into the driveway of the Okeechobee rental property early Saturday morning. Gio's family was already there unloading the Yukon. An older model silver Suburban was also in the drive way. It was pulling a festively painted food trailer featuring a giant red crab with a chef's hat, holding a lobster in one hand, and a hoagie roll in the other. The caption read *Charlie Crab's Lobstah Rolls*. *Lobster* was spelled with an *AH* at the end rather than the customary *ER*.

"Why did this guy bring his food truck?" Wynter asked.

"I'm sure we'll find out." Mason opened the door of the SUV. "Bring your things inside. Let's get settled in."

"Mace! How are you?" Francine's accent was thick and her voice nasally. She waved and clip-clopped over in her yoga pants and high heels.

"Who is that?" Wynter inquired.

"Gio's wife, Francine," said Mason. "Everyone calls her *Ceeny*."

"Why do they call her Ceeny?" asked Wynter. "Is that supposed to be short for Francine?"

Prairie eyed Francine's outfit and whispered to her father, "Whatever they call her, she's from Jersey alright."

"Shh." He dismissed the pointed remark and hugged Francine once she arrived.

"It's so good to see you!" Francine's eyebrows sloped down on the outsides in a show of sympathy. "I'm so sorry about Adrianna and your other two girls. How are you holding up?"

He'd been fine until she mentioned it. "We're all in crisis mode, I guess. We haven't really had a chance to sit down and process it all."

She turned to Prairie and Wynter. "Once we get settled, we'll put together a memorial. Does that sound good?"

Prairie nodded and snuggled up next to her father like she'd done when she was a small child.

"That's very kind," Wynter said. "I would like that."

"Thanks, Ceeny." Mason consoled Prairie who was experiencing a moment of sadness.

"Luca, put that down and come meet your new friends." Francine waved to her youngest son.

Luca left a plastic bin on the pavement near the Yukon and walked over. He looked to be about fourteen. Puberty was taking its toll on him in the form of a bad acne breakout. He looked Prairie and Wynter over, ignoring Mason.

"This is Mr. Lot and his girls," said Francine.

"Hi." Luca continued to stare at the girls, not looking at Mason.

"I'm Wyn, and this is Prairie." Wynter seemed less repulsed by the young ogler than Prairie.

Val came out of the garage and climbed up on the bumper of the Yukon to cut the strings binding a full-size mattress to the roof of the vehicle. "Can someone give me a hand?" He appeared to be calling his little brother, but Luca seemed oblivious to the request.

Wyn looked around. She seemed put off by the fact that there were no other volunteers. "Yeah, I can help." She left the group.

"I see that Charlie brought his food trailer," said Mason.

Francine put her hands on her hips. "Yeah. He brought all the dry goods he had in his stockroom from the restaurant. That will help out until we get this little farm thing going. Plus, the trailer has a propane kitchen. We can still cook if we lose power.

"The guy on the radio said we'll keep having brownouts and rolling blackouts. Lots of power companies were taken offline by the attacks. They're going to start diverting power from Florida and other areas that weren't affected so they can provide electricity to the parts of the country that are still in the dark."

Francine crossed her arms and looked around. She stepped away from Prairie and Luca. She spoke softly so they couldn't hear. "I'm afraid things are going to get really bad, Mace."

He took two steps in her direction. "We've got a plan. We'll get through it."

She nodded. "Thank you for telling Gio to get out of Jersey."

"I'm just glad he listened." Mason thought about his own family that had not heeded his warning.

"We owe you our lives," said Francine. "And those of our children. As a mother, I can't tell you what that means."

"Gio has helped me out recently too," said Mason. "A lot, in fact. You guys don't owe me a thing."

"Ceeny," Gio called from the house. "Come take a look at this kitchen and tell me what I need to get rid of."

"I'm glad you and Gio were able to reconnect. He missed you." Francine smiled, then turned to answer her husband's call.

Mason stood looking at the house for a moment, considering what this new chapter of his life was going to be like. He overheard a conversation between Luca and Prairie who were still nearby.

Luca watched his brother and Wynter take the mattress into the garage. "I guess if things get worse, it will be up to us to repopulate the earth. Val and your sister will probably hook up. That will leave you and me to do our part in…"

Prairie cut him off and shouted her response. "If you ever even *think* that about me again, I'll slap the taste out of your mouth. Got it?"

Luca lowered his head and his gaze. "Yes."

Mason turned away, trying to hide the fact that he'd eavesdropped on their exchange. He fought a grin and felt proud of Prairie.

Prairie stormed off to help with the mattress project.

Mason grabbed a few bags from the Interceptor and carried them inside.

"Let me get a couple of those." Gio came to his aid.

"Thanks." Mason handed him a duffle and a backpack.

Gio carried the bags to the master bedroom and placed them inside the doorway. "How was the trip?"

"Not many people on the road. Most of the shops we drove by were closed—even the grocery stores. We found gas down by Indiantown." Mason placed the remaining bags on the bed. He eyed the well-worn, leather-covered Bible on the nightstand. "We came by a big ranch on the way here. It's a couple of miles away. I saw cattle and orange groves."

"Yeah, I saw a lot of that on the way here," Gio replied.

Mason continued. "But this one has a big cross by the main gate. The name of the operation is Redemption Ranch. I'm thinking it might be some kind of church ministry."

Gio nodded. "And that all the people disappeared?"

"Maybe." Mason opened one of the two closets in the master bedroom.

"It'd be worth checking out," Gio said. "We can clear out the Crab's stuff from the food trailer and shove a cow in there."

Mason removed a long black plastic case from the top shelf of the closet, left by the home's previous occupants. "If they were a cattle operation, they'll have a livestock trailer somewhere." He took the case to the bed and opened it.

Gio looked on. "That's a twelve gauge. Do you know how to use it?"

"No. You take it," Mason said.

Gio took out the weapon. "I'll teach you the basics. The girls should learn too. You keep this one. We brought guns. The old man had some stashed in one of the safe houses down south."

"I suppose guns could come in handy if society comes unglued." Mason examined the pump-action weapon.

"Well, that's the one thing we got." Gio proceeded to show Mason how to rack the slide, engage the safety, and hold the butt of the gun to his shoulder.

Mason practiced the maneuvers for a while then placed the shotgun back in the case. "Want to take a ride over to that ranch?"

"Sure. Why don't you throw that in the back seat?" Gio walked to the doorway of the master bedroom. "Yo, Val! Saddle up. We're fixing to go round up some dogies."

Valentino answered his father's call. "You're going to get dogs?"

Gio huffed at having to explain himself. "No! Dogies. That's what they called cows in the old western movies. You know, *git along little dogie*?"

Valentino stared blankly at his father.

Prairie and Wynter trailed close behind Valentino. "Can we come?" asked Prairie.

Mason pressed his lips together. "It would be safer if you stayed here."

Wynter turned to look at the older man carrying a cardboard box into the kitchen. "We don't know these people. I'd feel safer with you."

Mason remembered her recent trauma. "Alright. But if we get out to look around, you two stay in the SUV."

Prairie and Wynter nodded. Mason tucked the pistol in the back of his pants and carried the shotgun to the door. "Come on. Let's get this over with."

"Ceeny, we'll be right back." Gio checked the chamber of his pistol, returned it to his inside-the-waistband holster, and pulled his shirt tail over to cover it up.

The five of them loaded into the Yukon. Mason watched as Wynter quickly got in the back seat, taking the middle position to cut her sister out of sitting next to Val. He saw the glares, felt the tension, but heard no squabbling which would have, at a minimum, betrayed Prairie's interest in the older boy.

Once out of the driveway, Wynter inquired, "Why are you guys carrying guns?"

"What? You ain't strapped?" Gio laughed. "This is how we always roll—unless I'm expecting trouble. Then I pack something a little bigger."

"Like an AK," said Valentino.

"That's my boy," Gio said proudly.

Mason knew all of this was a difficult transition for the girls, but he also knew they stood a better chance of long-term survival by having Gio and Val around.

The drive to the ranch took only about five minutes. Gio slowed down as they reached the property. "I don't see anyone."

Mason pointed to the cattle in the pasture beyond the first set of buildings. "Let's drive on back."

Gio turned onto the ranch's private road. "Looks like quite a few cows. I bet they've got more than a hundred."

"Someone is coming!" Prairie alerted. "It's a guy on a horse. I guess they didn't all disappear."

Gio laughed. "Check this character out. He looks like he came straight off the Marlboro cigarette billboard."

"Cigarettes aren't allowed to have billboards," Wynter argued.

"They used to," Mason corrected.

The young rider, who looked to be in his late twenties, slowed his horse to a walk. He wore a hat very similar to the one Ron, the real estate agent, wore. He had on a plaid shirt, jeans, boots, and had retrieved a lever action rifle from a scabbard that looked like it had been fashioned from duct tape. In fact, the duct tape scabbard was the only thing that differentiated the rider from a classical Western movie character. "You folks lost?"

Mason took the pistol out from behind his back and tucked it beneath his thigh before rolling down the window. "No. Actually we're new to the area." He saw that the cowboy was wearing a walkie-talkie on his belt.

Soon, a golf cart came rolling up with three more men. All were in their mid-thirties or younger. The driver was a young black man in his early twenties. Mason caught a glimpse of a shotgun across his lap. Next to him was an Asian man. He kept his hands low, so Mason could not tell if he was armed but suspected that he was. In the back seat was a Caucasian man with a bald head and not much of a chin. Likewise, Mason had no way of knowing if he was armed.

"So how can we help you?" the cowboy inquired.

"I was wondering if you were interested in selling any of your cattle?" Mason attempted to keep his tone as amiable as possible.

"Not likely," said the cowboy. "Money is going to be worthless, pretty soon. So, if you don't mind, I'll kindly ask that you remove yourselves from the property."

"Yo, Rhett," called the bald man. "Can I talk to you for a second?"

Rhett didn't say no, and the bald man got out of the golf cart.

Gio sat still, not moving the vehicle until the bald man had his say in the matter. The two conversed for a few moments. Then, Rhett came down from his horse and handed the reigns to the bald man. He still held the lever action rifle. "We might be willing to trade, *if* you have anything we need."

"What are you looking for?" Mason asked.

Rhett leaned against the Yukon and looked in the back. "Guns, ammo, solar generator, body armor, night vision, a good drone, chickens, pigs, a dirt bike."

"Mind if I consult with my friend for a moment?" Mason asked.

"Go right ahead." Rhett took a step back.

Mason rolled up the window and turned to Gio. "These guys know what's going on."

"Them and everyone else with a radio or a television," said Gio.

"How many guns do you have?" Mason quizzed.

"A few. But we might be able to parlay this situation into a better deal."

"What do you have in mind?" Mason asked.

Gio pointed to the cowboy. "He's obviously the guy running the show and he's packing a 30-30. That thing has six shots, max. And, he has to crank the lever every time he pulls the trigger. The shotgun in the driver's lap, it's a pump. That tells me these clowns don't even own a semi-automatic long gun. If they did, it would be here. They all came running out here as a show of force. Trust me, they brought the heaviest equipment they own."

Gio continued his evaluation. "See the Asian, how he's got his hands below the dash of the golf cart? He's holding a piece. Probably something big, but still, it's a pistol. And check out the bulge in baldy's front pocket. That's a peashooter, might be a .380 or a .25. But whatever it is, that's the bottom of the bucket. Otherwise, baldy would be packing more weight. These guys are sitting ducks out here with all their resources and this puny arsenal."

"Alright," Mason appreciated Gio's keen observation. "So what do you want to do?"

"Let me handle the negotiations," said Gio.

"Have at it." Mason rolled down the window.

Gio leaned over. "We've got Aks, and we've got ammo, but if I part with any, that leaves my group short on defense. And from the sound of things, you guys know as well as we do, things are only going to get worse from here. What I'd like to propose is that my group provides security for your operation and in turn, you keep us fed. As you can probably tell from my accent, I ain't much of a farmer, but I got guns, and I got shooters. I think we could make this little arrangement work."

Rhett shook his head. "What's to stop you from just killing us and taking everything for yourselves?"

The bald man spoke up. "Rhett, I think we should…"

The cowboy held up his finger. "Shut up, Turtle. I'm handling this."

Gio replied to the question. "Number one, what's to stop us from rolling up here in the middle of the night and taking what we want anyway?" Gio pointed to the lever action rifle. "That ain't gonna do it. How long does it take you to reload that antique?" Gio pointed to Turtle's pocket. "And what's he carrying? I wouldn't let my sister pack a sissy gun like that. We ain't stupid so don't try to bluff. If you had a stronger hand, you'd have played it when you came out here.

"And number two, why would I kill you? I don't know nothing about milking no cows. I wouldn't know where to begin. But trust me, things are about to get ugly all over. Them thugs from Miami and Orlando and Tampa are going to start streaming out of the cities like cockroaches. And if all you have to keep them at bay is that six-shot relic, a shotgun, and Turtle's little sissy gun, you're gonna be in a world of hurt."

Rhett glared at Gio as if not accustomed to his abrasive nature.

"Yo," called the driver. "I'm with Turtle on this one, Rhett. I think we need to hear the man out. I'm from Tampa. What he's saying about the gangs ain't wrong."

Rhett glanced at the Asian man. "Dixon?"

The Asian spoke perfect English with no accent albeit at an unnaturally fast pace. "Devron is right. It's only a matter of time. Let's at least listen to what they have to say."

Rhett seemed hesitant to enter into any further negotiations. He returned to his horse. Once back in the saddle, he pointed to the building near the road. "Follow me to the old church. Devron, follow them—and keep an eye on them."

CHAPTER 23

Thou wilt keep him in perfect peace, whose mind is stayed on thee: because he trusteth in thee.

Isaiah 26:3

Rhett hitched his horse to the metal pole of the portico at the entrance to the church. He knocked on the door. "Can't-Get-Right, It's me. We've got company."

Mason's eyes shifted to Gio, then to Prairie and Wynter. "Why don't you girls wait in the Yukon?"

"This concerns us," said Prairie. "We should have a say."

Gio seemed to share Mason's apprehension about other people being inside the church but not on the proposed solution. "It might be best if we all stick together, Mace."

Unhappy about the surprise, Mason sighed. "Alright."

A thin young man in his early twenties opened the door. He held a semi-automatic .22 rifle. "Me-me-me-me…"

"Megan?" Rhett asked. "Is she here?"

The stuttering young man nodded and stepped to the side so everyone could enter the church. Rhett led the way, through the vestibule and into the auditorium. A young blonde girl wearing tight jeans, western boots, and a midriff shirt was near the front. She hurried to Rhett's side and hugged him. "I went to wake up Can't-Get-Right as soon as I heard you call over the radio. Is everything okay?"

"Yeah." He gave her a quick kiss, then pointed for everyone to take a seat. "You did good."

Devron corrected Megan, "His name is *Billy*. Y'all need to quit calling him that."

"Devron, you're the one who gave him the nickname," said Turtle.

Mason took a seat on the front pew, signaling for Prairie and Wynter to sit next to him. He took some comfort in knowing his girls weren't the only females present.

Prairie looked at the nervous young man, then turned to Dixon, the caffeinated Asian who'd sat in the pew behind her. "Why do they call him *Can't-Get-Right*?"

"That movie," Dixon replied quickly. "*Life*, with Eddie Murphy. Can't-Get-Right was a character who couldn't talk—except that guy was a mute. Our Can't-Get-Right is kicking heroin, that's why he can't talk. Plus, he was on benzos. So it's going to be a while before his brain gets straightened out enough to function normally. He just got here a few days before the disappearances. Probably has another few weeks to get through the worst of his withdrawals."

Rhett wrinkled his brow. "Dixon, how about we iron out the details of this deal before we start getting chummy with our guests?"

"Yeah," Turtle chimed in. "Those chicks are too young for you anyway."

"Shut up!" Dixon scolded Turtle. "I was just answering a question."

"Alright! Alright!" Rhett held up his hands to calm the squabble. Then, he, Gio, and Mason discussed the particulars of the agreement.

Negotiations started with both sides wanting a deal that favored their side. Nonetheless, all seemed to understand the value of the arrangement and began making compromises in good faith. An hour later, they'd reached an understanding that all found amiable.

Rhett pointed toward the back of the property. "We've got five staff houses. Your group can have the one at the end of the row."

"That was Brother Dickie's house, so I need to go through it and get some things out before you move in," said Devron.

Mason shook his head. "Oh, I don't think we were planning to live here."

"Not live here?" Turtle asked. "You people are going to be providing round-the-clock security. Are you planning to commute every day?"

Gio lifted his shoulders. "We're gonna burn a lot of fuel going back and forth."

Val added, "Plus, we'll be easy targets when we're on the road."

"And if the only people at our house are the ones sleeping, who will watch over us?" Wynter asked.

Mason lowered his gaze. "Alright, I guess we'll bring everything over here."

Mason asked Rhett, "You said five houses?"

"Yeah," Rhett answered. "They were the residents of the Pastor and counselors who ran Redemption Ranch."

"Let me guess," said Prairie. "They all disappeared."

"Along with most of the guys in the program," Devron answered.

Billy stuttered, "It was, it was, it was…"

"The Rapture," Devron answered for him. Billy nodded to confirm that was what he'd been trying to say.

Mason ignored the discussion over the missing people. "We've got three more people to bring here, eight total. We'll be crowded all living under one roof. Could you give us two houses?"

Rhett shrugged. "Sure. Turtle and Dixon can share a house."

"Whoa!" Turtle protested. "I'm not giving up my house!"

Rhett cut him off. "You don't need a whole house all to yourself! You were in the dormitory with sixty other guys before the disappearances. They're two entire families with eight people total. Stop being so greedy. No wonder you were left behind."

"Oh yeah? You're still here too, aren't you?" Turtle looked at Megan. "You know what the Bible says about fornicators not inheriting the Kingdom of Heaven, don't you?"

"I'm going to crack your skull wide open!" Rhett's face flushed red, and he charged at Turtle.

"Easy!" Devron jumped between them. He grabbed Rhett and pointed to Dixon. "Get Turtle out of here before he gets himself killed."

Dixon put his arm around Turtle. "Let's go check out the houses. I'll let you pick which one we're going to live in."

"Fine," said Turtle. "But I get the master bedroom."

"Yeah, sure." Dixon led him out of the auditorium.

"Come on, baby, don't let that idiot get you riled up." Megan took Rhett's hand and pulled him toward the door.

Rhett's nostrils were flared out like a charging bull. He slowly regained his composure. He looked at Mason. "I'll be in the first house. Stop by when you get back. I'll help you get settled in."

"Sure thing." Mason wasn't thrilled about the less-than-ideal situation. "See you in a bit."

Devron waited for Rhett and Megan to leave. "I guess you've figured out by now that Redemption Ranch was a residential addiction recovery program."

Mason nodded. He didn't like having his girls around a bunch of people who had drug problems.

Devron continued, "Addicts tend to be pretty self-absorbed. After all, we've built our lives around making ourselves feel good—regardless of how that affects the people around us. As hard as it is to put down the bottle, the pills, the pipe, or whatever, it's even harder to put down those old behaviors, the selfishness, the rage, all of it." Devron sighed. "Especially without Jesus."

"So, you think it was the Rapture?" asked Prairie.

Devron lowered his gaze and nodded. "Like everyone else at the ranch who was left behind, I was just here to do easy time. I got busted selling crack and was able to get a court order to do the Redemption Ranch program instead of prison. Better food, more freedom, but I had no intentions of actually turning my life around."

Mason thought Devron sounded very sincere. "I appreciate what you're saying, but I'm not sure that's what happened. My family went to church, we tried to be good people. We're still here."

Devron smiled out of one side of his mouth. "Like Brother Dickie used to say, sitting in church doesn't make you a Christian any more than sitting in a garage makes you a car. And you could ask anybody who has ever set foot on this ranch. They all thought they were good people. But by whose standards? When I hold myself up to God's standards, I come up short. The Bible says all have sinned and fall short of the glory of God. Nothing I can do will ever make up for my sins and failures. Only the blood of Jesus can atone for that."

Prairie listened intently. "It sounds like you really believe all of it now."

Devron nodded. "Yep. Brother Dickie said this day was coming. He taught about the Great Tribulation just a few weeks ago. He pointed out everything that was happening and speculated that the Rapture could come at any time. When they disappeared, I knew. I was scared out of my mind, more afraid than I'd ever been in my life. Right then, I dropped down on my knees and cried out to God. I told him I was sorry for being so rebellious, for not turning my life over to Him before, and for every sin that I could remember. I felt ashamed that it had taken a cataclysmic event to make me repent, but after I finished praying, I felt this overwhelming peace wash over me. I never felt anything like it. Even though I know how bad things are about to get, I have this sense that everything is going to be okay, like I can just look right past the next seven years and into eternity." Devron looked toward the sky. A tear trickled down the side of his face. "I'll be with Jesus, and everything will be alright."

"Me-me-me…too." Billy's eyes were glassy, and he nodded his agreement with what Devron had said.

"What about Rhett, Dixon, and Turtle?" Wynter asked. "Do they believe in all of this?"

Devron lifted his shoulders and looked at Billy. "They know it was the Rapture. They know in their heads everything I'm saying is true. But whether or not they know it in their heart, that's between them and God." He sat in the pew and folded his hands.

"I don't understand," said Wynter. "How can you know something in your head and not know it in your heart?"

Devron thought for a moment. "Take capitalism, for instance. Everybody believes in it. I mean they all believe it exists, but that doesn't mean they all believe in it as a way of life. That's the difference between believing in your head and in your heart. Does that make sense?"

"Perfectly." Prairie nodded.

"Why did you say the next seven years?" asked Val.

"The Great Tribulation," Devron answered. "It's a seven-year period where God will pour out His wrath in the form of seven seals, seven trumpets, and seven vial judgments. It will be unlike anything the world has ever gone through. And it's already begun. The first four seals are the four horsemen of the apocalypse. The white horse, a conqueror bent on conquest, that's Ange de Bourbon, the Antichrist. The second seal was the red horse, war. The nuclear exchange between Russia and the US.

"Next was the third seal, the black horse, global famine and hyperinflation, a loaf of bread for a day's wages. The currency collapse had already started a hyperinflationary event. The nuclear exchange and ongoing tensions between the east and the west will create worsening supply chain disruptions, radiation took a lot of farmland out of production. Food prices are out of control and about to get worse."

Mason understood the young man's analysis of the coming shortages and skyrocketing prices to be correct. "You put all of this together yourself?"

"No." Devron shook his head. "Like I said, Brother Dickie taught us about all of this. I just didn't put much stock into it until now."

Val glanced at his father with worried eyes, then turned to Devron. "So that's three. What's the fourth horseman?"

"Death and Hades." Devron swallowed hard before continuing. "The pale horse. He will have the power to kill one-fourth of the inhabitants of the planet."

Mason tightened his jaw. "Given the economic collapse, radiation poisoning, supply chain issues, and the fighting over resources that are bound to come in the aftermath, a twenty-five percent die-off isn't hard to imagine."

Wynter crossed her arms. "A quarter of the global population would be two billion people. That's insane! Are you saying you believe in this antiquated prophecy?"

Mason wrinkled his forehead. "If a fourth of all humanity dies, it will be hard to deny. The other three seals seem to line up pretty well with what's happening."

Gio said, "I've gone to mass all my life; went to Catholic school and I ain't ever heard any of this."

Mason asked, "Devron, could you write down the passages that describe the Great Tribulation? I'd like to study it for myself."

"Yeah, sure. As a matter of fact, I'll get a copy of Brother Dickie's notes for you," said Devron.

"Thank you." Mason walked toward the door and signaled for his team to follow. "We need to go get our stuff and the rest of our people. I'd like to finish moving by dusk."

CHAPTER 24

So then faith cometh by hearing, and hearing by the word of God.

Romans 10:17

Mason rolled over the next morning, awakened by the sound of someone knocking. He threw off the covers and went to the door.

"Daddy, who is it?" Prairie came out of her room.

Mason checked the peephole before turning the latch. "It's Devron." He opened the door.

"Good morning," said Devron.

"Good morning." Mason shielded his eyes from the glaring sun.

"I wanted to invite you all to church."

"Church?" Mason surveyed the surroundings to see if anyone else was around.

"Yes, sir. It is Sunday."

Wynter had also emerged from her room to see what the commotion was about. "Is everyone else going?"

Devron turned to look at the other four houses on the small private street. "Just me and Billy—so far."

Mason politely declined. "Gio is going to be teaching us some shooting drills today. Plus, we have to put together our communications protocols for the security team. Maybe another time."

Before he could close the door, Prairie inquired, "Who is going to be preaching?"

Devron looked at the quiet little street behind him again, as if Billy Graham or Charles Swindoll might be walking toward the chapel. Seeing no one, he turned back to Prairie. "Um—I guess I will. Billy has a hard time getting his words out."

"Yeah." Prairie fought a grin. "What are you going to preach about?"

Devron seemed to scan his surroundings for a cue card. He pressed his hands in his pockets nervously. "I don't know, honestly."

Then, Wynter offered a suggestion. "What about the tribulation?"

"Oh," said Devron. "Maybe."

"Teach about that stuff and we'll come." Prairie looked at her sister. "Won't we?"

Wynter stepped closer to the door. "Yeah, I bet Val will come also. Did you ask them already?"

Devron looked down, as if suddenly unsure of his qualifications to teach. "Brother Dickie spent like six weeks preaching about all of that."

"We've got time," said Prairie. "How about you start with the four horsemen? That's probably about all we can handle for today."

Devron nodded. "I think I can do that."

"Great! We'll let Gio's family know about it and meet you over there," Prairie said with excitement.

"Alright. But give me like an hour to go over Brother Dickie's notes," said Devron.

Prairie rolled her eyes. "I'm still in my pajamas. It'll take me at least that long."

"Sure. No hurry. See you there." Devron waved and walked back toward his own house.

Prairie turned to Mason. "We've got all day to learn about guns. It's okay if we go to church this morning, isn't it?"

"I suppose so." Mason was likewise curious to hear what the Bible had to say about the coming waves of destruction.

***

Everyone from Giovanni's group also attended the impromptu service. Charlie the Crab sat next to Mason. He had stringy gray hair, a handlebar mustache, and a large potbelly. The nervous mobster smelled of last night's rum and his hands quaked. Gio sat between the Crab and Francine, with young Luca next to her. The girls sat in the adjacent pew, one on either side of Val. Billy, AKA Can't-Get-Right, sat by himself on the far end of the same pew.

Devron opened with a heartfelt prayer, then began reading from Brother Dickie's notes and the Bible. He started off stumbling over his words but soon found a more natural cadence.

After the service, Mason walked next to Gio. "What did you think?"

Gio shrugged. "This is all new to me. I never realized any of this was in the Bible. Devron makes a convincing case, but then again, I suppose you could read what you want into it."

"I'm not so sure about that," Mason countered. "The notes Devron was teaching from were written several weeks ago, and the Book of Revelation was written over two thousand years ago, long before anyone had heard of Ange de Bourbon, before the disappearances, before the nuclear exchange."

"So, you believe all of it?" Gio asked.

"Like you said," Mason replied. "Devron makes a convincing case. I did some reading last night in the Book of Revelation. I'll dig into it a little deeper after my security shift tonight."

Francine walked up and hugged her husband. "Sorry to interrupt, but Charlie and I need to head over to the kitchen. Gio volunteered us to be the cooks of the compound. We'll try to have something ready for lunch. Tell the others to head on over to the dining hall in about an hour."

"Sure thing," said Mason. "They'll be happy to have world-class chefs like you and Charlie."

She winked at him before walking off with Charlie. "I'll make sure you get an extra serving."

Gio waited until they were out of earshot. "Ain't no way I'm putting the Crab on security. As nervous as that guy is, he'd probably shoot himself in the foot—or worse."

"We need cooks. We've got a lot of mouths to feed," said Mason. "He and Ceeny might as well do something they enjoy."

Gio clapped his hands. "Okay, my kids and Mace's kids, let's go. Time to start familiarizing yourselves with the notorious AK-47. Follow me to the house."

Val protested. "I know as much about AKs as you do."

"Good." Gio laughed. "I'll let you teach the first class."

Val pressed his lips together. "You suckered me into that one, didn't you?"

Gio put his arm around him. "I sure did, kid."

Once back at the house, Gio handed out rifles to everyone and Val began explaining basic operations. Mason tried to stay focused, but his mind drifted as he watched Wynter and Prairie racking the slides and performing magazine changes. Seeing his remaining two daughters with guns in their hands reminded him how easily they could be snatched away.

Prairie watched Val's instructions on filling the magazines with bullets and began pressing round after round into her mag. "When do we get to shoot?"

"After lunch," said Gio. "But I like your attitude."

Wynter picked up a handful of loose rounds from the green metal box to load into her magazine. "So, what are the security teams going to be?"

Mason answered, "We're one squad and Gio's group is the other."

Gio nodded. "I'm kind of a night owl, so we can take nights and you guys take days."

"That's a twelve-hour shift, seven days a week," said Wynter. "It's going to be tough."

"It is what it is," said Gio.

Mason frowned. "She's right. We're going to get burned out fast."

"What options do we have?" Gio asked.

Wynter offered a solution. "Val and I could work together as a third team. That gives everyone an eight-hour shift."

"Why are you the one to work with Val?" Prairie wrinkled her brow. "When did you suddenly start liking boys again?"

Wynter tossed her magazine on the table and stood with her hands on her hips. "It's not about whether or not I like boys or any specific boy. It's about keeping us all safe. You included."

"Don't do me any favors," said Prairie. "I get by just fine on my own."

Wynter smirked. "Maybe I'm keeping Val safe from *you*."

"Oh, please!" Prairie rolled her eyes.

Luca offered a compromise. "Me and Prairie could be a team, Val and Wyn, then Mace and Dad for the last team."

Prairie scowled at the acne-faced Luca. "What did I tell you I'd do if you *ever*…"

Mason interrupted. "Okay, that's enough. Girls, take your guns, ammo, and magazines next door. You can finish loading your mags in your rooms. I think we all need a little alone time before lunch."

"Whatever." Wynter seemed the most embarrassed and was first to take her equipment and leave.

Luca watched Prairie like a scorned pup as she did likewise. Of all the disgruntled teens, Val seemed to be the only one enjoying the interaction.

Gio also appeared amused by the squabble. Mason walked out on the porch and signaled for Gio to follow. Once they were alone, Gio asked, "Do you have a solution to break us into three teams without triggering a civil war?"

"Maybe," Mason responded. "You and Val are the most proficient shooters. Since after dark is the time we're most likely to get hit, it makes sense to put you two on nights, from 11:00 to 7:00. I'll work evenings, from 3:00 to 11:00. I'll rotate the girls and Luca to work with me. That will allow me to evaluate all of them. The two who aren't on with me will take the morning shift, 7:00 to 3:00."

Gio grinned. "Luca will like that—especially when he gets to work with one of the girls."

"Yeah, sorry about Prairie being so mean to him."

"He'll get over it."

"And if you don't mind, help me keep an eye on Val and my girls," said Mason. "He's not the one I'm worried about, but…"

"Say no more." Gio called Val to come outside. "Son, come here. I want to talk to you."

Val walked out onto the porch. "What about?"

"Hey, listen. I know Prairie and Wyn are cute. You're out here, just you and them. But if anything happens between you and either one of them, I'll make you dig the hole before I put you in it. Understand?"

"Yes, sir."

Gio hugged his son. "You're a good kid. I love you. You know that, right?"

"Yes, sir."

"But I'll kill you if you disrespect me and go against my wishes on this. I mean it!"

"Yes, sir." Val nodded.

Mason was unsure if Gio was serious about the threat but took sufficient comfort in the fact that Val seemed to believe him.

***

After lunch, Rhett stood up. "Charlie, Mrs…"

Mason noticed he was looking at Francine. "Palermo."

"Right," said Rhett. "Mrs. Palermo. That was an unbelievable lunch. None of us would have ever put together a meal like that. We're happy to have you with us here at the ranch. But if you'll excuse us, Megan, Turtle, and I need to check on the cattle."

Just as Rhett finished speaking, the lights went out. He paused, looked up, then turned his attention to Mason. "Looks like the rolling blackouts have started. The man on the radio said they were coming. Your group best have your security plan ready and active by sundown. Something about the lights being out that seems to attract rats and cockroaches."

"We're on it," Mason answered. "We'll be running some shooting drills after lunch. From then on, we'll have two people on watch and four people on call at all times."

"Alright." Rhett put his cowboy hat on his head and led his team toward the door. "Let's hope it's enough."

CHAPTER 25

And then shall that Wicked be revealed, whom the LORD shall consume with the spirit of his mouth, and shall destroy with the brightness of his coming: even him, whose coming is after the working of Satan with all power and signs and lying wonders, and with all deceivableness of unrighteousness in them that perish; because they received not the love of the truth, that they might be saved. And for this cause God shall send them strong delusion, that they should believe a lie: that they all might be damned who believed not the truth, but had pleasure in unrighteousness.

2 Thessalonians 2:8-12

The days passed and the new members of the Redemption Ranch compound began to acclimate to the unfamiliar environment. Even so, Mason's group and the residents who'd been there before their arrival maintained separate social circles with minimal contact between the two tribes. The blackouts continued and the electricity was off more often than it was on.

One evening, roughly two weeks after they'd arrived at the ranch, Mason and Prairie came home from their security shift. Prairie leaned her rifle in the corner and dropped her shoulder bag containing her spare magazines. "I can't believe how hot it is. Eleven o'clock at night in October and I'm still sweating. Can you imagine what this place will be like in July?"

"I'm sure it will begin to cool off in November." Mason lit a candle, sat down on the sofa, and kicked off his shoes.

Prairie opened Wynter's bedroom door and peeked in on her. She closed the door and spoke softly. "I don't know how she can sleep when it's this hot."

Mason picked up the old Bible left behind by Brother Dickie and opened it to Revelation, just as he'd done for the past two weeks.

"Do you mind if I listen to the radio for a while?" Prairie asked.

271

Mason glanced up from the Bible. "Just a few minutes. We need to conserve the batteries."

"These are rechargeable," said Prairie. "Billy gave them to me. He said I could bring them back and he'd recharge them when the power is on."

Mason lowered one brow. "He said that?"

"That's what he was trying to say—between stutters, anyway. He's getting better. He strings together three or four words at a time now." Prairie powered on the small transistor and found the local GBC affiliate, the only station still on the air. The program was a re-broadcast of the British show, News Day with Diedre Collins, from earlier that evening.

"My guest needs no introduction; his name is one of the most recognizable on the planet. Please join me in welcoming the CEO of Gnosis, Amadeo Falcone."

"Thank you for having me, Diedre. It's a pleasure to be here."

"When I heard you were in London, I begged my producer to get you on."

"We do have offices here," said Falcone.

"You have offices everywhere, don't you?"

"Pretty much," Falcone laughed.

"So, we're being simulcast to radio as part of GBC's effort to keep the globe informed of what's happening. As you know, much of the Americas are without power or experiencing regular brownouts.

"For those listening on the radio, I have to tell you, Amadeo has brought the most adorable little kitten into the studio with him. And I'm going to add, probably the most well-behaved."

"Yes," Falcone replied. "This is Millie. Like you said, she is a kitten, but she also happens to be thirty-seven years old. That explains her behavior. She has a kitten's energy and likes to play, but she's gotten past some of that curiosity you might expect from such a small cat."

"How is that possible?" Collins inquired.

"Millie is from one of my projects called PerPETual."

"I've seen the commercials on TV," said Collins. "The logo is so clever. The *pet* in PerPETual is written in all caps. Excellent branding. You almost know what the company does without even reading about it. But it's a relatively new service, so tell us about it."

"Sure, but I'll have to start at the beginning or we're going to lose a lot of people."

"The floor is yours. Take all the time you need," Collins answered.

"When we talk about the soul, whether we're talking about a person or even an animal like Millie here, what we're really talking about is our essence—our memories, our personalities. Your soul is what makes you, you.

"At Gnosis, we've been able to map brainwaves, the little flashes of electrical impulses traveling between neurons. That's life. It's your own personal operating system. Everything else, the brain, the heart, the body, that's all just hardware and we can recreate it as needed. But your soul, that's the thing that's been so elusive, until now.

"Take Millie, for instance. We mapped out her soul, recorded her thoughts, her brainwaves, and made an electronic profile that would act as an envelope for her soul.

"Likewise, we were able to clone her physical body and then, when it was her time to go, we just uploaded her soul into the cloned body. In fact, this is her third go around on this planet."

Deidre Collins quipped, "So this cat really does have nine lives."

Falcone laughed at the corny jest. "Yes. If you figure one cat year equals about four human years, she's roughly 148 years old."

"Yet she's just a kitten. It's remarkable!" Collins praised.

"It really is, Diedre. But preserving your pets in perpetuity wasn't my only ambition with this project. PerPETual was actually designed to be a proof of concept for another project called iMortal, our neuro-upload cloning service for humans."

"You have *got* to be kidding me!"

"Not at all," said Falcone. "Gnosis has been on the bleeding edge of healthcare innovations for over two decades. We've developed an implantable brain chip that's been used to heal a myriad of ailments, particularly those that can be traced back to the brain. We've literally been able to make the lame to walk and the blind to see.

"Now it's time we offered eternal life. This has been the quest of all major religions, whether we're talking about Heaven or reincarnation, the goal of humanity has been to beat death. And we've finally accomplished that."

"But won't this be expensive?" asked Collins.

"It's not for everyone. But we have other more affordable options. Our Nuero-vana program offers a way to have yourself neuro-uploaded into our AI-created virtual paradise hosted on Gnosis's own quantum computer. Throughout the ages, we've had people claiming to be gods or prophets. Where they've fallen short is that either they don't have their own heaven, or they've been unable to prove its existence. But we've created our own version of Nirvana and it's something you can experience via virtual reality before committing to living there for eternity. And as you might have guessed, it's called Nuero-vana.

"But your version of paradise is very different from what your best friend's heaven might be like. We use all of the data collected throughout your lifetime of using social media sites affiliated with the Gnosis family of companies, your texts, email, pictures, videos, even your shopping habits, to tailor a one-of-a-kind eternal existence curated just for you."

Collins gushed, "You make is sound so special. I want to go to Nuero-vana! When it's time, of course. Unless I can afford to clone myself. But either way, I'm not in any hurry."

"Of course not," said Falcone. "But you can get started today if you'd like. We'll book you an appointment to have your soul backed up on our database—in case of any unforeseen accidents."

"You can do that?"

"Of course. And Nuero-vana is far better than the fictitious Heaven that you might have heard about in Sunday school. You'll still be able to stay in contact with friends and loved ones from beyond through traditional means such as email, text, and even voice calls. Or if they want, your friends and loved ones can come to a Neuro-vana Séance kiosk, where you'll be able to interact with one another through virtual reality."

Collins clarified, "So would I be correct in saying Nuero-vana is like Heaven and iMortal is your version of reincarnation?"

"Yes, but better. Especially iMortal. We can gene-edit your clone to be the best version of you. Plus, you can come back at any stage of your life that you want. You could come back as a ten-year-old, eighteen, twenty-one, up to forty years old. And if you were born with the wrong gender, we can fix that too. Gender can be edited at the clone's initial development level as easily as eye color, hair color, or any number of features."

Collins added, "For a fee."

He chuckled. "Clone technology isn't free. But thanks to a generous grant from the Bourbon family, Nuero-vana is."

"You're kidding!"

"Nope. I know it sounds cliché, but Ange de Bourbon is offering eternal life to anyone who will receive it." Falcone continued. "But on a more sobering note, we must realize, hundreds of thousands of people are suffering from radiation poisoning as a result of the nuclear exchange. And hundreds of thousands more are going to develop serious cancers that we have no means to treat. Beyond that, we'll be facing supply chain issues, starvation, disease, and all the usual suspects that come with the aftermath of war.

"My hope is that these suffering masses will see this free gift of salvation that Ange de Bourbon is offering and take him up on it. We'll be setting up transition centers in all the refugee encampments where people affected by the bombs and the fallout can come and move peacefully from this life to something far better. We'll offer a sedative and care for their final earthly needs.

"I believe we'll have entire families that choose to move on to paradise rather than deal with the pain and misery of…"

Mason stood up and turned off the radio. "This psychopath is trying to convince people to commit mass suicide! You can't put someone's soul into a computer!"

He felt his face getting white, he felt dizzy. Mason stumbled as he sat back down on the easy chair.

"Daddy, you don't look good." Prairie grabbed his hand. "What's wrong?"

Mason took a deep breath. "Gnosis. It was funded by In-Q-Tel."

"So?" Prairie seemed puzzled.

"Poseidon ran a fund for In-Q-Tel—a secret fund." He frowned. "I did this. I enabled this—monster, this liar. If Devron is right, Bourbon is the antichrist and Falcone is his false prophet, I helped to build the final world empire, the empire of the Beast."

Mason's walkie-talkie came to life with Gio's voice on the other end. "Mace, you better get out here. I got movement over by the cattle barn."

Mason pressed the talk key. "What kind of movement?"

"I don't know. All I can see right now is a couple of flashlights moving through the field."

Mason stood up and grabbed his AK-47. "Are you sure it isn't Rhett, or Turtle, or one of those guys?"

"They're all in bed. Besides, they know we shoot first and ask questions later. None of them are stupid enough to be wandering around out here without letting us know first."

"I'll be right there," said Mason.

"Meet me by the live oak hammock near the barn and come on foot. I don't want the sound of a four-wheeler to scare them off," Gio replied.

"Should I wake up Wyn?" Prairie grabbed her rifle.

"No. You stay here and guard the house." Mason opened the door.

"Daddy! You promised these people that we were all going to work together to keep the compound safe. I'm coming with you."

"I'm keeping that promise! You're going to stay here and shoot anyone who comes near the houses! Don't argue with me!"

She huffed and checked the chamber of her rifle. "At least call me on the radio to keep me in the loop."

He softened his tone. "I will. On second thought, wake your sister up. Both of you keep watch over the houses."

"I will." She gazed at him with worried eyes, "Be safe, Daddy."

Mason gave her a quick hug and headed out into the darkness. He followed the dirt road toward the cattle barn. The small patch of oaks soon came into view. Mason hurried toward the island of trees but could see no one.

"Psst!"

Mason raised his rifle at the noise. "Gio? Is that you?"

"Yeah, it's me. Put that thing down."

Mason lowered his weapon and walked toward the voice. He saw Giovanni squatting near a palmetto bush. "Where's Val?"

Gio pointed to the tree branches overhead. Mason looked skyward but saw no sign of Valentino. "What's happening?"

Gio kept his eyes trained on the cattle barn. "Looks like three of them. They killed a cow. They're butchering it up so they can load it into the pickup."

"I didn't hear any gunshots."

"They used a crossbow," Gio replied. "But they've got guns."

Mason frowned. "That's not good. If we let them get away with it, the ranch will become the local food pantry."

"You got that right," Gio replied.

"Trespassers with guns—we can't afford to try taking them alive." Mason squinted to get a better look at the midnight rustlers.

"Agreed," said Gio.

Mason glanced at the treetops. "Val can stay up there and cover us. We'll move in and eliminate the threat." His stomach felt sick at having to take a human life, but he could see no other solution.

"Got that?" Gio looked at the branches overhead.

"Yes, sir," a whispered voice replied.

Once Mason was able to zero in on the sound of Val's voice, he could see the young man perched on a limb with his rifle pointed in the direction of the activity around the pickup truck. Mason pulled the butt of the AK-47 into his shoulder and proceeded quietly toward the thieves.

Gio stayed close behind Mason. The two of them slowed their movement as they approached the slaughter site. Mason found concealment behind a patch of pepper trees. He watched the marauders long enough to see that one was standing guard and the other two were loading the back leg of the cow into the bed of the truck. "I'll take the guy with the gun. Then we'll try to eliminate the other two before they can get to their weapons."

Gio nodded his consent to the plan. Mason felt shaky inside. He raised the rifle. Felt nauseous, took aim. The man standing guard was young. Not much older than Wynter. A knot formed in Mason's throat. The boy looked in Mason's direction and furrowed his brow. Mason felt white hot, then ice cold, and pulled the trigger. The gun barked. The boy fell.

The other two bandits dropped the leg of beef and jumped out of the truck bed. They took cover behind the pickup. Gio charged toward the front of the vehicle, firing indiscriminately as he ran.

Mason froze, wished he hadn't done what he'd just done. Gunfire erupted from behind the truck. Gio retreated toward the barn.

Mason took a deep breath. "I'll feel guilty later. Right now, I have to keep Gio alive." He rushed toward the tailgate of the pickup, hoping to flank the cattle rustlers before they saw him coming.

The two of them continued to pursue Gio toward the barn.

Mason lifted his weapon again, fired, and missed. One of the bandits turned toward him with a shotgun. Mason let out a volley of shots, striking the man with the shotgun several times. He looked to see that the other man had also turned his attention in Mason's direction. The bandit's weapon was raised. Mason was out of time. Killing his assailant before he could pull the trigger was impossible.

POW! The shot echoed off of the barn wall.

CHAPTER 26

Woe unto you that desire the day of the Lord! To what end is it for you? the day of the LORD is darkness, and not light.

Amos 5:18

Mason felt ethereal, as if floating. His face felt cool, as if a refreshing breeze were blowing across it. *Am I dead?* He opened his eyes. He saw the threat lying sideways near the other downed shooter. *Maybe we killed each other*, he thought.

"You alright, buddy?" Gio walked toward him, keeping his rifle pointed at the two dead heaps on the ground near the pickup.

Mason looked down at his own body, unsure of his answer. He felt for holes, felt for blood. He ran his hand across his head.

Gio clicked on his flashlight and pointed it in Mason's eyes. "Let's get a look at you."

Mason closed his eyelids tight, turned away from the glaring beacon, and shielded his face with his hand. "Turn that off!"

Gio chuckled. "Yeah, you're fine."

Mason's breathing and heart rate began to regulate. He wrote off the bizarre sensations as a surge from his adrenal glands. "You shot that guy?"

"I didn't shoot nobody." Gio pointed to the corpses. "You got the guard, the first guy. Then you popped the goon with the shotgun, and Val hit the other guy from the tree."

Mason turned toward the live oaks. "Valentino saved my life."

Gio replied, "That makes you two even. Me, Ceeny, and Luca still owe you—for getting us out of Jersey before the bomb."

Mason signaled Gio to follow him. "We better sweep the area. Make sure no one else is around." They checked the barn as well as the immediate vicinity. Once the search was complete, they returned to the pickup where they found Valentino waiting for them.

Gio hugged the boy who looked disturbed over his role in the incident. "You did good, son. You did real good."

Gio picked up one of the knives the rustlers had been using to dissect the cow. "I say we decapitate them and put their heads on a pike near the front gate. That'll put out the message that we ain't the ones to mess with."

Unfortunately, Mason saw the wisdom in the grotesque act. "The time may come when we need to put up such a hideous billboard, but I think we're a little early in the game to be going full Barbarian. "Let's try to stay under the radar for a while longer. I don't want to draw the attention of law enforcement—local or otherwise."

"Alright then," said Gio. "I guess that means we need to dig a hole."

"Shovels are in the barn." Mason pulled the radio off of his belt. "I'll call Prairie and have her send Rhett over here to process the cow. No point in letting all this meat go to waste."

***

Early Wednesday afternoon, the entire group gathered at the outdoor pavilion for lunch. Charlie the Crab grilled steaks while Francine pulled potatoes from the coals of the nearby communal fire pit. Mason and his girls sat at the picnic table with Dixon, Rhett, and Megan. Gio and his boys shared a table with Turtle, Devron, and Billy. For the first time since Mason's arrival, the two groups seemed to share a cohesive bond.

Rhett's people appeared well pleased with the outcome of the prior night's trespass. Likewise, Mason's team was happy to be eating steak when the radio was reporting desperate situations all over America.

Dixon cut into his steak. "I can't believe you and Gio slipped up on those cats like that. You two are straight gangstas!"

"They're straight *stupid*, is what they are." Wynter cut a piece of fat from her meat.

Mason snapped, "That's very disrespectful. Don't ever talk about me like that again."

Wynter looked up from her plate with glassy eyes. "It hasn't even been three weeks since Mom died. You could have gotten yourself killed!" Her tone went from one of contempt to sorrow. "Then what would Prairie and I have done? We'd be completely on our own!" She dropped her utensils on her plate.

Mason understood her pain and scolded her no further. Prairie put her arm around her older sister. "She's right, Daddy. Our chances are better if we stick together. You should have waited for me to wake up Wyn."

He extended his hand across the table to touch Prairie's arm. "Okay. Next time, we'll stick together," he said, although he had no intention of honoring the commitment.

Wynter dried her eyes and toyed with her food as if uninterested in eating. "I'm working the evening shift with you tonight, Dad."

"Alright. That will be fine." Mason hoped lightning would not strike twice.

He heard the sound of a vehicle turning onto the dirt road of the ranch. He reached under the table and grabbed his AK. "Gio, looks like we've got company."

"It's the cops!" Turtle declared.

Rhett called out orders to his group. "All of you guys with felony charges, ditch your guns—quick!"

"Put them in the golf cart," said Francine. "I'll drive them back to the kitchen." Of the six, Megan was the only one in no hurry to dispossess herself of her firearm.

Mason left his rifle on the bench of the picnic table. "I'll go talk to them, see what they want. You guys cover me."

"Are we going to get into a shoot-out with cops?" Luca asked.

"It's not going to come to that," Mason assured.

"But if it does, you have to be tough!" Val firmly reminded his younger brother.

Mason spoke with the officers in the patrol car. "Can I help you gentlemen?"

The car came to a complete stop. The driver stepped out as well as another from the back seat and yet another man from the front passenger's seat. His uniform was similar to the deputies, but his badge read *Sheriff.* He was a tall, stout man, in his early sixties. He wore cowboy boots and had a mustache similar to Ron the realtor's. Unlike the deputies who wore semi-automatic pistols, he wore a shiny revolver on his belt with a long barrel. "Seems like you folks are living the high life out here; having picnics, eating steak."

Mason said nothing.

The tall man tightened his jaw. "I'm Sheriff Hackney. We got a report of some shooting last night. It's not uncommon for folks to do a little target practice around these parts during daylight hours, but when it happens at night, we look into it. Especially these days. We've had all sorts of trouble from folks coming through here from the cities. Looters, cattle rustlers, people going through orange groves and helping themselves, squatters trying to lay claim to properties where the owners are away."

Mason waited to see if the man would ask him a direct question.

Sheriff Hackney eyed the group sitting at the pavilion. "This property is on record as belonging to a non-profit called Redemption Ranch Incorporated. Are any members of the board or the director present for me to speak to?"

"No one has seen them for a few weeks, Sheriff." Being an attorney, Mason knew to keep his answers short.

"Lot of that goin' around." Hackney looked past Mason at the people still sitting beneath the pavilion. "Mind if I see your ID?"

Mason knew the conversation would deteriorate at a faster pace if he didn't cooperate. So, he handed over his driver's license.

"New York City," Hackney declared as he inspected the card. "Long way from home, aren't you?"

Mason assumed it was a rhetorical question and provided no comment.

"Are you in the addiction recovery program?" quizzed Hackney.

"No, sir."

Hackney continued the interrogation. "Were you employed by the ranch in any capacity?"

"Not previously."

"Then what gives you the right to be here?"

"I was invited—as a guest."

"By who?" Hackney narrowed his eyes.

"By the residents."

"You mean the people in the program—the dopers."

Again, Mason declined to elaborate.

"Those fellas don't have the authority to invite guests. Is that your family up there?"

Mason considered it might be easier to assume he was speaking only of Prairie and Wyn rather than explain how his mob buddy had also come down from New York. "Yes, sir."

Hackney nodded. "If those two pretty little girls up there were my daughters, I wouldn't want them around a bunch of crackheads and meth addicts. I don't know what them ol' boys told you, but most of them are here because they have to be. Either the judge sent them here, or they're on probation—ain't none of 'em here to get no merit badge for the Boy Scouts, you see."

Hackney waited for Mason to respond, but he did not. The sheriff seemed to take it as an act of disdain and scowled at Mason. "Anyway, being that they're wards of the county, and I'm the representative, I hereby declare myself administrator of this operation." He turned to the man behind him. "Deputy Watt, round everybody up. Run all their IDs. Anyone on probation, community control, parole, or court-ordered to be here is our prisoner. Anyone who isn't is free to leave. And I recommend they do so—right quick." He glanced back at Mason. "Start with this fella." He handed Mason's ID to Deputy Watt and then pointed to the other man. "Deputy Combs, help him out. Make sure everyone stays under the pavilion until we can sort out who's who."

Combs walked up to the covered dining area. "Sheriff, we've got guns up here."

"Well, collect them," said Hackney.

Mason held up his hand. "Hold on, we're not giving up our guns." He turned to Gio and the rest of his team and shook his head.

"Are you resisting the order of a law enforcement officer?" Hackney unsnapped the leather strap securing his oversized revolver.

Gio raised his rifle and held it on Hackney.

"I'm refusing an unconstitutional directive," said Mason. "This is private property, we were invited here by the residents, these are our personal firearms, and we've done nothing that warrants their confiscation."

Combs and Watt drew their sidearms. Val leveled his AK at Watt while Prairie and Wynter aimed at Combs.

"Oh, so are you a lawyer now?" Hackney let his hand rest on his pistol which was still in the holster.

"Yes, sir," Mason replied.

"Then you should know brandishing a weapon at a law enforcement officer is a felony."

Mason fought to keep his cool. "Is that your best attempt at de-escalation?"

Hackney huffed. "Combs, put your gun down. Get on the radio and tell them we have a situation out here at the ranch. You too, Watt. Put it down."

Combs holstered his weapon and reached for the speaker-mic clipped to his shoulder flap.

"Don't touch it!" Mason pointed at Combs. "Gio, if any of them reach for their radio, put 'em down. They'll have the whole department out here and this will turn into the Alamo."

"You've crossed the line Mr. City Slicker," Hackney said. "But you're a lawyer. You already know that."

Mason walked back to the pavilion to collect his AK. "Rhett, Turtle, Devron, get their radios, weapons, and cuffs. Then, restrain the officers."

"That's not going to happen. We're leaving. Come on, boys." Hackney turned toward the patrol car.

POW! Mason's heart jumped. He looked to see who'd fired the gun and who'd been shot. A trickle of smoke ebbed from Gio's rifle. The two deputies were pale white, but neither seemed to be bleeding. The sheriff appeared more red with anger than white, but he also appeared unharmed. However, he did look as though he appreciated the gravity of the situation.

Mason heard a low hissing sound. His eyes quickly located the source as the remaining air crept out of the patrol car's front tire.

Gio called out. "That was the only warning shot. Get your hands on the back of your heads."

Combs, Watt, and Hackney all complied with the order. Rhett and his team went to work securing the sheriff and his men.

"Good job," said Turtle with a sarcastic tone. "Now what are we supposed to do?"

Mason felt like a dog who'd finally caught a car. "Don't take that tone with me. You're no worse off than you were."

"How do you figure?" Turtle argued. "I had a repeat offender charge for crack-cocaine possession. Now I've added kidnapping cops to my sheet."

"He was about to turn this place into a prison camp," Mason defended. "He was going to take our guns and push my unarmed family out into a world that has come unglued." Mason glanced at his girls. "I couldn't let that happen."

"You did what you had to," said Rhett. "I understand. But still, we need to figure out what's next."

Mason hated the situation. "We can't stay here. Anywhere near here. They'll come looking for them soon enough. We need to be long gone by then."

"Gone where?" Prairie asked.

"I don't know. We may have to figure something out on the way." Mason looked at Hackney. "And we need to make it harder to find the sheriff and his men."

Gio shrugged. "We could take them over to the barn and tie them up. Most likely, they told dispatch where they were heading. The department's priority will be looking for the boss before they can concern themselves with hunting us down. I can use the patrol car to take them to the barn. It's still drivable. I'll just have to take it slow."

"Okay, that should buy us some time." Mason nodded. "Val, go get the Yukon and pick up your father at the barn. We need to be out of here in twenty minutes."

"Come on, Hop-along." Gio pointed his rifle at Hackney. "Get in the car. We're going for a little ride."

"What about us?" Megan asked with pleading eyes.

Mason looked at her. "You guys are welcome to tag along, but we've got nowhere to go."

Rhett turned to Dixon, Billy, and Devron. "What do you boys think?"

"Sounds like the sheriff plans on making this a slave camp," said Dixon. "I say we split."

Devron frowned. "I think Dixon is right. I don't want to stick around."

Billy stuttered, "My-my-my me-me-memaw has-has a place."

"Where? In North Carolina?" Devron asked.

Billy nodded. "Br-br-br-bryson."

"Is she there?" Rhett asked.

Billy lowered his gaze and shook his head.

"You think she was taken—in the Rapture." Devron put his hand on Billy's shoulder.

Billy nodded.

"Will we have room for all of us?" Mason asked.

Billy lifted his shoulders and gave a slight nod.

"We don't have anywhere else to be," said Prairie. "I vote we head to Memaws."

"Okay, but we need to be wheels up in twenty minutes," said Mason.

Rhett looked toward the equipment yard.

"What are you thinking?" Mason asked.

"Whether or not I can hook up the livestock trailer and have it loaded in twenty minutes."

Mason looked at the long silver trailer. "How many animals will it hold?"

"It's a twenty-four-footer. We might get a dozen if we're lucky. I was thinking nine cows, a bull, and a couple of horses. We'll put the horses between the bull and the cows. Otherwise, it might make for a bumpy ride."

Mason pointed to Prairie and Wynter. "Get our stuff packed and be ready to roll in twenty minutes. I'm going to help load the animals."

Rhett kissed Megan. "Pack our bags. I'll be by to pick you up."

"Okay." She ran toward the houses.

"What should we do?" asked Turtle. "Take the van?"

"Nope. Take the diesel pickups." Rhett answered. "We've got a couple of those big empty totes over by the orange groves. Go get one of them and fill it up from the diesel tank. Fuel might be hard to come by on the road." Rhett waved for Mason to follow him. "Come on."

Mason addressed Luca before leaving the group with Rhett. "Go to the kitchen. Tell your mom and the Crab what's going on. Tell them to load up as many dry goods as they can into Charlie's food trailer. Tell them we're leaving in twenty minutes."

Mason hurried to catch up with Rhett who'd already started toward the equipment yard. "Are the animals usually pretty good about getting into the trailer?"

"Nope."

"Should we maybe pray?" Mason could think of nothing else that might help expedite the foreboding process.

"If you believe in all that, be my guest." Rhett picked up his pace to the super-duty dually pickup.

Mason glanced skyward. He'd never prayed anything other than Hail Marys and Our Fathers.

"God, if you can hear me, we could really use your help. Please, God, help us load these animals and get out of here before the sheriff's department shows up."

CHAPTER 27

And when he had opened the fifth seal, I saw under the altar the souls of them that were slain for the word of God, and for the testimony which they held: and they cried with a loud voice, saying, "How long, O Lord, holy and true, dost thou not judge and avenge our blood on them that dwell on the earth?"

And white robes were given unto every one of them; and it was said unto them, that they should rest yet for a little season, until their fellowservants also and their brethren, that should be killed as they were, should be fulfilled.

And I beheld when he had opened the sixth seal, and, lo, there was a great earthquake; and the sun became black as sackcloth of hair, and the moon became as blood.

Revelation 6:9-12

Mason studied the side view mirror like a crystal ball that refused to reveal his certain doom. Rhett kept pace pulling the livestock trailer, with two more diesel pickup trucks from the ranch behind him, Charlie the Crab and his food trailer, and Gio's Yukon at the end of the convoy. Mason could see no one giving chase—yet.

Wynter sat in the front passenger seat of the Interceptor, turned halfway around, and faced the train of vehicles in their wake. "I don't understand why we're traveling through all of these little Podunk towns. We'd already be past Daytona if we'd taken the interstate."

"The interstates have license plate readers," Mason glanced at the road ahead then back to the side view.

Prairie examined a paper map in the back seat. "441 would have taken us all the way to Bryson City—without getting on the interstate."

"It would have taken us through Orlando." Mason forced himself to look away from the side view and pay attention to the road. "From what I've been hearing on the radio, Orlando has devolved into a third-world country. Traffic accidents are out of control because people are too scared to stop at traffic lights. They're afraid they'll be carjacked, kidnapped, or both if they stop."

"I guess it was only a matter of time before the chaos made its way down to Okeechobee," said Wynter.

"We got company." Gio's voice came over the radio.

Mason saw the red and blue lights in the side-view mirror. He pressed the talk key on the walkie-talkie. "I see them."

"It's a line of 'em," Gio replied. "At least eight. The guy in the front is trying to get beside me."

Mason switched to the right lane and tapped his brakes. Rhett and the other pickups sailed past him. Mason called over the radio, "Everyone, keep Rhett in the front of the line. We can't let one of these guys get next to him and pull a pit maneuver. Rhett will never regain control if they cause him to start weaving. He'll roll that trailer.

"Rhett, press as hard as you can. Head north when you come to Highway 27. We'll do our best to keep the patrol cars away from you."

"Roger that," Rhett replied.

Mason slowed until he was next to Gio so the patrol cars couldn't pass them. He checked the rearview. One of Hackney's deputies was inches away from his rear bumper. The deputy sped up. Boom!

"That jerk just hit us!" Prairie exclaimed.

"Dad, what are we going to do?" Wynter sounded upset.

"They're just trying to intimidate us," Mason said.

"Seems like they're trying to run us off the road," Wynter cried.

"Hang on," Mason warned. Wynter braced herself with her arm against the dashboard for another bump. Mason watched the patrol car speed up once more. He tapped the brakes just before the collision. The impact propelled Mason's vehicle forward but caused the patrol car to veer into the left lane and hit the car next to it. Both cars swerved, slowing down the entire procession and sending the assailing vehicle onto the grassy shoulder at a high speed.

"Nice work," Gio commended over the radio. "But that ain't going to be enough to stop them. Maybe we need to pepper their windshields with lead."

Mason glanced at Wynter, then Prairie. "If we start shooting, they'll respond in kind."

"Not if we spiderweb their windshields and they can't see where they're going." Gio looked across from the adjacent vehicle as he spoke into his radio.

"Let's give it some time," said Mason. "Maybe they'll give up."

Gio replied, "Mace, these guys are two counties past their jurisdiction. They ain't letting this thing go and they ain't playing by the rules."

Mason knew his old friend was right, but feared what would happen to his girls once the shooting began.

Wynter held her rifle in her lap. "I can do it, Dad. Just say when."

"Me too," Prairie added. "I'm ready."

Mason felt sick to his stomach over the thought of having his girls shoot at law enforcement officers. "Not yet."

He recalled the relative ease of getting the animals in the livestock trailer. He looked toward Heaven again. "God, I know I've neglected to get to know you or spend time with you over the years…"

"Who are you talking to?" Wynter asked.

"Shhh! He's praying!" Prairie scolded. "Bow your head and close your eyes."

"Psycho cops are trying to kill us!" Wynter retorted. "I'm not closing my eyes."

"Then at least close your mouth!" Prairie chided.

Wynter furrowed her brow but said no more.

Mason continued his petition. "We're in a real fix, Lord. I probably wouldn't ask for myself, but please, God, for my girls' sakes—help us."

The cab of the Interceptor became silent. The only sound was from outside the vehicle, the blaring sirens, the roaring engines, but no one inside the SUV said a word. Mason held his breath, wondering if God would grant him yet another miracle.

The chase continued for two miles. The deputies made no further attempts at bumping Mason's or Gio's vehicles. Rhett led the convoy onto the Highway 27 North exit lane. Mason slowed enough to let Gio get in front of him so the motorcade could continue in a single file. They raced forward, jockeying for position in order to keep the patrol cars from passing.

Mason and Gio drove side by side once more as they raced up the overpass which crossed above two sets of train tracks. Mason had the odd feeling of falling even though he was gaining elevation.

"Whoa!" Prairie cried out. "Did you feel that?"

"Yeah, what was it?" Wynter asked.

The whole of Mason's attention was focused on their pursuers, and he could not speculate on the cause of their shared sensation. The yellow lines on the pavement began to wave. Mason felt lightheaded, weightless for a moment, then off balance as if on a ship being tossed in the sea.

"Daddy! The road is moving!" Prairie declared.

Mason took his foot off the gas. The pavement fractured. The southbound lane fell away. He could see the abandoned rail cars beneath. The cement continued to crumble. Mason accelerated and swerved in front of Gio to keep from falling off the side of the failing overpass. Finally, the guardrail gave way. Mason could not be sure there was any asphalt below him at all as he careened down the opposite side of the overpass. He glanced to see Gio still behind him. Following Gio was a plume of dust and silt that lifted toward the sky as if propelled by a volcanic eruption. Charlie the Crab swerved ahead of him, his small food trailer tipping from left to right. Mason watched it lean and the wheels from one side leave the pavement. Mason tapped the brakes, trying to avoid hitting the Crab's trailer while not causing Gio to slam into his rear end.

Ahead of Charlie the Crab, Rhett veered into the grassy median, slowing down to avoid putting the livestock trailer on its side. Rhett remedied his course slowly by bringing the truck and trailer back onto the shoulder.

The other two pickup trucks pulled to the side of the road and gradually came to a stop waiting for the remainder of the caravan. Mason was eager for everyone to regain control of their vehicles so they could continue their escape.

"Daddy?" Prairie said.

Mason drove by the rest of his fellow fugitives hoping to set the pace for them to resume the getaway. "What is it, Sweet Pea?"

"The cops are gone," she said. "They never came out of the dust cloud."

Mason checked the rearview for a moment. Indeed, the silt plume was clearing, enough so that he could see the point where the overpass had been severed. No patrol cars were on his side of the railroad tracks.

"It's still happening," said Wynter.

Mason saw the powerlines swaying to and fro like a swing on a child's outdoor playset.

Turtle's voice came over the radio. "What's going on?"

Mason picked up his walkie-talkie. "Earthquake—and it's a big one."

The convoy halted while the roadway undulated like the waves on the sea. The experience felt surreal to Mason. He quietly observed the restless earth while it moved as if liquified.

"I thought Florida wasn't supposed to get earthquakes." Even Gio's voice had a tone of reverence in speaking of the phenomena.

Devron was the next to speak over the radio. "I believe this is the sixth seal. The whole world is feeling this earthquake."

Megan inquired, "Hey, Dixon. Aren't you from San Francisco? If Florida is feeling it like this, I can't imagine what the West Coast is experiencing."

"Yeah." Dixon sounded dejected. "I doubt I'll have much to go home to."

Once the earth's convulsions subsided, Mason spoke softly into his radio. "We should get going. We still have a long way to go."

They continued northbound on the buckled and cracked pavement. Most of the roadway was still drivable although they couldn't go much faster than twenty-five miles per hour due to multiple instances where chunks of asphalt jetted up as much as six inches. Many sections of the road were even worse, necessitating the motorcade to driving onto the grass, around the obstruction, and then back onto the pavement.

Mason led the caravan slowly up US 27 until they reached the Haines City interchange where, like the railroad overpass, the flyovers had completely collapsed. Mason rolled to a stop and picked up the radio. "We'll have to get off the exit, detour around the cloverleaf, and back on 27 by way of the other entrance ramp."

Haines City would prove to be only the first of many times they would have to utilize this maneuver. Prairie and Wynter assisted Mason by searching the map for potential pitfalls along the way, helping him to cleverly avoid a Florida Turnpike underpass that would have certainly collapsed.

Nevertheless, they eventually found themselves at an impasse; a point where the road they'd taken was blocked by the crumbled turnpike overpass. Mason stopped short of the first large cement boulder. He put the vehicle in park and got out to survey the obstacle.

The rest of the convoy stopped, and the others likewise exited their vehicles. Rhett and Gio walked up to Mason's location.

"We can move most of this debris." Mason pointed at the hundreds of concrete chunks obstructing the path forward. "It fragmented into manageable pieces when it broke away from the rebar." He pointed at the side of the overpass still propped up by the pier. "We need to clear our path at the highest point so we can get the livestock trailer through."

Rhett whistled loudly to get everyone's attention. "Let's get to work. We need all hands to help get the road cleared."

It took an hour to finally remove the obstructions. Everyone was hot and sweaty by the time they finished. Mason and the girls returned to the vehicle and led the way through the narrow path to the other side of the debris field.

Night hit them at White Springs, Florida, just south of the Georgia border. Mason called over the radio. "We'll pull off the road here. We've got some cover from the trees that will make us harder to spot by anyone passing through. We can let the animals graze, rest, and get back on the road in the morning. With the asphalt as rough as it is, it isn't safe to keep driving in the dark."

CHAPTER 28

And the stars of heaven fell unto the earth, even as a fig tree casteth her untimely figs, when she is shaken of a mighty wind. And the heaven departed as a scroll when it is rolled together; and every mountain and island were moved out of their places.

And the kings of the earth, and the great men, and the rich men, and the chief captains, and the mighty men, and every bondman, and every free man, hid themselves in the dens and in the rocks of the mountains; and said to the mountains and rocks, Fall on us, and hide us from the face of him that sitteth on the throne, and from the wrath of the Lamb: for the great day of his wrath is come; and who shall be able to stand?

Revelation 6:13-17

Thursday morning, Mason glanced at the rearview to see Wynter sleeping in the backseat. He smiled at Prairie in the passenger's seat before shifting his attention back to the crackled pavement in front of them. Prairie searched the staticky airwaves for any signs that civilization had survived the divine assault against the planet.

"Try switching to AM," Mason suggested. "It travels farther."

Prairie followed his advice and continued scrolling through the frequencies. "I got something!"

"This is GBC," said a voice muffled by the white noise of interference. "Scientists say yesterday's global mega-quake was the inevitable result of global warming which caused the planet's sub-surface temperatures to rise and tectonic plates to swell causing pressure to build up. A massive upheaval was triggered by a confluence of multiple subduction zones and convergence zones releasing simultaneously.

"Currently, all major metropolitan areas on the earth are without power. This broadcast is being aired from a subterranean, US continuity of government facility at Cheyenne Mountain, Colorado. With assistance from the Global Order

Council, GBC is able to use satellites to reach various affiliate stations around Europe and the Americas, operating them remotely in the instances where those stations are running on generator power.

"Unfortunately, our ability to disseminate information may be short-lived as we face a multitude of issues that could interrupt future broadcasts. The most obvious is the limited supply of fuel in the generators at stations currently acting as repeaters for GBC. The other is a separate threat.

"It seems when misfortune comes it often arrives in waves. It would appear the Earth's normal path orbiting around the Sun intersects with a meteoroid field that was previously thought to be inconsequential. Astronomers have been tracking this massive ocean of cosmic rocks which they thought was comprised of smaller particles for several years. However, the space debris contains much larger asteroids that appear to be made up of iron-nickel alloy, which will be far more destructive than the originally anticipated water, methane, and carbon meteors.

"While scientists doubt many of these objects will survive Earth's atmosphere, a barrage of such space rocks will wreak havoc on GPS and communications satellites as they all exist outside of the planet's atmospheric protection."

Wynter had woken up and was listening to the broadcast from the back seat. "Is that why we saw all of those shooting stars last night?"

Mason mumbled his reply. "The stars of heaven

fell unto earth… It's part of the sixth seal."

"Dad, tell me you're not buying into all of that," she said.

Prairie scolded, "Tell me you're not still in denial. Can't you see everything is lining up perfectly with what the Bible has to say about the end of the world?"

Wynter argued, "You can make the Bible say whatever you want it to."

"No, you can't!" she countered. "It specifically talks about a global earthquake and falling stars."

Wynter found Brother Dickie's old Bible which Mason had been studying. She flipped through the pages of Revelation. "What about this part? *The sun became black as sackcloth…* You can't pick out pieces and ignore the parts that don't support your narrative. It doesn't work like that."

Mason raised his voice, "Knock it off, both of you. This could be the last news report we get for weeks. We need to pay attention so we can glean as much information as possible." He turned up the volume.

The GBC reporter continued his static-plagued commentary. "Yesterday's seismic event also triggered volcanic eruptions around the globe with some of the largest being in the Hawaiian Islands, Japan, Rolanda, Washington State, Iceland, and Italy. Heavy ash plumes are creating near-blackout conditions around Mt. St. Helens, Katla, Vesuvius, Kilauea, and Fuji.

"Under normal conditions, the smoke and ash associated with volcanic eruptions would dissipate as it was blown by the wind away from the source, but because of the sheer number of concurrent eruptions, meteorologists believe this could create a haze around the world that will mimic night-time conditions around the clock in terms of visibility and temperatures. It is uncertain when the eruptions will cease."

"The sun became black as sackcloth," Prairie said to her sister.

Wynter made no reply.

***

That afternoon, Mason stopped the vehicle at the Ocmulgee River. The bridge was out, and the river was wide. He got out and walked to the precipice of the collapsed crossing. Gio soon arrived at his side. "Ain't no driving around this one."

Mason stared at the murky waters. "The girls saw it on the map. The nearest crossing is over thirty miles from here and that bridge is probably out also."

Rhett was the next person to join them. "It's gotta be a hundred feet across. It ain't like we can drop a couple of trees with the chainsaw and fabricate a bridge."

"Could the horses swim it?" Mason asked.

"Sure, cattle too," Rhett answered. "But we're not getting the vehicles to the other side."

Mason climbed the guard rail and led the group down to the river's edge. He took off his shoes and waded out into the water. He reached the midpoint and could still touch the bottom. Mason continued to the opposite bank.

"At least we know it's crossable," called Gio.

Mason returned to the south bank. "This is the heartland. My guess is that a lot of people around here were taken in the Rapture. We should be able to find vehicles nearby. We can ferry our supplies across, load them into the borrowed vehicles, and continue our journey."

"I can get the horses," said Rhett. "That will make the vehicle search go faster. I'll volunteer to be on the vehicle location team."

"I'm already wet," said Mason. "So I'll come with you. Gio, you coordinate the others. Have them start hauling gear to the opposite bank."

"What if you don't find us another ride?" Gio quizzed.

"Then we'll walk," said Mason. "But either way, we need those supplies on that side of the river."

Rhett retrieved the horses, then he and Mason mounted up to find suitable transport for the group. Mason held the saddle horn and blew a kiss to his daughters. "I'll be back. Gio, watch out for my girls while I'm gone."

"You don't even have to ask." Gio smiled. "I'll take care of them just as if they were my kids."

Mason followed Rhett's lead across the river and up the bank of the other side. They traveled about a mile when they arrived at an old farmhouse. A yellow Labrador rushed toward them barking as if defending his territory. Mason's horse reared up and neighed.

"Lean forward!" Rhett instructed as he rode

closer and grabbed the reigns of Mason's beast. "Whooaaa! Easy! Easy!" He succeeded in calming the horse, but the dog continued barking.

"Down boy," said Mason.

"Want me to shoot 'em?" Rhett asked.

"I hope that won't be necessary. Seems like he's keeping his distance. Let's go to the house and see if anyone is home." Mason spoke gently to the agitated dog and continued riding up the dirt driveway.

As they got closer to the house, the dog's barking turned into crying and whining. Mason looked around the yard. "Chicken feathers—all over the place. Looks like someone has been a bad dog."

"Either that or a hungry dog," said Rhett.

Mason slowly dismounted. "Which might be the case if his master disappeared." He held out his hand for the Lab to sniff. "It's okay, boy."

The dog gave a high-pitched yelp. He looked around and whined as if confused about what he should do about the intruders.

"Everything is going to be alright." Mason saw an empty dog bowl and picked it up. This agitated the animal even more. He barked, howled, and gave another high-pitched yelp. Mason found the water spigot on the side of the house and filled the bowl. The dog began lapping up the water as if severely dehydrated.

Mason stroked the bemused animal for a while before getting up and going to the door. He knocked but no answer came.

Rhett hitched the horses to a nearby tree and came to the porch.

"It's unlocked." Mason checked the handle.

Rhett nodded. "Let's check it out."

Mason opened the door. "Hello?"

The dog ran in the open door and turned to look at Mason.

Mason scanned the living room. The leg rest of the recliner was extended. On the end table beside the easy chair was a pair of reading glasses sitting next to an open Bible. "They're not here, are they, boy?"

The dog seemed sad about the people being gone but relieved to no longer be alone.

Rhett said, "There's a Ram 2500 in the drive. They've also got a tractor hitched to a flatbed wagon next to the barn. Let's see if we can find the keys."

"You look for the keys," said Mason. "I'm going to get old Harlan here some dog food."

"How do you know his name is Harlan?"

"I don't. But from the looks of the feathers all over the yard, it's safe to assume he likes chicken."

Rhett pressed his lips together. "Harlan—as in Harlan Sanders."

Mason walked into the kitchen and found a can of wet dog food. "It will be getting dark by the time we finish moving our gear across the river. We'll bring everyone back here to rest for the night. They'll be tired and wet. This will be a good place to make camp."

***

The next morning, Mason managed to back the

pickup truck containing the 275-gallon fuel tote into the river. On the north bank, he used the tractor to back the flatbed wagon into the river. He offloaded enough diesel from the tote to float it across the river and onto the wagon. He secured the tote to the wagon with rachet straps allowing them to bring the precious fuel cargo along for the journey.

The sky was black from the volcanic ash spreading around the country. Nevertheless, the sojourners set out to continue the expedition. The convoy now consisted of a pickup truck filled with supplies, a tractor pulling a flatbed wagon, two people on horseback driving the small herd of cattle, and a yellow Labrador who was quickly picking up the skill of keeping cows on the straight and narrow.

The lack of a livestock trailer put the entire procession at a glacial pace. Despite the limitations, everyone in the group agreed that they needed to stick together.

Mason assisted Rhett with driving the animals for the first leg of the trip. He switched places with Megan at noon and rode on the flatbed wagon with his girls.

The faint glow of daylight had completely vanished by 5:00 PM Friday. The travelers had covered only twenty-five miles for the day. Mason studied the map with Rhett next to a campfire. "It's going to take us two weeks to get to Bryson City at this rate."

Rhett replied, "Our options are to look for a livestock trailer, split into two groups, or sit back and enjoy the ride."

"I'd be content to do the latter," said Mason. "But my concern is that people are going to start getting more desperate. The longer we take, the more unsafe it will be to travel."

Gio joined them by the fire. "Things were hard enough before the power went out."

Mason considered the alternatives. "Let's pick a destination point for tomorrow. Somewhere about twenty-five miles from here. The people riding the wagon behind the tractor can provide security for the cattle drive. Then, a couple of us can take the pickup to scout ahead. We'll look for a trailer."

"It's a good idea, but you aren't likely to find anything longer than sixteen feet that will go on a standard hitch," said Rhett. "Larger trailers usually have a gooseneck hitch that goes in the bed of the truck."

"Which we don't have." Gio frowned at the pickup.

"Even if we did, the pickup bed is filled with our food, supplies, and luggage," Mason said. "How many cows could we fit in a sixteen-footer?"

"We might squeeze all the cattle in, but not the horses," said Rhett.

"But you could move faster on horseback if you weren't driving cattle, couldn't you?" Gio inquired.

Rhett shrugged. "Maybe fifty miles a day. These are work horses. They're in good shape, but that's about the max, especially going day after day."

"Fifty miles a day would cut our travel time in half," said Gio. "We could get to Bryson in six days."

"If we don't come to any more bridges that are

out." Mason studied the map. "We'll almost certainly have to take a detour around Sinclair Lake."

"The horses wouldn't," said Rhett. "They can swim. I can take them and meet up at a rendezvous point on the other side of the lake."

"As much as I hate to split up, that would save us some time," said Mason.

"I say it's worth a shot." Gio tossed a stick into the fire.

"Alright," Mason said to Gio. "You, Val, me, and the girls will scout ahead tomorrow for a livestock trailer. We'll leave the supplies on the wagon in case we run into trouble during the search."

"You should check farm supply stores," Rhett suggested. "But also keep your eyes open for stockyards. You'll always find trailers in those places."

"Good call. I'll catch you guys in the morning. I'm going to get a spot to sleep under the wagon before they're all taken." Mason grabbed a blanket and settled near the rear of the wagon beside his daughters. Harlan, the yellow Lab, managed to squeeze into the slim space between Mason and Prairie.

CHAPTER 29

And whereas thou sawest the feet and toes, part of potters' clay, and part of iron, the kingdom shall be divided; but there shall be in it of the strength of the iron, forasmuch as thou sawest the iron mixed with miry clay. And as the toes of the feet were part of iron, and part of clay, so the kingdom shall be partly strong, and partly broken. And whereas thou sawest iron mixed with miry clay, they shall mingle themselves with the seed of men: but they shall not cleave one to another, even as iron is not mixed with clay.

And in the days of these kings shall the God of heaven set up a kingdom, which shall never be destroyed: and the kingdom shall not be left to other people, but it shall break in pieces and consume all these kingdoms, and it shall stand for ever.

Daniel 2:41-44

Mason's team was not successful in finding a cattle trailer on Saturday, but they continued their forward scouting mission on Sunday morning. Days were dim, as if in a perpetual twilight. The nights were pitch black, as if inside a deep cavern. The number of refugees traveling along 441, either by foot or bicycle, was higher than they'd seen since leaving Okeechobee.

"Daddy, it's two girls hitchhiking. They're the same age as Wynter and me. We have to stop and give them a lift," Prairie begged from the back seat.

Mason looked at the two pitiful young girls as he drove by. "We can't, Sweet Pea. We have a limited amount of fuel that must get us to Bryson City."

"What if that were us?" Wynter asked. "Wouldn't you want a nice family to give us a ride before some perv picked us up?"

Mason tried to ignore the sick feeling in his stomach. He glanced at Gio who was shaking his head. Mason frowned, knowing he had to at least offer. He pulled to the side of the dusty road.

The two teens hurried to the pickup. Mason rolled down his window. "We can offer you a ride north, maybe a couple of towns. But we can't go out of our way. We don't have extra fuel."

"Okay." The first girl looked like the older of two sisters. "We just need to get to the camp."

"I don't know where that is," said Mason. "But I can drop you at the closest spot along 441."

"It's in Dublin," said the younger girl. "It's only about ten miles up the road."

Prairie rolled down the back window. "What kind of camp?"

"Refugee camp," said the older girl. "Haven't you heard?"

Two people rode by on bicycles and the younger girl pointed at them. "That's where everyone is heading. Supposedly, they have food, medical services, shelter, and running water. It's at the Laurens County rec center. You know, where they have the baseball diamonds, the water park, soccer fields and all that."

"Where they have the fireworks on the fourth," added the older girl.

"We're not from around here," said Val.

"It doesn't matter," said the younger girl. "Anybody can go. The Global Order Commission set up the camp. It's the only one around. Next closest is in Macon. We'll show you where it is."

"No thanks," said Mason. "But we'll drop you off when we get close."

Prairie asked the girls, "Since you two seem familiar with the area, do you know where we could find a stockyard?"

"What's that?" asked the younger girl.

"A place where they sell livestock." Mason felt impatient over wasting so much time. "Go ahead and get in the back of the truck. Just slap the wheel well when we're getting close to the place where you'd like us to drop you off."

The older girl pointed north. "We have a livestock auction on Laurens School Road. It's right before I-16. But it's not the type of place you can just go buy a cow. And I doubt they'll be holding auctions anytime soon, with everything that's happened."

Mason felt suddenly excited. "Yeah! Perfect. That's what we're looking for!"

"Well, it's about two miles before the camp." The older girl looked disappointed, as if she'd just talked herself out of a ride. "I guess we can walk from there."

"No. We'll take you where you want to go. Just tap on the side of the truck near the place I should turn for the auction. I'll make a mental note of it and head that way after we drop you off."

"Sure thing!" the girl said with renewed optimism.

"Thanks, Mister." The younger smiled, walked to the back, and climbed into the truck bed with her sister.

Mason continued northbound on 441 until he heard one of the girls slap the side of the truck bed. He stopped and turned toward the back.

The oldest girl was pointing west. "The livestock auction is right up yonder," she yelled.

Mason waved out the window and continued along 441. When they arrived at the I-16 overpass, he noticed that the debris from the earthquake had been cleared with heavy machinery.

"Looks like the Global Order is trying to get things back to normal," said Gio.

"I'm afraid to ask what's their definition of normal." Mason proceeded cautiously until he heard the girls in the truck bed slap the wheel well once more.

The girls jumped out with their backpacks and walked up to the driver's side window. "Thanks for the lift."

Mason nodded. "Thanks for the information. You two be safe."

"We're in good hands now," said the oldest.

The younger added, "It's going to be great. And even if it's not, you can elect to have yourself uploaded into Neuro-vana. They have an entire tent dedicated to the Gnosis Immortal Project."

Mason shook his head. "Don't fall for that. It's a lie. Your soul isn't something that can be inserted into a computer."

"That's misinformation." The older girl scowled at Mason and put her arm around her little sister. "Come on, Kelly. We shouldn't be talking to these people."

Mason felt sad for the teens who had bought into the enemy's deception.

"We should offer to bring them with us," Prairie suggested.

"For one thing," said Mason. "We're not guaranteed to reach our destination. And secondly, I don't think they'd be interested in trying to get there."

"Your dad is right," said Gio. "You can't help people who don't want to be helped."

Mason turned the truck around and headed south.

Shortly after passing through the cleared debris of the I-16 overpass, Val said from the back seat, "A Humvee turned onto 441. It looks like they could be following us."

Mason checked the side-view mirror and saw the military vehicle. He pressed the accelerator. "That's the last thing we need."

"They're speeding up!" said Wynter.

Mason turned sharply onto Laurens School Road and gunned the engine. "If they turn here, we'll know we have a problem."

"Look!" said Prairie. "There's the stockyard."

Mason quickly turned off and raced down the dirt road toward the rear of the auction site.

"There's our trailer." Gio pointed at a sixteen-foot aluminum stock trailer.

Mason frowned. "Okay. That's why we're here. It's not like we're going to outrun a Humvee anyway." He backed up to the trailer.

Gio grabbed his AK. "How about Val and me head over to the barn? We'll keep an eye out to make sure these Global Order goons don't get in the way of our operation. If everything goes smoothly, you can pick us up once the trailer is hitched."

Mason opened his door and got out. "Good idea. Girls, take your weapons and follow Gio."

"Daddy! I want to stay with you!" Prairie pleaded.

"Do what I asked, please!" Mason insisted. "If you're with Gio, you can help if I get in a jam. If you're with me, you'll be part of the problem."

Wynter handed Prairie's rifle to her sister. "Come on. We have to hurry or they'll see us."

Prairie took her AK and looked at her father with worried eyes. "Be safe, Daddy."

"You too." He swallowed hard. "Now go!"

Mason watched the four of them sprint toward the cattle barn. He heard the noise of the Humvee approaching. Mason squatted and began lowering the hitch jack onto the ball of the mount. The Hummer slowed down on the dirt road and drove over to the livestock trailer where it came to a stop.

Three soldiers exited the vehicle. Their uniforms looked like US military but with new insignia. "Is that your trailer?" asked one of the soldiers.

Mason figured in this world, he had as much claim to it as anyone else. "Yes, sir."

"Mind if I ask what you're planning to do with it?" The soldier stepped closer.

Mason looked up at the new decal on the door of the Humvee. It was the initials for the Global Order Commission, GOC. The O had the silhouettes of North and South America as well as those of

Europe and Africa. It also had longitude and latitude grid lines running over it as if it were a globe. "Not to be rude, but that's none of your business."

"It is my business, actually," said the soldier. "Come over here. We want to talk to you."

Mason completed his task of securing the trailer to the hitch. "I can hear you just fine where I'm at."

"I'd like to check you for weapons—for everyone's safety." The soldier pulled his rifle up to his shoulder.

Mason's heartbeat quickened. "This is Georgia. People are allowed to carry weapons. They don't even need a permit. You don't have the right to question me or search me. In fact, what gives you the authority to act as law enforcement in any capacity?"

"Global Order Commission Emergency Powers Act 24 makes it a high crime against the Commission for civilians to possess firearms of any type. There's a two-week amnesty period, but that's contingent upon Global Order citizens complying in good faith and turning in those firearms upon finding out about Act 24.

"Emergency Powers Act 24 also grants sworn military personnel jurisdiction over all Global Order territories. Citizen, you are hereby informed about Act 24. Now, are you going to cooperate or are we going to be forced to detain you?"

Mason walked backward to draw the soldiers into Gio's firing line. "I don't know. Let's say I do have a gun. If I turn it over, are you going to let me take my trailer and be on my way? Or is it going to be another command, and another, and another?"

The soldier followed Mason at the pace he'd set. "Let's get one thing clear. This isn't a negotiation, and you aren't in a position to dictate terms to me about how I do my job."

"I refuse to comply. I'm going to get in my truck and drive away." Mason hoped they'd let him leave.

The soldiers all raised their guns. The leader yelled at Mason, "Get on the ground! Do it now! I'll shoot!"

Mason's mouth went dry. He saw their fingers slip past the trigger guards on their weapons. He put his hands in the air and slowly went to his knees. Mason forced himself not to look at the cattle barn and risk giving away his team's position.

"Face down!" The soldier walked closer with his weapon trained on Mason. "Fruge, check him for weapons. Brainerd, put the restraints on him. I'll cover you."

Brainerd pushed Mason's face into the dirt and grabbed his right hand. He pulled it down to his back and tightened the plastic restraint around his wrist.

"He's got a pistol!" Fruge pulled the Glock from Mason's waistband.

"We'll be running into a lot of these sorts down here in Georgia," said the lead soldier.

"It's better than being up north and dealing with radiation." Brainerd tried to feed Mason's left hand into the restraints.

Mason resisted, not wanting to have his hands encumbered once the shooting began.

Brainerd tugged harder. "Stop fighting me or I'll Tase you!"

POW! Blood spurted from the neck of the lead soldier, and he fell sideways onto the ground.

"We're under attack!" Fruge scurried for cover.

Mason rolled onto his back taking Brainerd over with him. He wrestled to get his hands free. Gunfire erupted from the cattle barn. Mason saw the Glock that Fruge had dropped during his retreat. Brainerd seemed uncertain about whether he should pull his rifle around from his back or try to keep Mason from reaching the pistol. The two of them scrambled for the Glock, both reaching it simultaneously. Mason grabbed the handle and Brainerd took hold of the barrel.

"Call it in!" yelled Brainerd.

Fruge fired wildly at the barn with his M-4 on full auto. "If I stop shooting long enough to call it in, we'll be done for. You call it in!"

"I'm kind of in the middle of something here!" Brainerd attempted to wrench the pistol from Mason's hands.

Mason could not get the barrel pointed at his assailant, but hoped firing the weapon would allow him to get control of it. He pulled the trigger; the pistol barked.

"Ahh!" Brainerd cried out in pain.

Mason pointed the gun at the soldier and pulled the trigger again. Click! Nothing happened. Brainerd holding the slide when the gun fired had caused the shell to stovepipe in the ejection port. The pistol was jammed.

Brainerd spun his rifle to the front and tried to get far enough back from Mason to get a shot off. Mason closed the distance and pushed Brainerd to the ground. He lay on top of him and racked the slide, trying to clear the jam. He pushed the gun to the soldier's temple and fired again. Still nothing. The jam was clear, but no new round had entered the chamber.

Brainerd pushed him off, then kicked him back with his foot. Brainerd raised the rifle at Mason. He fired, but missed. Laying on his back, Mason jerked the slide back once more. Brainerd fired again. Dust kicked up from the ground next to Mason's head. Dirt went in his eye. His ears rang. He could hear nothing. Mason pulled the trigger. This time, the recoil pulled the barrel toward the sky. Mason placed the front sight back over his target and held the gun tight. He took the slack out of the trigger but noticed his attacker was dead. Blood oozed out of Brainerd's right eye socket and the soldier lay limp on the ground.

Mason spun the pistol around to Fruge. He was dead also. Mason looked up to see Wynter and Prairie running across the stockyard. They were yelling but he couldn't hear what they were saying.

He couldn't hear anything except the ringing in his ears.

CHAPTER 29

And when he had opened the seventh seal,
there was silence in heaven about the space
of half an hour. And I saw the seven angels
which stood before God; and to them were
given seven trumpets. And another angel
came and stood at the altar, having a golden
censer; and there was given unto him much
incense, that he should offer it with the
prayers of all saints upon the golden altar
which was before the throne. And the smoke
of the incense, which came with the prayers
of the saints, ascended up before God out of
the angel's hand. And the angel took the
censer, and filled it with fire of the altar, and
cast it into the earth: and there were voices,

and thunderings, and lightnings, and an earthquake. And the seven angels which had the seven trumpets prepared themselves to sound.

Revelation 8:1-6

The ringing in Mason's ears continued, but he could hear Prairie's voice as she approached. "Gio was shot! Bring the truck!"

Mason's stomach sank. He feared the worst. Nevertheless, he checked to see that the soldiers were all truly neutralized before leaving the scene. Once confident that they posed no further threat, he jumped in the Ram along with Prairie and Wynter and raced to the cattle barn.

Mason didn't shut off the engine or close the truck door. Rather he rushed to the location inside the barn where Val was holding his father's head in his lap.

Mason knelt beside his old friend. Blood oozed from Gio's chest.

"Hey, Mace." Gio opened his eyes and forced a smile. "Did we get 'em?"

"Yeah, you got 'em. And we got the trailer. What do you say we get out of here?" Mason gripped Gio's hand.

Gio closed his eyes and shook his head. "I think I'm going to rest here for a minute. But while I do that, why don't you go see what you can get off those goons? They probably have some high-dollar gadgets."

"How about we help you to the truck and go?" Mason replied. "We'll get you comfortable and find someone who can help you out. I'll stop by the Humvee on the way out and see if they have a medical kit."

"I appreciate what you're trying to do here, Mace. But what I really need is a few minutes with my boy here." Gio glanced at Val. "I need to give him a message for Ceeny and Luca too. All I need from you is to know you'll look out for them."

"You know I will." Mason felt a knot forming in his throat but was not ready to give up on his old friend. "Still, I think we can get you fixed up."

"I appreciate that, Mace. But when you know, you know. The Lord's been good to me—too good, in fact. My ticket should have come up a long time ago, the business I was in. I'm grateful He gave me the chance to see all of this—end of days and whatnot; so I would believe."

Mason's concern shifted from Gio's temporal well-being to his eternal. "So you've made peace with Him? You've put your faith in Jesus?"

"Yeah, that's part of what I need to speak to Val about. I love you, pal. Take care of Ceeny and my boys. Now, if you don't mind…"

Mason gritted his teeth to hold back the tears. "You got it, Gio. I'll see you soon."

Gio grinned. "Yeah, seven years or less, right?"

Mason lost control of his emotions but managed to eke out a smile as he waved goodbye to his old friend. He motioned for Prairie and Wyn to follow him out of the barn so Val and Gio could be alone for a few precious final moments.

"Can't we do something to help?" Prairie asked.

"I don't think so, Sweat Pea." Mason felt helpless.

"What are we going to do?" Wynter asked.

"I'm going to honor Gio's final request. I'm going to strip those soldiers of anything we can use." Mason signaled for the girls to follow him across the field to the Humvee.

Upon arriving, Mason assessed the scene. He looked in the rear of the vehicles. "Plenty of ammo." He opened a small black case.

"What's that?" Wynter inquired.

Mason read the booklet inside. "Night vision."

"That might come in handy," said Prairie. "Especially considering it's dark most all of the time."

Mason looked back at the fallen soldiers. "I think these units attach to their helmets. We should collect those also. In fact, take their entire uniforms."

The radio inside the Humvee came to life. "Patrol Bravo Three, this is Laurens County Base. What's your location?"

Prairie stood by her father. "Do you think this was Patrol Bravo Three?"

Mason watched the light on the radio come back on. The voice sounded again. "Please respond, Patrol Bravo Three. Did you make contact with the white pickup you were following?"

Mason nodded. "Yeah, I think it was."

The radio came back on. "All patrols, Bravo Three's last known location was 441 heading south of the interstate. Can one of you head that way and see if you can get eyes on them? Also, be on the lookout for a white pickup truck. They didn't give a make."

Another voice came over the radio. "This is Patrol Bravo Six, we're about seven miles north of the interstate. We can head that way if no one is closer."

"Roger that, Bravo Six. Let me know if you spot them."

Mason clapped his hands. "We have to move!"

"Are we still getting the uniforms?" Wynter sounded frantic.

"Yes! Hurry!" Mason went to work on the first soldier while the girls each stripped one. They tossed the weapons, helmets, and uniforms into the Humvee and got inside. Mason jumped in the driver's seat and found the keys still in the ignition. He looked toward heaven. "Thank you, Jesus!"

He started the engine and raced back to the cattle barn.

"Should I put all the gear in the pickup?" Wynter asked.

Mason jumped out of the Hummer. "No. Leave it. We'll take the Humvee too."

"Daddy, they have GPS on these vehicles," Prairie protested.

Mason hurried into the barn. "If they could locate the vehicle with GPS, they wouldn't have the other patrol out looking for it. The satellites probably got knocked out by the meteors."

When he got inside, Val was crying over his lifeless father. Mason knelt beside him. "Val, we need to get your dad into the truck. You'll have all the time you need to mourn his loss, but we have to go. More soldiers are on the way."

Val nodded and stood up to help Mason, Prairie, and Wynter get the heavy corpse into the bed of the Ram. Val stayed in the back with Gio. Mason pointed to Wynter. "You drive the Ram. Stay close behind me. I'm going to find us a route back to the group that keeps us off 441."

"They have a map in the Humvee." Prairie ran to the passenger's side of the vehicle. "I'll navigate for you, Daddy."

Mason did not want to leave Wynter in the cab of the pickup by herself, but he could think of no better option. "Okay, fine. Get in!"

They loaded up and sped away from the stockyard, kicking clouds of dust in the air as they escaped the brutal hands of the new global empire.

***

Mason intercepted Rhett's team moving slowly along 441 just north of Cedar Grove. They managed to get the cattle drive off the main thoroughfare and found another abandoned farm where they could lay low. They remained at the farm until the chatter over the radio concerning the search for the missing Humvee subsided.

The following morning, they found a peaceful location on the old homestead to bury Gio and held a brief memorial for him before getting back on the road.

On Tuesday, they found a two-horse trailer which they hitched to the Humvee. This allowed them to travel much faster and the journey moved along steadily until they reached a river in north Georgia which they could not find a way around. They managed to get the tractor and wagon across a wide shallow spot but could not get the truck to the other side. They were able to pull the trailer across with the Humvee and use it to tow the cattle. But Rhett had to ride the horses the rest of the way. He rode them one at a time, while the other horse followed with no rider. This kept them from getting tired as fast and the convoy progressed more rapidly than it otherwise would have.

***

They reached their destination eight full days after leaving Okeechobee. Since the property had belonged to Billy's grandmother, he handed out the room assignments for the three-bedroom farmhouse, granting priority to the females in the group. He gave the master bedroom to Ceeny, Val, and Luca. Mason and his daughters would share one of the upstairs bedrooms while Rhett and Megan would take the other. This left Billy, Dixon, Turtle, Devron, and Charlie the Crab to divvy up the living room.

Upon their arrival, Mason climbed out of the Humvee and carried his pack to the porch of the old farmhouse. Harlan the dog followed him quietly as did Prairie and Wynter. No breeze blew through the treetops. No crickets or tree frogs chirped. The rest of the group was tired, like Mason, and didn't speak a word while hauling their belongings into the house. Despite the activity, Mason couldn't remember a time in his life when he'd experienced such silence. Even the water in the creek they'd crossed on their approach didn't make a sound. The quietude was extraordinarily peculiar.

Half an hour after their arrival, lightning flashed across the sky, illuminating their surroundings as if by the midday sun. Soon, roaring thunder cracked and shook even the boards of the old farmhouse's porch. Harlan whined and squeezed up next to Mason's leg.

After the rumbling of the thunder had subsided, the porch continued to vibrate. The support beams propping up the roof of the porch swayed. Mason grabbed Harlan by the collar and walked him down from the porch. "It's an earthquake. Everyone, get away from the house."

They all scurried down and into the pitch-black yard. Mason shined his flashlight on the farmhouse as it continued to wobble like a drunkard. The sound of a heavy tree crashing in the nearby forest could be heard. Mason directed the beam of his light toward the disturbance but could not see the tree. Soon, the undulation of the earth abated.

Turtle was the first to speak. "It must have been an aftershock."

Devron corrected him. "It was the seventh seal."

"What comes after that?" Prairie snugged up close to her father as if for protection.

"Seven trumpet judgments." Mason had read through the Book of Revelation several times and knew the coming plagues by heart.

"What's that?" asked Wynter. "Will it be like the seals—like what we just went through?"

"Worse," Devron answered.

"Much worse," Mason added. "Much, much worse."

DON'T PANIC!

Inevitably, books like this will wake folks up to the need to be prepared, or cause those of us who are already prepared to take inventory of our preparations. New preppers can find the task of getting prepared for an economic collapse, EMP, or societal breakdown to be a source of great anxiety. It shouldn't be. By following an organized plan and setting a goal of getting a little more prepared each day, you can do it.

I always try to include a few prepper tips in my novels, but they're fiction and not a comprehensive plan to get prepared. Now that you're motivated to start prepping, the last thing I want to do is leave you frustrated, not knowing what to do next. So I'd like to offer you a free PDF copy of *The Seven Step Survival Plan.*

For the new prepper, *The Seven Step Survival Plan* provides a blueprint that prioritizes the different aspects of preparedness and breaks them down into achievable goals. For seasoned preppers who often get overweight in one particular area of preparedness, *The Seven Step Survival Plan* provides basic guidelines to help keep their plan in balance, and ensures they're not missing any critical segments of a well-adjusted survival strategy.

To get your **FREE** copy of *The Seven Step Survival Plan*, go to **PrepperRecon.com** and click the FREE PDF banner, just below the menu bar, at the top of the home page.

Thank you for reading *The Days of Lot, Book One: Seven Seals*

Stay tuned to **PrepperRecon.com** for the latest news about my upcoming books.

Can't get enough post-apocalyptic chaos? Check out my other heart-stopping tales about the end of the world as we know it.

The Beginning of Sorrows

For nation shall rise against nation, and kingdom against kingdom: and there shall be earthquakes in divers places, and there shall be famines and troubles: these are the beginnings of sorrows.

Mark 13:8

When Agent Joshua Stone is called to a high-level meeting at the Department of Homeland Security, he learns about a new global order which will be transitioning into power. Stone is read in on the plan for a single planetary government and a world-wide cashless-currency, which will step in to fill the void left by the failing monetary system. To win wide acceptance by the nations of the world, the old system must first be allowed to fail, bringing about a state of global chaos never before seen by mankind. Once desperation has taken the place of pride and hubris, humanity will beg for the proposed one-world empire led by the charismatic tech guru Lucius Alexander.

The Days of Noah

In an off-site CIA facility outside of Langley, rookie analyst Everett Carroll discovers he's not being told the whole truth. He's instructed to disregard troubling information uncovered by his research. Everett ignores his directive and keeps digging. What he finds goes against everything he's been taught to believe. Unfortunately, his curiosity doesn't escape the attention of his superiors, and it may cost him his life.

Meanwhile, Tennessee public school teacher, Noah Parker, like many in the United States, has been asleep at the wheel. During his complacency, the founding precepts of America have been systematically destroyed by a conspiracy that dates back hundreds of years.

Cassandra Parker, Noah's wife, has diligently followed end-times prophecy and the shifting tide against freedom in America. Noah has tried to avoid the subject, but when charges are filed against him for deviating from the approved curriculum in his school, he quickly understands the seriousness of the situation. The signs can no longer be ignored, and Noah is forced to prepare for the cataclysmic period of financial and political upheaval ahead.

Watch through the eyes of Noah Parker and Everett Carroll as the world descends into chaos, a global empire takes shape, ancient writings are fulfilled, and the last days fall upon the once-great United States of America.

Black Swan: A Novel of America's Coming Financial Nightmare

America's financial doomsday. A wayward son. The epic struggle to survive.

Country music icon Shane Black is this year's headliner for the New Year's Eve bash in Times Square, but when violent riots break out, he'll need more than a six string to escape the maelstrom.

After decades of abuse as the world's reserve currency, the US Dollar's day of reckoning is at hand. Without a functioning monetary system to purchase basic goods, society rapidly descends into abject chaos. Protests, looting, and bloodletting take the place of civility in a country which is coming unhinged.

Thrust into an apocalyptic gauntlet of terror, Shane must resort to savage brutality to get out of Manhattan alive.

Seven Cows, Ugly and Gaunt

In *Book One: Behold Darkness and Sorrow,* Daniel Walker begins having prophetic dreams about the judgment coming upon America for rejecting God. Through one of his dreams, Daniel learns of an imminent threat of an EMP attack which will wipe out America's electric grid and most all computerized devices, sending the country into a technological dark age.

Living in a nation where all life-sustaining systems of support are completely dependent on electricity and computers, the odds of survival are dismal. Municipal water services, retail food distribution, police, fire, EMS and all emergency services will come to a screeching halt.

If they want to live, Daniel and his friends must focus on faith, wits, and preparation to be ready . . . before the lights go out.

Cyber Armageddon

Cyber Security Analyst Kate McCarthy knows something ominous is about to happen in the US banking system. She has a place to go if things get hectic, but it's far from the perfect retreat.

When a new breed of computer virus takes down America's financial network, chaos and violence erupt. Access to cash disappears and credit cards become worthless. Desperate consumers are left with no means to purchase food, fuel, and basic necessities. Society melts down instantly and the threat of starvation brings out the absolute worst humanity has to offer.

In the midst of the mayhem, Kate will face a post-apocalyptic nightmare that she never could have imagined. Her only reward for survival is to live another day in the gruesome new reality which has eradicated the world she once knew.

Ava's Crucible

The deck is stacked against twenty-nine-year-old Ava. She's a fighter, but she's got trust issues and doesn't always make the best decisions. Her personal complications aren't without merit, but America is on the verge of a second civil war, and Ava must pull it together if she wants to survive.

The tentacles of the deep state have infiltrated every facet of American culture. The public education system, entertainment industry, and mainstream media have all been hijacked by a shadow government intent on fomenting a communist revolution in the United States. The antagonistic message of this agenda has poisoned the minds of America's youth who are convinced that capitalism and conservatism are responsible for all the ills of the world. Violent protest, widespread destruction, and politicians who insist on letting the disassociated vent their rage will bring America to her knees, threatening to decapitate the laws, principles, and values on which the country was founded. The revolution has been well-planned, but the socialists may have underestimated America's true patriots who refuse to give up without a fight.

ABOUT THE AUTHOR

Mark Goodwin holds a degree in accounting and monitors macroeconomic conditions to stay up-to-date with the ongoing global meltdown. He is an avid student of the Holy Bible and spends several hours every week devoted to the study of Scripture and the prophecies contained therein. The troubling trends in the moral, social, political, and financial landscapes have prompted Mark to conduct extensive research within the arena of preparedness. He weaves his knowledge of biblical prophecy, economics, politics, prepping, and survival into an action-packed tapestry of post-apocalyptic fiction. Having been a sinner saved by grace himself, the story of redemption is a prominent theme in all of Mark's writings.

"He brought me up also out of an horrible pit, out of the miry clay, and set my feet upon a rock, and established my goings." Psalm 40:2